‘Happy Daze’ Are Here Again

By Julie Ann Mulvey

Dedicated to all of you who have been kind enough to support me so far x

Prologue

The large bright lights in the big festival hall quickly start to dim, and the loud beat of the music thuds, as the tall blonde supermodel struts confidently down the catwalk, in a stunning low cut peach taffeta and lace creation, with a diamond studded belt and long flared skirt, closely followed by a dark haired supermodel in the same outfit in rose pink.

The whole of the assembled crowd at this exclusive Paris fashion event gasp audibly as the models stride up and down, posing for effect every so often as dozens of flashbulbs go off at the side of the stage, while the worlds press fight one another for the best shots of these incredible outfits.

The cut glass accent of the female announcer can be heard loudly above the hubbub of the specially invited audience, crammed full of the most well-known and influential people in the fashion industry.

"And now, the latest collection from 'House of Maynard', Birmingham, England."

The crowd applaud loudly in appreciation.

"And the head of the organisation, the chief designer herself is here with us tonight, please give a warm welcome to Miss Johanna Maynard! Take a bow Johanna, come on, get up....."

21 year old Johanna Maynard comes to with a jolt. Annoyingly for her the instruction 'Johanna, get up' has not come from the announcer at a Paris fashion show, but from her overbearing father Trevor shouting up the stairs in his broad Birmingham accent, imploring her to get out of bed.

"Come on, shift yourself," he bellows, "Me breakfast won't make itself."

Johanna turns over, trying to block out his loud demands, burying her face in the pillow. The noisy bellowing doesn't cease. "Are you listening to me Johanna, get up this minute, we're waiting for you down here."

Wearily, she opens one eye to look at the clock. It's 6.30am. Generally, the call doesn't come as early as this, but as today they are heading off for a week's holiday in Wales she reluctantly gets herself out of bed, annoyed that her precious dream had been rudely disturbed.

She has this same dream almost every night, whilst knowing in her heart it'll never become a reality. Johanna is a very talented artist indeed, drawing the beautiful fashion designs of her dreams and stunning caricatures to go with them in her sketch books in secret, knowing full well her selfish parents Trevor and Muriel would most likely destroy her precious artwork if they ever found out about it. The only way her secrets can ever be played out is in private, where every day she lovingly fills her sketch books with drawings at any time she gets a moment to herself.

Johanna's books are full of her incredible works of art, beautifully crafted drawings. Despite Trevor and Muriel always stating that nothing would ever come of their youngest daughter, she is a highly intelligent, and supremely gifted artist, in possession of an astonishing photographic memory.

Whilst at school, she shone brightly in her art lessons, day after day dreaming of becoming a top fashion designer working in London, Paris or New York, showing off her creations to the most influential fashion houses, and enjoying a high flying career.

Johanna's teachers actively encouraged her passion for design, coveting her work and showcasing it often, something that completely bypassed Johanna's ignorant parents no matter how many times they were told or shown her stunning artwork.

During Johanna's final year at school, with her teachers telling her over and over again how she must enrol at a top art college and then go on to university to study fashion design, Trevor made sure that there was never any prospect of this. He drilled into Johanna relentlessly that it was her obligation to go out and get a job to bring money in to keep them, and that going to 'a lah dee dah college like a pouffe' was not even a remote possibility. A distraught Johanna had to break the news to her careers teacher that she was leaving school at 16, and not continuing on with her education, as both she and they had wanted. Her teachers were as devastated as she was, imploring her to get her thoughtless parents to change their mind, that to drop out would be a terrible waste of her incredible talent. It couldn't happen, as Trevor and Muriel were far more interested in what wages Johanna would be bringing home, so the lazy, feckless twosome didn't have to bother going out to work for themselves.

By this time Johanna's elder siblings, her brother Rodney and sister Christy, had already fled the family home, both of them getting married in quick succession. Their parents' reaction to this was to ensure Johanna didn't do the same, employing a selfish plan to keep her as their personal slave. They make her dress in clothes designed to make her look half a dozen years younger, ensure that she never wears make up or jewellery, and has her long mousey hair tied back in a pony-tail on a permanent basis. They also make sure that contact with anyone her own age is severely restricted, not wanting Johanna to grow up and leave home as Rodney and Christy did, determined to keep her in servitude.

A miserable existence, but one Johanna now accepts as normal, just getting on with her parents bidding while working full time on the checkout of a local supermarket.

She puts on her usual outfit of a Disney t-shirt and shorts, that would look better on a 12-year-old. To the outside world she looks like a young girl, a minor, certainly not a grown woman of 21; a deliberate move on her lazy, selfish parents' part.

Johanna appears around the kitchen door, as her father and mother sit there waiting to be waited on, as they usually do.

"Put the kettle on Johanna, and get some bacon under the grill, there's a good girl," says Muriel, forcefully, "Oh, and bring those cases down as well, the van keys are on the sideboard."

Silently she does exactly as her mother asks, never daring to question her mean, unreasonable demands.

Within 15 minutes, her parents are greedily tucking into their bacon sandwiches and slurping large mugs of tea, while Johanna is dragging their heavy cases down the stairs to be stowed in back of their rusty old minibus. This same scenario is played out twice a year every year, prior to heading off to 'Happy Daze Leisure Park' located in the Pembrokeshire seaside resort of Portwynne. Trevor drives the van, Johanna pays for the diesel, and the rest of the family are collected from various parts of Birmingham; Rodney and his wife Sandra, with their twin boys Karl and Mikey, Christy and her husband Neil Hassall, and finally Trevor's elderly mother Eunice.

The other family members are fully aware of the cruel treatment meted out to Johanna, and none of them approve at all, but angry denials from Trevor and Muriel any time concerns are raised, plus kindly Johanna's insistence that no-one need fuss, quell this. Her sister Christy is angrier than anyone that nothing has been done to help Johanna escape her mean parents' clutches, and has been secretly plotting a way of doing this, knowing that getting some money together would be a start as Johanna herself has no savings, with every penny of her wages dutifully handed over to Muriel week after week.

For the past two years Christy had been putting every spare penny she could find away in a secret savings account at the Building Society, with the intention of saving up £500, before signing it over to Johanna so she can put down a deposit on a flat, and to help give her a proper start at last. Sadly, all Christy's best laid plans have fallen by the wayside. At one point she had almost £400 saved up, but when husband Neil was put on short time at the local steelworks she had to delve into the pot to make ends meet, all the time not revealing to her husband where the extra funds really came from, pretending she had received tips and bonuses from her job as a part time barmaid at a local hotel.

More recently, just as she had started to build the savings back up again, came a demand from Trevor to pay their share of the holiday fund. Christy and Neil had seriously considered not coming to Happy Daze for a second holiday, having already spent a week there only two months before, preferring to save what little money they had for themselves. This sparked a furious rant from Trevor, knowing fine well that neither he nor Muriel would be getting another week away unless a further £150 was found.

Reluctantly, Christy dipped into the secret account again, this time leaving just £75 in the kitty, nowhere near the £500 she estimates it would take to fund Johanna's escape.

A week prior to this latest getaway, Rodney and Sandra, Christy and Neil, all went out for a meal and an urgent family conference. They were all agreed on one thing. Their parents' gravy-train needs bringing to a rapid halt, and that things need to change swiftly.

Apart from the money to stay at Happy Daze being totally funded by them and Johanna, from the second they arrive in Portwynne, until they leave, Trevor and Muriel never offer to pay for a single thing, expecting their jollies to be completely paid for by their offspring. The only other person that isn't expected to pay is Eunice, despite her being more comfortably off than the rest of them put together thanks to a generous pension courtesy of her late husband and his many years working for British Rail.

Over dinner, the four of them make a vow that before their week at Happy Daze is out Trevor and Muriel will be sat down and told in no uncertain terms that their 'free' holidays are no more, and that their treatment of Johanna will no longer be tolerated. Christy didn't let on about the secret account at the Building Society however, wanting this to be something she did for herself, praying that sooner or later the £500 will be saved up and handed over to her younger sister.

Johanna returns to the kitchen. "The cases are all locked away, dad," she confirms, "What time are we going?"

"Another half an hour, and make sure you've got your purse, will you, because we need diesel," says Trevor, as he sits at the kitchen table, belching and rubbing his fat belly, "Go on, then. Make us another brew, don't just stand there idle, doing nothing."

Again Johanna does as is asked of her, without a second thought. Once her parents are enjoying their freshly brewed mugs of tea again Johanna retreats to her bedroom, getting her own belongings together. Both her case and her handbag have secret padded compartments sewn into them by her, to ensure her sketch book and expensive pens, that she purposely hid money away to get, are safely hidden away should Muriel or Trevor decide to search them.

She glances sadly around her bare bedroom while grabbing a few meagre bits and pieces to take away with her, the childish outfits, not a single dress or skirt amongst them. Again Trevor shouts loudly up the stairs. "How much longer Johanna, we're waiting to go here, hurry up for Christ sake, what the hell are you up to?" She makes sure her books and pens are safely hidden away before slowly making her way down.

Just after half past eight the three of them are in the minibus heading off to the petrol station, prior to collecting the rest of the Maynard family. "'Happy Daze' are here again," chuckles Trevor, as the minibus splutters its way towards the west coast of Wales.

Chapter 1

With its beautiful, golden sandy beach and glorious sea-views, the sleepy seaside town of Portwynne on the Pembrokeshire coast was one of Wales' best kept secrets for many years. But when Welsh entrepreneur Louis Peyton bought thousands of acres of real estate around the bay to build 'Happy Daze Leisure Park' in the early 1960s, it wasn't only the landscape that changed. Overnight many thousands of tourists from all over descended for their annual week or fortnight away, to the dismay of locals who had long enjoyed their quiet way of life.

But now, some twenty years on, and with the local economy booming, the residents are a little more forgiving, as many businesses make fortunes on the back of this very popular holiday destination.

"Thank you for holidaying at Happy Daze, Portwynne. We hope you enjoyed your stay, come back soon, safe journey home," booms the loud voice of Alun Williams through a hand held megaphone, as several early birds depart, hoping to beat the busy Saturday morning holiday traffic.

His loud Welsh drawl resonates as busses and cars, many with children waving out of the windows, make their way off the large main car park and out of the resort at the end of their stay. The sun is burning high in the sky, and as all these people leave, very soon many more will arrive from all four corners of the country.

When Louis Peyton first opened his holiday parks, basing his model on very similar ones already dotted about the British Isles, his idea was to provide a mixture of high class facilities and entertainment, for low-budget prices. Currently, they have never been more popular, particularly with families with little or no money, as year on year Peyton's Leisure Parks undercut their rivals significantly.

The downside to this is the small, cramped chalets, many of

them poorly maintained, that visitors are housed in during their stay, with Louis caring more about entertainment and catering rather than the comfort of his guests.

He is ably assisted by his ever faithful personal minder, Elvis Mansfield, a tall, strapping ex-Royal Marine, who has worked for Louis for more than 10 years, and this loyalty is repaid handsomely, with Elvis earning more a week than a lot of the Happy Daze staff earn in one summer.

Back in his tiny staff chalet, Johnny Major is putting on his pale blue blazer, striped tie and his name badge, while smoothing down his white slacks ahead of another long day entertaining the masses, alongside Alun and the other leisure park entertainers known collectively as 'Seasiders'.

This is so far removed from the career Johnny had enjoyed up until a year ago. A very experienced song and dance man, with six of his own highly rated, and popular TV series' behind him, he found himself thrown on the entertainment scrap-heap after a new young programme controller was employed at regional station North West Television. The maverick youngster immediately swept clean with a new broom, labelling shows such as 'Johnny's Variety Showcase', which had been one of the stations most watched programmes, as 'old hat and out of touch in 1980s Britain'.

In an unpopular move, Johnny and a lot of the other household names, who had been employed at the station for decades, were replaced, while many others had simply resigned in disgust at the treatment of these big stars, who had made the station fortunes over many years.

With the cancelation of his show pretty much signalling the end of his television career, Johnny found the going extremely tough. Returning to the Working Mens clubs where he initially started out as a youngster in the 1950s, he quickly discovered that much of Clubland had either gone, or had completely changed beyond recognition, with what venues still remaining simply not wanting the nostalgia-feelgood act Johnny was well known for, preferring younger and modern performers and singers instead.

His lifestyle also went swiftly downhill as a consequence. When 'Johnny's Variety Showcase' was attracting over 20 million viewers at its peak, and making him very well-off in the process, Johnny, his wife Olivia, and their three young children moved into a spacious cottage deep in the Welsh countryside, set in many acres of land, enjoying all the trappings of their wealth, with a large new car every twelve months, and the children sent to be educated at exclusive private schools.

Once the television work and the money that went with it completely dried up, the Majors had to quickly sell their house for a fraction of its value, replace the car with something a little cheaper to run, and the children forced to return to mainstream education. All of this greatly frustrated Olivia who had very much enjoyed their lavish lifestyle, the expensive trips to the beauty salon, the spa holidays, and didn't take too kindly at the families now meagre living standards.

She took this out on Johnny, causing their marriage to now be at breaking point. Struggling to find decent paid work on the club circuit, and even considering dropping out of show-business completely, a chance meeting in a local pub with Louis Peyton lead to the promise of guaranteed work between Easter and the beginning of October, with accommodation and all meals thrown in, and the opportunity to entertain the many thousands of holiday-makers passing through the gates of Happy Daze.

Louis was very shrewd, knowing full well that Johnny would still be a big enough draw to have families from all over descending on Portwynne, and he was quick to take full advantage of this familiar celebrity, using him to front a modest advertising campaign on radio and television at the start of the year, and having his image plastered throughout Peyton's brochures and on large billboards all over England and Wales.

Johnny quickly found this new line of work challenging and

tiring, with 14 hour days, 6 days a week, every week, very hard going indeed, but the warm response from the public had been enough to justify accepting the job, along with a decent sized pay packet. He's not too unhappy at being away from Olivia's non-stop nagging either, but the family pay him visits when they can, and the wages are substantially more than the scraps he was earning at the odd club that would employ him.

With it being a Saturday, it's a very busy day ahead bidding farewell to guests leaving, or warmly welcoming newcomers. Johnny is looking forward to today a little bit more than usual as some close friends of his are coming to Portwynne for a week's holiday.

A month earlier, completely out of the blue, Johnny received a letter while at Happy Daze from his old friends Colin and Liz Chesters, a couple he had known for many years. Colin was a well known performer like Johnny, doing stand-up comedy, and had also been treated harshly by the new regime at North West Television, seeing the two shows he appeared on cancelled in quick succession.

The Chesters' had been a little more prudent than the Majors down the years though, they never moved from their modest semi in the Manchester suburbs, and all three of their children, Colin's daughters from his first marriage, and his son from his marriage to Liz, went to state schools in the borough. Once Colin was out of full time TV, an early victim of the same cull that saw Johnny's career vanish, they were financially secure. No mortgage and no worries, enabling Colin to have the luxury of taking things easy while enjoying life with his beloved wife and children.

Liz has known Johnny since she was a youngster, when they lived in neighbouring villages in the South Wales valleys. It was when he was recruited to perform at Liz's 18th birthday party in the early 1970s that Johnny was finally spotted by a top TV producer, and fame beckoned. Although he and Colin didn't work on the same TV programmes together, it was through Liz they became good friends, but more recently they had all fallen out of touch somewhat. That was until Liz had been made aware of Johnny's new career, after her cousin, still living in South Wales, saw a brochure for Peyton's Leisure Parks in the window of a local travel agency, with a large photo of Johnny on the front of it. She also saw some of the adverts on television. She told Liz who and what she'd seen on a 'thought you might be interested to know' basis, nothing more, but Liz, intrigued to see how Johnny was doing now, persuaded Colin to forego their regular family holiday in Blackpool for a week on the Pembrokeshire coast instead.

Johnny has Liz's letter in his pocket, as he makes his way to the staff canteen for a quick breakfast. He reads it again fondly, making sure he'd got the date right, that today was definitely the day his old friends were arriving. He was gladdened that they were taking the trouble to holiday at Happy Daze specially to see him, something Liz had made quite clear in her correspondence. Both Liz and Colin guessed that Johnny's new job might not be the career he really wants, but seeing a familiar face or two wouldn't do him any harm.

Saturdays at the leisure park are very much routine, with Johnny and some of the other Seasiders spending the early part of the day by the front gate waving off the leavers, then from 12 noon onwards wending their way around the Reception Hall, greeting new arrivals as they queue up for the keys to their basic, no-frills accommodation.

Colin and Liz set off soon after 8am for their 4 hours journey between Manchester and the West coast of Wales. With Colin's daughters, Charlotte and Eleanor, in the back, either side of their younger half-brother Jamie, the five of them excitedly head off for their week by the seaside. The traveling on this very hot day starts to get a little weary for the youngsters.

"Are we there yet?" asks 7-year-old Jamie at least a dozen

times during the journey, to the annoyance of the other passengers.

"Shut up, Jamie," implores 12-year-old Eleanor, herself a little fed up of the long trip, elbowing her brother in the ribs.

"Yes, Jamie give it a rest, we'll be there soon enough," says 17-year-old Charlotte, as they pass a large roadside billboard advertising Happy Daze, complete with a photo of Johnny smiling broadly, and brandishing a Peytons flag.

They arrive at the leisure park just after 12.15, and make their way onto the main car park. Liz looks around at the many buildings, a theatre in the shape of a large marquee, another building that appears to be a bar, along with a shopping arcade and other amusements. Quite a big place this, she muses, having never been to a leisure park before and not knowing quite what to expect. They had already seen a large outdoor swimming pool complete with sun loungers and an outdoor stage, and many hundreds of other holiday-makers wandering their way around.

The Maynard's rusty old minibus pulls up noisily behind Colin's Jaguar on the car park, just as him, Liz and the children are getting out. Liz looks on in horror at this large tank-like contraption, belching out its diesel fumes, and glances a little disdainfully at the scruffy looking people getting off the bus.

Mikey and Karl, fully familiar with Happy Daze, immediately run off towards a nearby large sports field with a football, which they start to happily kick about. Jamie's eyes light up at the sight of two boys his own age doing what he likes to do best when at home. "Mum. Can I go and play football with those boys?" he asks. Liz doesn't particularly like the look of any of the people getting off the bus, and isn't so sure.

"You don't know who they are, you can't just barge in like that," she says.

Trevor Maynard has overheard the conversation. "He'll be alright, bab," he shouts over to Liz, in his strong Birmingham accent. Liz blushes slightly, hoping no one noticed her looking down her nose at them.

"Let him go if he wants to," says Colin, chuckling, "But stay on the grass, and don't wander off anywhere else." Jamie quickly dashes off to make his acquaintance with the Maynard boys.

Charlotte and Eleanor stand looking around at the unfamiliar surroundings. A large fun fair can be seen and heard in the distance, which appeals to them. "Can we go to the fair please dad?" asks Eleanor.

"Yes, alright then, we'll come straight to you when we've got the keys to the chalet," says Colin, "Make sure you stay together though, please." The girls stride off happily, in the direction of the rides.

Trevor is stretching his legs alongside the bus, as the others continue to get out, with Rodney currently helping his elderly grandma Eunice down the step. "Lovely day for it," Trevor calls across to Colin and Liz, not immediately recognising Colin as someone he would have seen on television. Muriel is a little quicker off the mark however.

"Hey!" she shouts, "I know who you are. You're what's-his-face, comedian chappy. Or you look very much like him in any case." Colin used to be recognised in public all the time, but not so much now which he's not too unhappy about, preferring to be an ordinary family man off screen. He smiles politely back at her, nevertheless. "You here working then?" asks Muriel.

"No," confirms Colin, "Just here for a family holiday, same as you."

"Oh, I see," replies a slightly bemused Muriel, not really understanding that TV stars might just be ordinary humans as well, with normal lives and families.

"Where do we go from here then," says Colin to Liz, while looking around. Again it's Trevor who shouts up noisily.

"That building over here mate," he states, pointing towards a large white building with a big Peytons sign on the front, Underneath, a slightly smaller sign can be made out saying 'Reception Hall'.

"Thank you," says Colin, "May as well leave the cases in the car for now, Lizzy, until we know how far away the chalet is."

"Ok then," smiles Liz, "What time does it say on the booking form, for checking in."

Trevor shouts up yet again, just as Colin is retrieving the paperwork from his inside jacket pocket. "You can go and register now, but the chalet won't be ready until 3 at the earliest. We always go for a few bevvies, and some fish and chips while we wait, the bar in that building over there allows kids in during the day. The Jolly Roger it's called."

"Thank you," says Liz, a little annoyed at Trevor's constant interruptions.

"I take it you not been here before then," continues Trevor.

"No we haven't, it's our first visit," replies Colin, wanting nothing more but to get away from this loud mouthed Midlander. They quickly stride past the Maynard family, hand in hand, in the general direction of the Reception Hall, merely calling over to Jamie to stay where he is, and that they would be back for him in a few minutes.

Chapter Two

Johnny and several other Seasiders are now in the Reception Hall, along with a long queue of holiday-makers waiting in line to be attended to at a large hatch, behind which sisters Dolly and Val Mason are dealing with booking forms and other assorted paperwork, ensuring the right keys are handed to the right guests.

Colin and Liz wait patiently in the queue. As they look around, they see many different people of all shapes and sizes, some with luggage, others with pushchairs or young children running around. They soon spot Johnny down the front between the heads, as he can be seen to be shaking hands warmly and laughing along with a tall, thin elderly gentleman.

"Have a lovely week Mr Reynolds," says Johnny, his voice loud enough to be heard over the squealing kids and general chitter chatter of the queue. As the old man goes back to his place in the line Johnny notices Colin and Liz queuing up and bounds over to them quickly.

Liz feels more than a little embarrassed, as he happily ignores two dozen others nearer the front of the queue in his haste to get to them. Colin is also not keen on this extra fuss, happy to have waited his turn for Johnny's attention. No such luck.

"Colin, how are ya mate," smiles Johnny enthusiastically, shaking his hand firmly and giving him a fond man hug. Others in the queue look on at this floor show, some of them noticing it's Colin stood there, and start to nudge one another.

"Look who that is, never knew he was on here, didn't say so in the brochure," can be heard from the people who recognise him.

"Elizabeth, lovely to see you thanks for coming," says Johnny, giving Liz a big hug and a kiss on the cheek, "How are you both? How are the kids, how are your mum and dad keeping, Liz?"

"Everyone is fine," says Colin, quietly interjecting, trying to deflect attention away from themselves, "Looking forward to a weeks rest."

"Not much chance of that here," says Johnny, laughing, "It's all go go go at Happy Daze, you know, loads to see and do." Finally, he does lower his voice slightly. "I have to warn you though, the accommodation here is a little basic - it's clean of course, but a bit small perhaps, certainly nowhere near as grand as the places we were used to in the good old days, know what I mean Col," he says.

Liz glares at Johnny in amusement. Not once had the Chesters family embarked on the expensive foreign holidays, or stayed at the five star hotels that Johnny and Olivia purportedly frequented at the height of his fame, their modest guest-house holidays in seaside resorts such as Blackpool and Fleetwood more than enough to keep them happy.

"Anyway," says Colin, "It's really good to see you Johnny, I'm sure we'll see plenty more of you this week."

"Yes, every day except for Monday, my day off," he confirms.

"Best get back to it then," says Liz, wanting Johnny to pay rather more attention to the other holiday-makers in the line, as he's paid to do, "We'll see you during the week, that's for certain."

"Yes, you will," smiles Johnny, shaking Colin's hand again, "I'll see you both some more." With that he strides back to the front of the queue.

The elderly gentleman Johnny greeted earlier wanders across, tottering gently on a walking stick, with his wife similarly frail right behind him. Both have quickly recognised Colin and are keen to speak to him. Mr Reynolds holds out his bony hand to shake, which Colin does, politely.

"Well, this is a lovely surprise," says Mr Reynolds, "I mean, they always have proper good turns on here, but I wasn't expecting to see you, how lovely this is, good old Louis Peyton, he never lets us down, quality entertainment all the way."

"Oh, I'm not here performing," confirms Colin, "Just for a holiday with my family, and to catch up with Johnny."

"Oh, well that is a shame," replies a clearly disappointed Mr

Reynolds, "I thought with you being here that you were going to be the Midnight Cabaret in the Jolly Roger this week, pity that, you were good years ago."

"Thanks," says Colin, looking to see Liz smother a giggle.

"Anyhow, I won't keep you any longer, cheerio for now," says Mr Reynolds, as him and his wife make their unsteady way back towards the exit.

"Years ago?" says Liz, "It's not that long ago, goodness me, making you sound ancient!"

"Oh well," says Colin, "Nice to know someone still remembers me anyway, not that I really want too much of that while we're here to be honest."

Another 15 minutes goes by before they finally reach the front of the queue. Dolly Mason greets Colin and Liz like old friends, despite neither of them having a clue who she is. "Here they are Val, look," she says, smiling widely. Her sister also sports a big grin, while busily attending to someone else. "It's so lovely to see you both, it really is a treat," says Dolly, "Johnny showed me your letter, proud as punch he was when he got it."

"Oh, very nice," says Liz, a little annoyed that her personal correspondence had been shared about with complete strangers.

"He's been counting down the days, haven't you Johnny," Dolly confirms. Johnny has reappeared and is standing alongside Liz, smiling from ear to ear.

"I most certainly have," he beams, "It's such a thrill to see the pair of you after all this time, I can't tell you how much I've been looking forward to today." He's swiftly interrupted by a young boy, no more than five years old, tugging at the hem of his blazer. Johnny puts on all the Seasider charm he can muster, and goes to speak to the boys parents, who are stood further back in the queue.

Colin hands the booking form over, while Dolly fetches an envelope with their keys in and some paperwork to sign.

From the back of the queue a familiar sounding voice can be heard. "Look at the state of this bloody queue, it gets worse and worse every time we come, too bloody slow them sisters, they want telling the pair of 'em. Completely useless." Trevor Maynard is the complainant.

The rest of the queue of people, including Liz, turn around. Liz rolls her eyes when she sees who's making the needless remarks and turns back to face the desk. She can see the look on Dolly's face has turned from joy to aggravation in five seconds flat. "Is it that time of the year again already," she mutters, "flaming 'Wagon Train'. That's all I need."

Due to their frequent stays at Happy Daze the camp staff are very familiar with the Maynards indeed, sneakily referring to them as 'Wagon Train', as generally all of them traipse around the camp together in a tribe-like fashion.

Dolly and Val both know Trevor and Muriel Maynard well, neither of them fond of Trevor's bombastic manner, or his body odour. It was only a few years since Dolly caught them out, trying to pay children's rates for Johanna by altering her date of birth year on year, keeping her at age 14. Eagle-eyed Dolly had spotted early on that Johanna shared the same birthday as her, and had calculated how many years younger than her she was. As the gap appeared to widen year on year, Dolly did some cursory checking, finding the original paperwork from their first visit in 1974 when Johanna genuinely was 14. Every visit since had seen her year of birth go up by one. A strongly worded letter from Louis Peyton about identity fraud, and a request to see Johanna's birth certificate prior to any future bookings being accepted soon did the trick, and they never tried to disguise her true age on the booking form again, although they do make sure she's not usually seen by either Dolly or Val at any time during their stays.

"There we are Colin," says Dolly, smiling, this over-familiarity not impressing Liz much as everyone else up until now had been spoken to formally, as Mr or Mrs so and so. How impolite to be on first name terms with someone she thinks she knows because he's been on television, muses Liz. "Now, you are in Primrose Block, which is up the bank from here, you go past the fair, it's a big yellow coloured building, you won't be able to miss it. Chalet Number 114," says Dolly.

Colin signs the paperwork, allowing him and Liz to quickly bid the Mason sisters good day, keen to get back to Jamie and the girls before unloading their car. They head out of the building taking no notice of a few rubber-neckers, including Muriel.

Dolly can see the Maynards getting nearer and nearer the front and is dreading it, hoping that Val is free before she is. No such luck as Val gets stuck with a family who have a discrepancy on their booking form, meaning Trevor and Muriel are left to her. Trevor leans over the desk leerily, as Muriel gets some paperwork from her handbag.

"Well, hello Dolly," laughs Trevor in a sing-song voice. Dolly is used to his unfunny joke and takes no notice, while holding her breath, with Trevor being as un-fresh as usual. Muriel hands over three booking forms, as the others are already in the Jolly Roger reserving 'their' table.

"Now how many more times Mrs Maynard," says an exasperated Dolly, "The rest of your family need to collect their own keys and sign their own forms. We are here until 7 o' clock, if they can see their way clear." Louis Peyton employs a very strict security policy to safeguard against thieves, the named person on the booking form has to sign for their own keys. The Maynards attempt to flout this policy on every visit, leaving Dolly wondering why they even bother trying.

She quickly hands back the two booking forms that aren't theirs. "Oh come on Dolly, petal," says Trevor, leaning even further over the desk to Dolly's total disgust, "We'd miss our table in the Jolly Roger if our Rodney and the others didn't go and save it for us, we can't have that can we, let us sign for them, it'll be alright, seeing as you know us."

"It's against Peyton's security policies, as you well know Mr Maynard," says Dolly sternly, "so please ensure your Son and Son in Law come over here to sign for themselves when they can. Let me get your envelope."

"I hope you reserved our usual abode, in Primrose Block," states Trevor, knowing fine well that their request for the same three chalets every stop is always honoured.

"Yes, Chalet 115 in Primrose Block, as always," confirms Dolly.

"Are you absolutely sure we can't sign for the others?" asks Muriel, pushing the two extra forms back across the desk, "It'll be much quicker, you know."

"No," implores Dolly, moving the forms back again, not wanting to risk her job for them. Reluctantly the Maynards take their own chalet keys only and return to the Jolly Roger.

By the time Liz and Colin get back to the playing field Jamie is on his own, sat on the grass with his back against a goalpost with the twins nowhere to be seen. "I thought you'd forgot about me," he moans, seeing his parents striding up, "Those boys had to go."

"So I can see," says Liz, "Sorry we were ages, there were a lot of people queuing besides us and we had to wait."

"They gave me some football stickers," smiles Jamie, holding up three, "I told them that we go to watch United, dad, and they give me these. Look."

"Very nice, but you shouldn't have taken them," says Liz, as overprotective as ever.

"Where's the harm," says Colin, "Anyway, let's go and find your sisters at the fairground, before they think we've forgotten about them too."

Trevor and Muriel arrive back at the Jolly Roger to find the rest of the clan in their usual haunt around two large tables they deliberately push together, to the annoyance of the bar staff and other people trying to squeeze past this giant obstacle.

"Get the beer and grub in, our Rodney," bellows Trevor, plonking himself down on a chair, "Large fish and chips for me and your mother, and whatever everyone else wants, come on Rodney, get your wallet out, what are you waiting for?"

Rodney and Christy exchange a look, knowing that this is the last holiday where his demands will be heeded. "No bother dad, just going now," he replies quietly, before making his way to the bar, well used to this routine.

Johanna is sitting quietly on a small stool, feeling more than a little fed up. She is also well aware how the afternoon will pan out, her greedy parents stuffing their faces and slurping down beer, none of which they ever pay for. Then at 3 o'clock on the dot her father will throw the keys to the bus in her direction, telling her to get the cases took up to Primrose Block, not once offering to help. Also she hasn't seen Johnny yet, which is making her particularly miserable.

After their previous visit back in May, where they met Johnny for the first time, Johanna was at first merely star struck, but by the end of the week hopelessly infatuated, following him around at a safe distance, or simply turning up at every event he hosted. Of course he never remotely noticed this ordinary plain looking young girl, and Johanna wasn't particularly bothered in any case. Just seeing him was enough for her. Even when she shyly asked for his autograph on the Friday night he looked straight through her like she was invisible.

None of this stopped Johanna's secret crush however, but never admitting anything to her sister Christy, or anyone else at all. The only place her secret desire is played out is in her sketch-book, which she lovingly fills in with her beautifully drawn caricatures, mostly of Johnny, and also of a tall red-haired model who wears her many fashion creations. Johanna dreams that the model she frequently draws will be her someday.

As ever, she has to watch her father and mother noisily

tucking into their large fish suppers, making her feel nauseous, as she prefers far healthier meals. 3pm arrives and Trevor has the bus keys out in a flash, tossing them across table nearly taking out Johanna's bottle of coke, complete with straw.

"Go on our Johanna, you know the drill, go get them cases, there's a good girl," says Trevor, while quickly gulping down yet another pint of beer. Reluctantly she gets to her feet, knowing to put up any sort of resistance would be futile, and quickly shouted down.

Christy is out of her seat straightaway. "I'll give you a hand, sis," she smiles.

"Oh sit down, Christy, what ya doing, she's alright, leave her to it," booms Trevor, "Get us another beer instead, make yourself useful."

"No, dad," says Christy defiantly, the only person who ever matches her father blow for blow, "It's not fair to make Johanna do it all."

"What? She doesn't mind, do ya bab," says clueless Trevor.

"It's alright," says Johanna, timidly making her way towards the doors.

"No it's not alright," snarls Christy, in hot pursuit of her younger sister.

Chapter Three

Johanna is already half way across the main car park before Christy finally catches up with her.

"I don't know why you let them get away with this all the time," says Christy, knowing fine well her younger sister would never question any order from Trevor and Muriel, no matter how unfair or belittling.

"It's fine, don't worry about me," sighs Johanna, as they reach the bus. She gets the keys out, unlocks the rear doors and retrieves two large cases, along with her own bags. Christy gets her luggage out as well, now in possession of the chalet keys that Neil went over to the Reception Hall with Rodney to collect.

"You shouldn't have to put up with this, I mean look at you," moans Christy, despairing at Johanna's cartoon t-shirt and child-like shorts, "It's cruel to make you wear these daft clothes, and have you fetch and carry for them all the time, it's ridiculous."

"It doesn't matter," replies Johanna, as she locks the bus up again, "I'll come back for Grans case when I've took these."

"No you won't, I'll get Neil to take it up later," says Christy, kindly, "But you don't have to put up with this treatment, and if I had my way you wouldn't have to, I mean it." It's taking all of Christy's resolve to not reveal her long-standing plans, about the secret account at the building society, and the £500 target.

Johanna hears her sisters kind words, no-one has looked out for her more than Christy has, but no matter what happens her parents always have the final say, and what they say goes.

As the two of them make their way up the bank, past the fair and onwards to Primrose Block, the Chesters family pass them coming the opposite way, having spent some time at the fairground, with Charlotte, Eleanor and Jamie all having the time of their lives, enjoying the many rides and amusements and the loud pop music blasting out, before going back to the car to retrieve their luggage, completely unnoticed amongst the hundreds of other people milling about, most of them also making their way to their accommodation now it's past 3 o'clock.

Within ten minutes Johanna and Christy are climbing the metal steps up to the first floor of Primrose Block, a large building three stories high, painted in a garish yellow colour. "Just dump the cases in the chalet, and we'll go back to the pub," says Christy, "I'll even treat you to a glass of wine when we get there, how about that!" Johanna looks at her sister gloomily, knowing fine well their parents would never allow her a proper drink, and there's a chance that Christy might get in trouble if the barman thinks she's buying drinks for a minor, even though she's 21 and plenty old enough.

"It's ok, you don't have to do that," says Johanna, turning the key in the lock of chalet 115, the same one they always stay in on every single visit to Happy Daze.

Christy makes her way to chalet 117, where she and Neil are housed for the week. As soon as Johanna closes the door behind her she delves into her handbag, carefully unlocking the secret padlocked and padded compartment that can't be seen from the outside, containing her latest sketch book and set of coloured pens. She sits at a small table in the living area and starts to draw, putting the finishing touches to a caricature of Johnny in his light blue Seasiders outfit which she had started before they came away. Her books are full of these cleverly drawn portraits.

Johanna isn't concerned that her precious artwork won't see the light of day, more than happy to keep her drawings a secret.

Christy bangs loudly on the chalet door. Johanna quickly puts her book and pens back in the secret pocket in her bag. "Are you ready?" asks Christy, as Johanna answers the door.

"Yes, just about," she replies, wishing Christy had been a little slower in turning up. Just as they talk in the doorway the Chesters family make their way up the stairs behind them, heading for Chalet 114.

Colin doesn't take a blind bit of notice of the two girls stood nearby as he unlocks the door, which creaks loudly as it opens, but

Liz recognises both Johanna and Christy straightaway and her heart sinks.

Charlotte is last through the squeaky door, closing it behind her. "You know who those girls are, don't you," sighs Liz.

"What girls?" asks Colin, putting the cases down as Johanna and Christy walk past the window.

"Those two," replies Liz, pointing, "They were with that loud mouthed man from Birmingham, don't you remember?"

"Oh, him. I didn't take much notice to tell you the truth, Lizzy," admits Colin.

"Well, you know what that means, of course," says Liz, "We're going to be next door to them. That is one thing we could well do without."

"Take no notice of him, Lizzy," says Colin, looking around the sparsely furnished chalet, "We'll be out a lot of the time in any case, we probably won't see much of him at all."

Liz also glances around the small room. Two single beds, doubling as seating, a smallish table with a couple of rickety looking wooden chairs, one cupboard with a very small electric kettle on the top, and nothing else. The inside is painted a slightly less bright yellow than the exterior walls of Primrose Block. Like Johnny had told them, it's clean and tidy, but not very big at all. The bathroom is also tiny, with a small bath, toilet and washbasin tightly squeezed in. A tiny bedroom with one single bed and a cupboard, and a second slightly bigger bedroom with a double bed and a small wardrobe. 'Ok, the holiday was cheap enough,' Liz thinks, 'should have expected the accommodation to be equally cheap, oh well, need to make the best of it.'

After a couple of hours more, where Jamie and Eleanor make full use of a large nearby play-park and swings, and while Liz and Charlotte get on with the unpacking, allowing Colin to have a rest and a study of the events programme, the five of them go over to the dining hall for their evening meal.

Before opening his leisure parks, Louis Peyton had owned several successful restaurants, and where certain parts of Happy Daze are on the basic side, the catering arrangements are most definitely not. A large selection of hot and cold food, all beautifully prepared, served in notoriously big portions. Liz looks at the menu and is staggered, barely believing the wide choice of different meals available. "Well, who would have thought this?" she says, "Everything and anything near enough. Good heavens."

She glances across at a neighbouring table where a middle aged couple are both enjoying a large plate of salad each. "Well, we won't go hungry this week, that's for sure," she laughs.

The waiter comes over to take their order, a young ginger haired Irishman by the name of Barnaby Walsh. He's wearing pristine kitchen-whites, and a pale blue bandana.

"What'll it be," he says in his strong Dublin brogue.

The family all make their choices and Barnaby swiftly disappears to the kitchens. No more than five minutes after ordering he reappears with the meals requested. Liz has ordered spaghetti and meatballs, and this appears in a huge round bowl piled high, with a large basket of garlic bread. Just looking at this massive feast over-faces her. For Colin, his Shepherd's Pie covers almost half a large platter, while four different vegetables make up the remainder. An enormous gravy-boat appears with this. The childrens meals are a little smaller, which Liz is glad of. It's bad enough she'll not manage all of her own meal, she didn't really want this replicated across the others as well. She wonders how much waste food the place must get lumbered with.

The fish fingers, chips and beans for Jamie, and the two slightly smaller plates of Shepherd's Pie for the girls, are more like the size of portions that Liz would prefer. She makes a mental note to ask for a smaller meal next time.

Just as they begin to tuck in, an all too familiar voice can be heard booming across the dining hall.

"I have a complaint to make, young man," shouts Trevor

Maynard in Barnaby's direction, to the embarrassment of the rest of his family, aside from Muriel who is seemingly unconcerned as usual. "I am not going to get fat on these tiny morsels," he moans at the top of his voice.

Liz looks at her own massive bowl of spaghetti and accompanying bread basket, and can't believe anyone had been served less. She also recalls him saying something about having fish and chips. 'Surely he can't be hungry already unless they didn't bother,' she thinks.

Barnaby is giving Trevor as good as he's currently getting. "Now listen here sir," he says, forcefully, "You have had the same sized portions as everyone else, and nothing less. Usually we have folk saying we over feed them, not the other extreme. I am not allowed to bring you or anyone else a second main meal."

"How dare you," shouts Trevor, as the rest of the dining room stare in horror, "I'm a paying customer, and the customer is always right, so run along little boy and bring me another one of these."

"I will do no such thing, now if you want a pudding that is fine, but you've had your main meal and won't be getting another," insists Barnaby. Trevor is now on his feet, looking like he is about to grab poor Barnaby by the throat.

"Sit down dad, for pities sake, stop showing us up," pleads Christy.

"Not until I'm brought another dinner," snarls Trevor, nastily, "Come on, I'm waiting, bring me one." No one in the room can quite believe what they are seeing and hearing; what an obnoxious man, using bully-boy tactics to gain extra meals he's not entitled to.

By the doorway, welcoming guests into the dining hall, is Chief Seasider Marissa Black, also from Ireland, and as such very protective of Barnaby. She hears the rumpus and swiftly leaves her post by the main entrance.

"It's ok Barnaby, I'll sort this, go and serve some others," she says. Barnaby is quietly glad Marissa has his back, in the face of this needless tirade. "Now what appears to be the problem Mr Maynard?" asks Marissa, as Barnaby scurries away.

"What's the problem?" shouts Trevor, "The food in here, that's the problem, not enough to keep a gnat alive and you know it."

"Shut up dad, these plates are massive, don't talk stupid," says Christy, struggling to finish her plateful of lamb casserole.

"But I pay to stay here, so if I want extra portions then that is my right," he replies. The irony of that statement isn't lost on any of the others, knowing fine well he never stumps up a single penny.

"No one is getting extra portions," states Marissa, "One meal per person, per sitting, nothing else."

"That's bloody outrageous," splutters Trevor, "It barely touched the sides." Looking at his wide girth, Marissa doesn't doubt this, but is happy to stick to the rules.

"It's still only one per person, so if you will please sit down Mr Maynard, and stop disrupting everyone else."

She heads back to the main entrance, just as other holidaymakers are arriving for dinner. Finally defeated, Trevor sits back down.

"Why do you have to make a show of us like that, dad," says Christy.

"Yes, Trevor, no need for all that," says Eunice, herself struggling to finish an oversized bowl of minestrone soup.

Johanna sits quietly, enjoying her childrens sized portion of salad, but as embarrassed as everyone else at her fathers' rude behaviour. She looks out of the window and sees Johnny walking past, making his way down to 'Peyton's Pavilion' where he is appearing in a family stage show that evening. Her heart quickens at the sight of her handsome crush, and she blushes slightly, while hoping no one else noticed.

Chapter Four

Prior to making his way to the Pavilion, Johnny had somewhere else he desperately needed to be.

A few weeks into his job as a Seasider, thanks to the unforgiving hours and non-stop hard work, he was at the point of total collapse, all but ready to tell Louis to shove his job, and head straight back home to Olivia and the kids. Completely shattered, he'd had enough. He confided in Alun Williams, telling his fellow Seasider of his plans to quit, that he couldn't keep up the brutal pace, and that the non-stop exhaustion was getting far too much for him to bear.

Alun quickly had an answer for this, eagerly telling him how he got through the tiring shifts and massive workload. "Go and see Bo-Bo," he told him. Robert 'Bo-Bo' Boston runs a small bookmakers on the first floor of the large entertainments building in the centre of the park.

Bo-Bo has a very shady past indeed. He was employed as the manager of Louis Peyton's new 'Betting Lounge' at the start of the previous season, on the back of a heavily doctored CV crammed full of untruths.

He duped Louis into thinking he'd been a successful Rails Bookmaker, who had sold prestigious pitches at numerous racecourses for a tidy profit. Nothing could be further from the truth. He did frequent the races, but as a failed punter, squandering all his money on useless tips, and running up huge gambling debts with those stupid enough to fall for his 'Here's my hand, here's my heart' routine when requesting credit for wagers.

Once the debts were starting to be called in, Bo-Bo swiftly went to ground, setting up home with his new young wife in Portwynne where he knew no-one, and more importantly no-one knew him.

A less than vigilant Louis Peyton never bothered to check the false references, quickly drawn in by Bo-Bo's smooth patter, but at the same time was also desperate to get someone in, after being unable to fill the post of Betting Lounge Manager with only a few days to go until the park re-opened for the summer.

Ever since then, Louis has literally been taken for a ride, being financially screwed over by his employee, the daily figures constantly being manipulated, as Bo-Bo uses his dishonest nature to make a small fortune out of holiday makers unfortunate enough to lose their money in the Betting Lounge.

This big time money laundering is also supplemented by a neat line in drug pushing. Bo-Bo's air-headed wife, Krystal, currently works as a PA at a local medicine factory, 'Colviles Pharmaceuticals' where she is able to get her hands on tablets of any quantity, in return for certain 'favours'. Colviles Financial Director and their Head of Sales are the current recipients of her favours, in return for a plentiful supply of 'Colviles Uppers', a popular, but powerful prescription stimulant.

Bo-Bo sells these ill-gotten gains on for a princely sum to Peyton's frazzled staff, whilst turning a blind eye to his wife's extra-marital activity.

Alun tells Johnny about Uppers, how effective they are, and how these will resolve his lethargy, albeit for a price.

"I'm losing nothing by trying, I suppose," says Johnny "I'm not sure how much more I can take otherwise, this tiredness is killing me."

He paid Bo-Bo a visit, requesting a small supply of Uppers. £20 changed hands in return for half a dozen of these small yellow pills, with Bo-Bo telling Johnny in no uncertain terms to take no more than one at a time, and only if completely necessary, given their potency.

It wasn't long, however, before Johnny was taking several in one go, sometimes more than once a day, happy with the effect it had on him, his exhaustion a distant memory, but not realising he was slowly getting hooked in the process. Not that Bo-Bo cares, happily taking Johnny's money off him, despite the request for

Uppers now coming almost every single day.

Bo-Bo has already closed the betting lounge for the night, and is fiddling the paperwork and takings as he does every single day as a matter of routine. He chuckles to himself at the ease of being able to pocket anything up to £400 at a time, with Louis blindly assuming that the Betting Lounge is ticking over fine, and not realising that if it was run honestly this enterprise would actually be one of his biggest sources of revenue.

Johnny softly knocks on the door. Bo-Bo freezes for second, wondering who is there. Lately, Elvis Mansfield had been taking a closer than usual eye on proceedings, and Bo-Bo is bothered he may share any suspicions he might have with Louis. "Who is it?" he calls out.

"It's me, Johnny," comes the reply.

Bo-Bo lets out a large sigh of relief, happy that it's not Louis' minder sniffing around, but his best customer instead. He unlocks the door to let him inside.

"Can I have another half a dozen, if you've got them?" asks Johnny, as Bo-Bo locks the door behind him and strides back to the counter. Quantity is not a problem, as supply is plentiful. But the frequency that Johnny requests these tablets is becoming alarming, even for dishonest drug dealing Bo-Bo.

"Christ, Johnny, that other lot didn't last long," he says, recalling it was only the day before he bought his previous dozen Uppers.

"I'm stockpiling," lies Johnny, completely out of tablets already and panicking.

"Well, I've just had a new batch brought in, so yes you can have another six – but you know what I told you, no need to take any more than one at a time, strong stuff they are," implores Bo-Bo. He can tell that Johnny is completely addicted to Uppers, but is worried that if anyone found out about his ongoing dependency, and who was behind it, that would lead Louis straight to his door, and then his lucrative sideline, and his job, would quickly be snuffed out.

“I know, and I am careful, of course I am, but grateful for the pick me up,” confirms Johnny, a little sheepishly.

Bo-Bo opens the safe behind the counter, and quietly removes a false wall at the back behind which the pills are hidden. “There you go,” he says, “That’s twenty quid, Johnny.” The money and the box of tablets change hands.

“How’s business, then,” says Johnny, looking around, meaning the Betting Lounge, in an attempt to divert the talk away from drugs.

“Slow,” says Bo-Bo, untruthfully, “No money around, Johnny, it’s nothing short of dire in fact. No money around at all.” Many guests are more than happy to have a holiday flutter, trying to win extra spends for their stay, but predictably most of them end up losing more than they win. These profits should be in Louis Peytons bank account, instead it is being used to line Bo-Bo’s pockets.

He quickly hustles Johnny towards the door, keen to get back to cooking the books prior to a night out with Krystal, spending his stolen wealth.

Once Johnny is back outside, he immediately diverts to his chalet, swallows another three Uppers and sets about his nights work.

After their eventful evening meal, the Chesters family make their way down to 'Peyton’s Pavilion', a large theatre complex at the front of the leisure park in the shape of a marquee, for the nights show. There is a full page spread devoted to 'Peyton’s Family Showtime, starring Johnny Major and the Seasiders' in the events programme, and they are all looking forward to this performance. The theatre foyer is busy, some folks are heading towards the auditorium and others are grabbing quick refreshment at a large bar area, packed with people.

It's an hour before the show, so Colin and Liz opt to get a round of drinks and sit around a table in a specially cordoned off area for families. After this, the five of them go into the theatre, wondering if they could get seats all together. They're unlucky, as the place is already heaving with people. Best they can do is three seats directly behind two others. Colin, Liz and Charlotte sit behind Eleanor and Jamie, about half way back.

The Maynards, minus Christy and Muriel who have gone off to play bingo instead, will be sat three rows from the front. Trevor had sent Johanna, Mikey and Karl on ahead to ensure their 'usual' seats in the theatre were saved, to the annoyance of others wanting to sit near the front, wanting to know how these children are getting away with putting cardigans and bags on eight seats in the same row.

A complaint from an elderly woman with poor eyesight, thus needing a seat as near the front as possible, didn't get far once the person she complained to, Seasider Alun, recognised Johanna and decided the fuss Trevor would make if he found his seats occupied was worth finding the lady alternative seating instead, politely asking two youngsters on the front row if they would kindly make way for a partially sighted lady. They quickly agree to move to allow the lady and her husband to sit down.

Trevor and the others turn up at the Pavilion with less than five minutes to go until the performance. The Chesters' don't notice them striding down the aisle past them as the lights in the auditorium have been lowered, and the orchestra at the front is already striking up.

Colin looks down towards the stage while quietly reflecting on his own career in entertainment, over 20 years appearing in venues just like this one. For a moment he wishes he was back there, memories flooding back of a summer season in Blackpool almost a decade before, where Liz was managing a show he appeared in. It was during that unforgettable season that they first got together, getting married early the following year. Such precious memories, he thinks, looking at pretty Liz sat alongside him.

She turns to face him, and smiles knowingly. "Do you miss all this, the performing?" she asks.

One look at Liz, Charlotte next to her, and Eleanor and Jamie in front is all it takes. "I don't, and I wouldn't go back to performing full time for all the money in the world," he smiles, "I love you and the kids too much, the thought of being away for months on end doing what Johnny does now fills me with dread. I couldn't be any happier with the life I have now."

Liz smiles fondly, glad that they were prudent enough to have put enough away to not have to worry about making ends meet. In recent months Colin had been offered gigs after-dinner speaking thanks to a contact who runs a local business, and these have been lucrative. Two of these engagements a month is more than enough to provide a decent standard of living for the family.

The curtains open to reveal six scantily clad dancers in feather head-dresses, cavorting across the stage enthusiastically. Just like Johnny's television show, remembers Liz. She's not wrong. When Louis Peyton invited Johnny to work at Happy Daze it was on the proviso that a show almost identical to 'Johnny's Variety Showcase' would be performed. 20 million viewers can't be wrong, insisted Louis.

Indeed, in a recent interview with him in a local Pembrokeshire paper Louis was quite forthright in his condemnation of what he called 'television for the brain dead', as the expensive and extravagant television variety shows of the 60s and 70s, were being quickly replaced with cheaper versions. "Come and see the real thing at my leisure park," he went on to say.

The man sat the other side of Colin nudges him. "Look at them smashers on there," he says, suggestively.

Colin nods, out of politeness not agreement. He looks across at the man's wife, not too unattractive herself, and wonders how any man could prefer the dancers to their own partner. He holds

Liz's hand protectively, knowing he's never so much as looked twice at another woman since he fell in love with her at first sight, across a television studio floor ten years before.

The dance routine ends to loud cheers and wild applause, as they split down the middle to allow Johnny, in his trademark white tie and tails, to bound onto the stage. A very talented dancer in his own right, he took up performing in the local Working Mens clubs in South Wales in the 1950s, having been inspired by the likes of Fred Astaire and Gene Kelly.

The audience continue to cheer enthusiastically, as this instantly recognisable star starts one of his well-known routines.

Johanna is quickly taking a mental snapshot, excitedly planning the next drawing of her favourite subject. She smiles up at him adoringly, but due to the bright lights Johnny is unable to see past the front row, although he appears to be looking at the whole audience as he dances about, theatrically. As far as Johanna is concerned there is only her and Johnny there, as she daydreams.

He bursts into song halfway through his routine, and again this is enthusiastically received. His opening number alongside the other dancers is wrapped up in spectacular style, as he is lifted shoulder high by the two tallest of them. Everyone cheers loudly as he's gently placed back on the stage, while coming to the front to give an extravagant bow.

As the cheering dies down something completely unexpected happens. He gets heckled. "Load of old cobblers this, bloody rubbish," shouts Trevor Maynard, to the horror of not only the rest of his family, but the whole of the theatre, not understanding how such a talented performer could be shouted at so unkindly for no reason at all.

Johnny glares in the general direction of the nuisance maker, although unable to see exactly who the culprit is due to the bright spotlights. Johanna is devastated that her father could be so nasty towards the man of her dreams.

"Pack it in our Trevor," hisses his mother Eunice, sat two

seats away from him, "No need for any of that."

"Every need, load of old twaddle," he repeats, "No wonder he's not on telly no more, best thing they ever did was cancel his show."

Johanna wants to burst into tears, believing that Johnny will now totally shun them all for the remainder of the week, unaware he can't actually see who the heckler is. Alun Williams strides purposefully across to where the Maynards are sat.

"If the show is not to your liking Mr Maynard," he states, "The exit is that way." He points up towards the back of the auditorium.

"You what? I paid good money for this holiday, if the entertainment isn't up to scratch I should be allowed to say so," insists Trevor.

Rodney, who doesn't usually challenge anything his father says, quickly speaks up as he can see his wife Sandra rolling her eyes, knowing Trevor hasn't paid anything at all. "Sorry, Alun," he says leaning across, "Leave it out dad, you're making a prat of yourself, and showing us all up at the same time."

"Whatever happened to freedom of speech," retorts Trevor, as Johnny tries desperately to pick out were the trouble is coming from.

"Last chance Mr Maynard, I don't want to have to eject you," implores Alun. Trevor sees no choice, doesn't fancy being thrown out, so elects to keep quiet.

As the moment passes, Alun returns to the front, puts his thumb up to Johnny to state all is now well, and the show can continue.

Liz looks down towards where the Maynards are sat, quite a bit nearer the front than them. She can't quite see them but can pick out Trevor’s voice anywhere. "How can one person cause so much disruption," she whispers to Colin, "Ridiculous."

Colin shakes his head. He recalls having any number of put downs for the drunken hecklers he sometimes had to deal with, and wishes Johnny could have found a witticism of his own to stop the mouthy Midlander in his tracks. "We've only been here a few hours," whispers Liz again, "And he's done enough to make me want to go home already."

Colin puts his arm around Liz's shoulders reassuringly. "He's probably had too much to drink, Lizzy," he says, "He won't be that brave if Johnny comes looking for him afterwards."

The show starts again with Johnny cheerfully telling the audience how hard the Seasiders have been practising their various talents to bring them a top class hour and a half of entertainment. And so it was, with various acts being performed. Marissa Black turns out to be a very talented singer, two male Seasiders put on a Laurel and Hardy routine, which goes down very well. Three female Seasiders perform a medley of 60's girl-group songs. All in all, a very entertaining show, and as the grand finale takes place with Johnny, the dancers and the other performers taking a bow, all memories of the earlier interruption have been successfully banished.

The Chesters' leave the Pavilion in good spirits, having all enjoyed the show immensely. Still finding their way about, they look around for the Family Centre, the main entertainment building. The Maynards also leave at the same time, but in a slightly less cheerful mood, fully aware that Trevor's unkind outburst spoiled the night not just for them, but for many others too. They meet up outside with Muriel and Christy, back from a losing night at the bingo, before splitting into two groups, with Trevor, Muriel and Eunice going over to the adult surroundings of the Jolly Roger, while the others head to the Family Centre.

Johanna is very down indeed, and her black mood doesn't go unnoticed by her older sister Christy. Once they are inside the Family Centre she takes Johanna over to one side.

"What's the matter, has something happened, you look upset?" she asks her, kindly, "You can tell me, you know."

Johanna gets a little tearful. "It was dad - don't say anything

Christy, please," she begs.

"Of course I won't, but what did he do?" demands Christy.

"He started shouting at Johnny, while he was on the stage," says Johanna, struggling to hold her tears back.

"Unbelievable, what the hell for?" says an exasperated Christy.

"Said his act was rubbish, and he was glad it was cancelled off the telly," replies Johanna, as a tear escapes.

"Oh no," says Christy, giving her clearly distraught sister a hug, "Johnny means a lot to you, doesn't he, don't think I haven't realised, you know." Not once had Johanna mentioned her secret crush to anyone, and can't understand how Christy has guessed. More tears fall, as she nods. "Hey, it's ok, I won't say anything," confirms Christy, "He is very nice looking though, no getting away from it."

"He doesn't take any notice of me," says Johanna, glumly.

"Well, he's busy all the time isn't he, and there's lots of other people for him to speak to, he can't notice everyone," replies Christy, while seeing over Johanna's shoulder that Johnny has arrived in his usual Seasiders outfit and that he's currently dancing with a very pretty lady to the sound of the Family Centres resident band, Dave Busby & Busbys Canyon.

She doesn't say anything to Johanna, instead leading her over to the table where the others are.

The Chesters family find a table, but decide they won't be staying late as Liz can already see that Jamie is getting tired.

Johnny, having finished his dance, comes over to Colin and Liz's table and pulls up a chair. "Hello everyone, did you come to the show?" he asks them, cheerfully. Liz wonders where the heck Johnny gets all his energy from, blissfully unaware that this is due to him currently being high on his latest overdose of Uppers.

"We did, great start to the week, well, except for your interruption of course," says Colin.

"Oh yes, him," says Johnny, frowning, "Who was it? Couldn't

see a damn thing from the stage, the lights were that bright."

Liz wonders whether she should pretend she doesn't know, as she sees Colin glance across at her. She decides it's best to be truthful. "Some chap from Birmingham, think I heard your mate call him Mr Maynard?" recalls Liz, "Actually, I think he may be in the next chalet to us or nearby, I saw some other girls who were with him when we went back before."

"Maynard?" says Johnny, knowing the name from somewhere, but having only met the family briefly on their last visit, and having spoken to thousands of others in the meantime can't bring him to mind, "Nah, can't picture him, never mind."

Colin has a word of advice. "Next time you get a pillock like that shouting you down give 'em this, works every time. 'Sorry mate, I can't understand what you're saying, I'm not a native Moron speaker.'"

Johnny laughs heartily. "I'll remember that one, cheers Col. Anyway, while I'm here, I wonder if your charming eldest daughter would like to dance with me."

Charlotte blushes profusely, but manages to nod her head in affirmation. Johnny employs this tactic of inviting those who he believes are the 'pretty' ones up to dance, as he thinks it keeps the plain ones from bothering him. Charlotte gets up and is soon being spun around the floor.

Back at their own table, Johanna looks across sadly as Johnny is dancing with Charlotte, wishing it was her. Christy can read Johanna’s mind, knowing fine well it will never happen, having only ever seen Johnny dancing with the best looking ladies. As Trevor and Muriel never allow Johanna to wear make-up or the latest fashions then she will always miss out, thinks Christy unhappily, wishing she could get her hands on the five hundred pounds that would help transform her younger sister’s life.

A flushed Charlotte returns to the table, unable to stop smiling. "Did you enjoy that?" asks Liz, feeling very happy for her.

"Oh, that was amazing mum," says Charlotte, "Lucky old

me!"

Liz spots Jamie almost falling asleep at the table, so they quickly drain their glasses and decide to head back to the chalet. Before they get halfway there, Charlotte has a suggestion. "Look, it's still quite early," she says, as she looks at her watch reading just gone half past nine, "I can take care of Jamie and Eleanor, why don't you two go and have a drink somewhere, have a bit of time to yourselves."

Colin smiles at Liz, rather liking the idea. And as they have left the two youngest in the care of their older sister on numerous occasions, there are no concerns whatsoever. "Ok, but only if you're sure," says Liz, smiling.

"It's fine, mum, we'll see you later," says Charlotte, as the three of them go back to Primrose Block.

Colin and Liz turn around and head hand in hand back towards the centre of the park, in the direction of the Jolly Roger.

Liz spots the now more than familiar frame of Trevor Maynard as soon as they walk through the doors. "Oh, let's go somewhere else," she moans, "He's the last person I want to see." Colin knows the only other place to go would be the Family Centre they just came from, but wanting to be amongst grown-ups in a proper bar, not somewhere playing cheesy pop music to keep children entertained, decides otherwise.

"Ignore him, he doesn't know us, let's get a drink," he says, striding towards the bar, wanting nothing more than a quiet hour or so with his beloved wife before going back to the chalet.

Unfortunately, they are spotted by Muriel who is quick to shout up. "Look who it is, that comedian chappy again," she says, loudly.

"Oh yeah, so it is," says Trevor, equally as loud.

Colin turns, and nods politely before turning back to pay for, and collect, his and Liz's drinks off the bar. What he hears next, however, takes him completely by surprise. "Pity it wasn't you in that show, bloody good comic you were as I remember," states

Trevor, "You didn't need to dance round like a fairy, like that Welsh pouffe."

"Thanks," says Colin over his shoulder, while Liz is looking for an empty table in what seems to be a very busy bar.

"Come and sit with us," shouts Trevor, "Plenty of room here, it's alright."

Liz is less than keen, wanting to spend some precious time alone with her husband, and not in the company of strangers. By the look of it though almost every other table is fully occupied, leaving Colin and Liz with little choice, so they take two stools around the same table as Trevor, Muriel and Eunice.

To Liz's surprise the Maynards come across as quite normal, not the boorish loudmouths they've been so far. Colin and Trevor chat happily about comedy and football, while Liz asks Muriel and Eunice about activities to do during their stay at Happy Daze.

Whilst they are all deep in conversation, Johanna appears to let the others know her and the rest of the family are going back to the chalets. Liz looks up in astonishment. There are signs pinned up all around the walls stating 'Adults Only After 7pm', 'surely this young girl is no older than Eleanor,' she thinks, completely unaware Johanna is actually a grown up woman.

"Alright bab," says Trevor, "We'll be right with ya, I'm just finishing this pint off." He notices Liz looking quizzically, as Johanna goes back outside. "It's ok, love," he says, "She is old enough to be in here, just got a thing about wearing dolls clothes, just a fad." Liz doesn't know what part of that, if any, is true.

Having mentioned to the Maynards that she and Colin are neighbours, all five of them make their way back to Primrose Block together, saying a cheery goodnight on the front. Once back inside they discover that although Jamie is in bed, the girls are still up talking. Just as well, as the squeaky front door probably would have woken them up in any case. After telling them to put the light out and go to sleep, Colin and Liz go to their own room, with the two of them looking in on a snoring Jamie beforehand.

As they lie in bed together, they reflect on a very eventful first day in Portwynne. "What a strange day that was," whispers Liz, mindful of what look like paper thin walls.

"I know," Colin whispers back, "I'm certain the rest of the week will be quite normal though, in fact I'm sure of it." He kisses Liz lovingly, with the idea of a quiet but amorous end to the day.

The second he makes a meaningful move towards her though the barely-there mattress and thinly sprung bedframe make such a loud squeaking noise that they both guess it would be heard throughout their chalet and probably the whole of Primrose Block.

The idea of intimacy is swiftly abandoned, to their mutual frustration.

Chapter Five

Sunday morning, and the sun is high in the sky once again, promising a very hot summers day.

Johnny is making a quick call to Olivia in the telephone box at the end of the staff chalet line. He's a little upset that she didn't come to Happy Daze with their children this weekend, but as it had been her Mothers birthday she had elected to spend Saturday with her instead.

"Livvy? It's me, are you ok, how are the kids?" he says down the phone.

"Everyone is fine," states a less than enthusiastic Olivia, trying to smother a yawn. It's got to the stage where she couldn't care less whether she hears from Johnny or not, having got used to him not being around. She's extremely frustrated at not being able to have the opulent lifestyle she had got used to when Johnny was earning five star wages, and also the one person who warned him at the height of his fame not to be complacent, that he should consider modernising his act, that one day the viewers, or the producers, may get a little weary of his song-and-dance man performance.

He didn't listen, and the axe eventually fell.

As much as she loves being a mum to their three children, not having a nanny to fall back on for respite any more also gets her down. To her mind it's all Johnny's fault for not re-inventing himself, while not considering the fact that having his show cancelled was more down to the new hierarchy at NWTV, and not because of something he did wrong.

His show still was still attracting millions of viewers when it ended.

"I missed seeing you all yesterday, did Gladys have a nice birthday?" replies Johnny.

"Yes, it was a lovely afternoon, pity you couldn't be with us, Johnny," says Olivia, sneeringly.

"Oh, don't start all that again, I can't just down tools on a Saturday afternoon can I," he moans.

Olivia looks disinterestedly out of the window, can hear their three sons noisily playing outside. 'Don't know why he bothers ringing' she thinks, while drawing on a cigarette. She simply isn't interested in her husband any more, and wants to call time on their marriage. Recently, she has been enjoying the attentions of her young next door neighbour, Rory, with neither Johnny nor Rory's fiancée aware of their illicit romps.

"Well, everything is going ok here, well almost everything," says Johnny, "I got heckled while I was on stage last night."

It's all Olivia can do not to laugh out loud. "That's awful," says Olivia, with a sly smirk on her face, meaning nothing of the sort.

Johnny can tell this conversation quickly appears to be going nowhere. "Are you sure you're alright?" he asks, a little concerned.

"I'm fine, I told you, stop going on will you," she replies.

"Look, I'll be down on Monday, about lunchtime," says Johnny.

"Oh yes, of course, you can't be here all day, thanks to that slave driver you work for," spits Olivia. Louis Peyton is notorious for getting work out of his staff even on their day off. Johnny has to attend a weekly meeting with his boss prior to being able to get away.

"I can't help that," insists Johnny, "Look, I know working here isn't ideal, Livvy, and I would much rather be at home with you and the kids all the time, but without this job I don't know what we'd do."

Olivia is gazing out of the window again, barely listening as she can see her young lover over the fence, mowing his lawn.

"Are you still there, Livvy?" asks Johnny.

"Yes, I'm here," says Olivia, putting her cigarette out and wanting to get off the telephone, "But I've got to go now, I promised the boys I'd take them to the park before lunch."

Johnny feels guilty, knowing he should be there taking them out himself. He glances around at the leisure park, wondering if this job is really worth sacrificing his marriage for.

Despite it being his day off, Elvis is interrupted by an early morning phone call from Louis, whilst trying to rustle up some breakfast in his flat above one of the many amusement arcades on Portwynne promenade. Elvis of course could stay in one of the staff chalets on the camp for free, but knowing how, in his opinion, 'downright dangerous' some of them are, and how little Louis does to rectify matters, prefers to rent out this small one bedroomed abode instead.

"Morning Elvis," says Louis down the wire.

"Morning boss," replies Elvis, trying to keep his eye on his frying pan of eggs and bacon while stuck on the telephone, "What can I do for you?"

"I'm a bit worried," says Louis, a little quietly. The previous day he had been at one of his other leisure parks, and had not been dropped back at his South Wales mansion until late. As such, he had a large brandy and went straight to bed, ignoring a small pile of letters that had been posted through his door. Now he is going through this correspondence, and one letter in particular has caught his eye. An anonymous correspondent, someone who claimed to have spent a recent holiday at Happy Daze, making accusations that most of the Seasiders and other staff are on drugs, being peddled by someone else employed there. Nothing more than that, but for Louis more than a little alarming.

He reads this letter to Elvis, who by this time has to briefly leave the phone to stop his breakfast from spoiling.

"Why would someone make these spurious claims?" splutters Louis, unaware that his employees are being worked to the point of meltdown due to the long hours, compounded by his tactic of getting them to do a small shift on their designated day off as well.

Elvis is no fool, doesn't doubt the information for one minute and, ironically, would put money on where any drugs have come from. With no concrete proof however, he can't rightly mention Bo-Bo's name in all this, aware that foolish Louis trusts him, believing him to be a successful businessman like himself, and not a lying, sneaky, charlatan, who has been mugging him for months.

"What did you want me to do, boss?" asks Elvis, while seeing his eggs and bacon starting to go cold.

"Put some discreet feelers out, speak to Marissa, or Johnny, or anyone, see if they know anything or if they have heard any rumours, if it is true it's probably the younger members of staff I would imagine," states Louis.

Elvis rolls his eyes, suspecting if anyone is taking drugs it's the going to be the older ones to keep them from all out exhaustion. "Will do boss," he replies, happy to comply.

"There's probably no truth in it," says deluded Louis, "Probably someone from a rival holiday company trying to dig non-existent dirt." Unbeknown to him the letter is from an ex-employee of Colviles, recently made redundant by them, acting on a grievance and inside information.

Back at Happy Daze, Colin and Liz get up, after a restless night thanks to the noisy bedframe, to find the others already awake. Charlotte is outside on the landing chatting to Johanna, who is patiently waiting for the rest of her family to be ready for breakfast. Johanna keeps nervously looking over her shoulder, knowing that Trevor and Muriel would not approve of her making a new friend, but has quickly decided she likes Charlotte enough to take the risk.

"So, how old are you?" asks Charlotte kindly, believing her to be no older than 12 year old Eleanor.

Johanna takes a deep breath. "21," she admits quietly. Charlotte can't believe her ears. "Don't say anything, please,"

Johanna whispers.

"I won't, of course I won't, but why do you dress like this then? It's the sort of stuff my little sister wears," says Charlotte, casting her eye over Johanna's t-shirt with Snoopy and Woodstock on the front.

Johanna starts to get a little emotional. She can tell immediately that Charlotte can be trusted, so quietly continues. "My parents are very controlling, I don't have any choice," she states. Charlotte recalls how Trevor had behaved in the dining hall and at the theatre, and isn't altogether surprised.

"But surely if you're 21 surely you can get away from them?" asks Charlotte.

"No chance, they account for every penny of my wages the second I get them," Johanna replies.

"That's dreadful," says Charlotte, feeling very sorry for her.

Trevor and Muriel come out of chalet 115. They both glare at Charlotte nastily, while quickly scurrying Johanna away, with Eunice following close behind. Charlotte looks on, shaking her head in astonishment before going back inside, happy to keep Johanna's secrets to herself.

"What is she like then, your new friend," smiles Liz.

"She's ok, seems very nice," replies Charlotte, giving nothing more away for now.

Like most things in the life of the Maynards, another day of routine beckons. Trevor, Muriel, Eunice and Johanna going off for the very early breakfast sitting, to allow the three elders to go straight back to Primrose Block and their beds afterwards, while waiting for the Jolly Roger to open its doors at noon.

All of this gives Johanna a precious few hours to herself, which she is grateful for. Having checked the events programme, it states that Johnny will be on the big sports field with the other Seasiders, co-ordinating a sports event, along the line of a school sports day, where youngsters up to the age of 12 are invited to compete against others their own age in running races, obstacle courses and other events. As she will be with the other family members, neither Trevor or Muriel think anything of this or prevent her from going, more bothered about a lazy lie in ahead of another afternoons beer.

A large crowd has quickly formed on the sports field, with many families keen for their children to take part in the mornings events, and there is a table with certificates and small gold trophies on for the winners of each race.

Johanna deliberately stays as far away as possible from the main group of people, sitting down on the grass where she can get a good view of Johnny without being disturbed by anyone else. She gets out her sketch book ready to draw her latest picture of him, having already completed one of him in last night's stage-wear while she was sat in her bed the night before, unable to sleep as Trevor and Muriel's snores were resonating loudly throughout the chalet.

On this morning he's in sportswear, a polo shirt in the same light blue colour as his Seasiders blazer, and a pair of white shorts and trainers. The other Seasiders are similarly dressed, and are busily directing the children and their parents to where they need to be, putting their names down for the various activities that are taking place.

Johnny can be seen chattering happily with Liz and Eleanor, who at just three weeks short of her 13th birthday is one of the oldest children taking part. Very quickly Johanna gets her pens out and starts to draw, first Johnny, then little Eleanor. It doesn't take Johanna long to draw Johnny, having done numerous caricatures of him before, so each one getting easier and quicker to complete. She concentrates more on Eleanor, making sure that the picture is as realistic as possible, preserving her precious memories.

Barnaby Walsh is making his way back to his staff chalet after completing his duties serving breakfasts. He decides to take a shortcut across the sports field, and looks across at the large crowd of people gathered there. He notices Johanna sitting on her own, while wondering why she isn't with them, entering the races herself. Like most others who don't know any different he assumes she is no older than 12 or 13. He spots that she seems to be drawing something in a book, so to be nosey he hovers quietly behind her, looking over her shoulder, wondering what she's doing.

Johanna is concentrating that hard she is totally unaware she is being watched at such close quarters. Barnaby can't believe his eyes, looking at the drawing of an instantly recognisable Johnny. 'Did she really draw that?' he wonders in amazement. Seeing her busily sketching the child Johnny is speaking to confirms she definitely did.

He can't keep his thoughts to himself any longer, these pictures are genius. "Wow!" he proclaims out loud, causing Johanna to almost jump ten feet in the air with the shock.

She quickly abandons her portrait of Eleanor and stows her book and pens back in her bag. "What do you think you're doing?" she asks, extremely flustered, "Sneaking up on me, you shouldn't do that."

"Sorry, love," says a slightly sheepish Barnaby, knowing it would have been polite of him to make his presence known, "But those pictures are incredible, how do you draw like that?"

"You haven't seen anything," protests intensely private Johanna, looking at the grass, blushing.

"Don't talk daft, love," says Barnaby, kindly, "I've never seen drawings like it, I can tell that was Johnny straightaway."

"It's a secret, you didn't see anything, ok?" implores Johanna.

"Ok, but why hide your talent away like that, what do your schoolteachers say, they must be aware how good you are?" he replies, unknowingly.

"I'm not at school anymore," confirms Johanna, leaving Barnaby to scratch his head, not quite understanding. "I'm 21, if you must know, I have a full time job, I draw when I have free time, but it's a secret," she goes on, "Happy now?"

Barnaby's chin almost hits the floor. 21? She can't be a year older than me, he thinks, well I never did. "Oh, sorry, I thought you were younger, I didn't realise," he says.

"It's alright, everyone else thinks the same," replies Johanna, unable to bring herself to look at him.

He sits down on the grass beside her. "Well, your secrets would be safe with me," says Barnaby, "Can I see those drawings again? Please? I won't tell anyone, I promise."

He seems safe enough, thinks Johanna. "Ok then, but you mustn't tell anyone, if my parents found out they'd take my pens and book off me, and throw them away," she says, gloomily.

Barnaby thinks this is extremely strange, given she's 21 years of age. He then remembers who her parents are, and suddenly things start to fall into place.

She gets her sketch book out again and shows him her latest pictures, while not letting the book out of her hands. "You are really, really talented," says Barnaby, "but forgive me for asking, and you don't have to tell me, but are your folks really as strict as all that?" He casts his eyes over Johanna's t-shirt, her child-like baggy shorts and scraped back pony tail.

She sighs. "Yes, they are," she admits, "I'm only here now because they've gone back to the chalet for a sleep until the pub opens."

"That's terrible, do they make you wear these clothes?" asks Barnaby. Johanna nods sadly, as he looks at her drawings in awe. "These are incredible, thank you for sharing them," he smiles, "I won't mention anything to anyone, but you really shouldn't hide these away you know. I bet Johnny would be thrilled to see them."

A sudden gust of wind blows the pages of the book over quickly, displaying a drawing that Johanna had no intention of ever showing anyone. Once again it's a lifelike caricature of Johnny in a top hat and tails, this time in a dance-pose with the flame haired model that Johanna draws in her own image.

The model is wearing a striking gold and green ball gown, with a dark green bodice. Barnaby can barely speak at the sight of this intimate portrait. “Oh my god,” he splutters, as Johanna looks at the ground in horror, hands trembling. No one was ever supposed to see this. “Who’s the redhead? She’s so lifelike, she must be real!”

Johanna cannot bear to reveal the truth. “I copied her out of a magazine, don’t know who she is,” she lies, fearing Barnaby would probably ridicule her if he knew the redhead was supposed to be her.

“Blimey, I wouldn’t mind seeing her in real life,” smiles Barnaby, immensely taken with Johanna’s drawing.

Johanna turns the pages back again, and starts to put the finishing touches to her portrait of Eleanor, as Barnaby continues to look on. A loud cheer can be heard in the distance as the first of the running races is taking place. Barnaby gets to his feet. "I won’t disturb you any longer, erm," he says, remembering he doesn't know her name.

"Johanna," she confirms.

"I'm Barnaby, perhaps I'll see you later on?" he replies.

"Yes, probably, goodbye Barnaby," says Johanna.

He strides off towards his chalet after an almost surreal five minutes.

At the other end of the sports field, Liz and Charlotte are busy cheering on Eleanor, as she wins her running race against other 12 years old with ease. She comes back to them with a small gold cup and a certificate. "Look at this mum," she beams.

"Well done, Eleanor, clever you," says Liz, smiling, "Wait until your dad finds out." Colin and Jamie have spent the morning playing snooker in the camps Games Room, despite Liz insisting Jamie also take part in the races. Sadly, unless there is a football involved Jamie isn't remotely interested!

Eleanor is looking back over her shoulder where Marissa, Johnny and the other Seasiders are busily rounding up the next group of participants. "Mum, I want to be a Seasider!" she proclaims, smiling.

Liz laughs. "Whatever brought this on?" she asks.

"They have so much fun, look at them!" says Eleanor, enthusiastically, looking across at Johnny and the others smiling and laughing while going about their work.

"They also have very long days, and hardly ever get home to see their families," says Liz, putting a realistic spin on things, not wanting her 12 year old step daughter getting any big ideas.

"So what, that’s nothing, I can cope with that, it’ll be easy," smiles Eleanor, while staring intently at Marissa who is currently holding hands with Mikey and Karl, taking them to the start of the obstacle course.

"Oh, I don't doubt it," replies Liz, trying to lead her away, with difficulty.

“Oh mum, can’t we stay a bit longer,” pleads Eleanor, looking back.

“No!” states Liz, forcefully. They go off to find the missing males, ahead of an afternoon on Portwynne beach.

Standing nearby are Rodney, Sandra, Christy and Neil, all there to cheer on the twins as they complete the obstacle race, neither of them winning. They saw Johanna sitting away from everyone else, but weren't able to make out what she was doing, neither did they notice when Barnaby was keeping her company. Christy looks at her watch and sees it’s 5 minutes to 12. Looking up she can see Trevor, Muriel and Eunice ambling up, with Johanna who saw them coming behind them in pursuit.

As the large party heads off towards the Jolly Roger, Alun and Marissa are stood nearby watching. They start giggling and muttering about 'Wagon Train', as the Maynards disappear into the distance.

Elvis arrives at the front gates of Happy Daze just after noon, knowing that trying to get information out of senior Seasiders would most likely be a fruitless pursuit. Even if they were aware of drugs being peddled, he believes they won't tell him in fear of their jobs, with them knowing anything they admit to would be fed back to Louis at the earliest opportunity.

First place he heads for is the cafeteria, knowing that by this time of day some of the Seasiders will be getting a quick bite to eat before the afternoons events. By the time he arrives, only Johnny is left there. Elvis suspects if anyone is taking drugs it may be him, remembering how run down he had been after only a short while in his job, then all of a sudden he's dashing around all over the leisure park with boundless energy. He approaches him, and takes a seat across from where Johnny is busily finishing a sandwich.

"Hello there, Johnny," smiles Elvis.

"Afternoon, Elvis, how are you?" Johnny replies, cheerfully, "Everything ok?"

"Yes, and no," says Elvis, lowering his voice, "I'm after some information, in complete confidence."

"Sure, how can I help?" asks Johnny, unsuspecting.

"Louis has been sent an anonymous letter, someone telling him there's drugs on the site, have you heard or seen anything?" says Elvis, trying to read the answer from Johnny's face.

Johnny tries not to panic, or give anything away. Instead he gives a nervous, giggle. "Drugs?" he says, "Don't think so, unless it's some of them youngsters, all night partying – I was wondering how they did it, could be that I suppose, I really don't know."

Elvis can tell immediately that Johnny is definitely covering up something, given his nervous and vague answer. "Any idea where they might be getting the drugs from, if it's true?" he asks, holding his breath.

"I really have no idea, I don't know anything, I was only speculating," says Johnny, again a little unconvincingly, now wishing Elvis would clear off.

"Ok, then," replies Elvis, "Not to worry in that case, but please keep a watch out will you, Louis would be grateful." He gets up to go, as a sweating Johnny breathes a massive sigh of relief.

Next, Elvis needs to track down Marissa. This is a little more awkward, as Elvis and Marissa are currently in a serious relationship, neither of them keen on Louis finding out as he has long forbidden any fraternising between his employees. If he knew two of his most loyal staff were sleeping together, they have no doubt that Marissa would be quickly sent packing to a different Peytons Leisure Park miles away, or even worse be sent back home to Ireland. The pair of them go to great lengths to ensure no-one else amongst the staff know either.

Elvis heads inside the Family Centre, remembering that she conducts a 'Mother & Baby' contest on a Sunday afternoon. He decides to get a beer and sit down near the front, where he can see Marissa addressing the largish crowd. She spots Elvis amongst the audience and smiles involuntarily. He grins adoringly back. 'Beautiful' he thinks, as Marissa cheerily invites this weeks contestants onto the dance floor.

Elvis knows that getting a few minutes of her time will be a tough ask, but is happy to wait.

Once all the Mothers have been spoken to, it's time for the judges to deliberate, and an opportunity for Marissa to go over to where Elvis is sat waiting.

"Wasn't expecting to see you until later," she smiles, "What a nice surprise!"

"Couldn't keep away," replies Elvis, mentally undressing her. Marissa blushes slightly, can always tell when Elvis has 'things' on his mind.

"I haven't got long," she says, trying not to make their mutual attraction too obvious to everyone else.

"I just needed a quick word, Louis has sent me if you must know," he confirms. Marissa looks slightly worried, hoping that their boss hasn't sussed out their ongoing relationship. "It's nothing much, it's just he's heard that there might be drugs on the site," confirms Elvis.

Marissa is fully aware, although doesn't partake herself. "Look, I can't talk about this now," she whispers, "I'll tell you later." They have already got an arrangement whereby Marissa will be going over to Elvis's flat for a short while immediately after her afternoon shift, and before her evening one.

She scurries back to the dance floor to wind up the contest.

Chapter Six

Portwynne forms a glorious part of the Pembrokeshire coastline, with its golden sands and clear blue sea. Along the promenade are a dozen brightly coloured beach huts, built there in a joint venture between Louis Peyton and the local council. Most of the owners of the huts are sat outside them, soaking up the sun.

On this very hot day the beach is completely packed, leaving the Chesters family with difficulty finding somewhere to sit. Eventually Liz finds a spot just big enough for two hired deckchairs for her and Colin, and two large beach-towels for the others. Charlotte takes Jamie off for a paddle, as Eleanor elects to sunbathe alongside her father and step mother.

Meanwhile, back at Happy Daze, Johanna has managed to get away from the rest of her family, wanting nothing more than a quiet afternoon at the beach with her sketchbook and her pens. When she stated she wanted to go out for a wander in the sunshine, Trevor quickly told her no. Neither him or Muriel are ever keen on Johanna going off on her own, never happy with her being out of their sight or away from the others, worried that one day she might decide to keep walking and not come back.

Christy tells her parents quietly she will follow Johanna at a safe distance, if that'll do. Trevor reluctantly agrees to Johanna's request. "Oh, alright then, but don't go far and come straight back, do you hear me?"

A delighted Johanna makes her way out of the Jolly Roger, with Christy a minute behind her.

Christy is assuming that Johanna is probably only going off to where Johnny happens to be, remembering on their previous visit that by the end of the week wherever he was Johanna was not far away. To her surprise though Johanna is heading straight for the front gates. Christy carries on following, wondering what her sister could possibly be up to. Hovering at a safe distance, she watches as Johanna does nothing more than sit on the wall that surrounds part of the beach completely unnoticed, as thousands of other people wander down the promenade behind her.

She quickly delves into her handbag for her book and pens, wanting to sketch a quick drawing of the beach huts, the beach itself, and the people on it. Christy looks across, wondering what on earth Johanna is doing. She finds it difficult to tell from distance, although she thinks she can see her scribbling something in a book. Perhaps she is writing a diary, thinks Christy, getting ready to leave, happy that Johanna will simply come back to the Jolly Roger when she's good and ready.

Just as she's about to walk off, however, Christy can see an elderly couple who are pointing, and trying to look over Johanna's shoulder at whatever she is doing. That's a bit odd thinks Christy, striding over, intrigued as to what the old couple can see her sister doing. Several other people are also standing looking as well, as Johanna carries on drawing without a care in the world.

As a small crowd starts to form, Johanna is aware she is being watched but confident it's only strangers simply carries on drawing.

Christy makes her way through the bystanders, and gets the shock of her life. "Oh my god," she states in surprise, as she sees a beautifully drawn scene of the beach huts and the holidaymakers on the sand, a vivid portrait of what is right in front of her.

Johanna quickly closes her book in horror, now convinced her secret will be shared with the rest of the family, resulting in her parents removing, and possibly destroying her work.

"Hey, don't stop," says Christy, smiling widely, "That drawing is incredible, look how many other people were enjoying it as well."

"You'll tell mum and dad, and they'll stop me," says Johanna, a little tearfully.

"No I won't, you know you can trust me," confirms Christy, knowing full well that Trevor and Muriel would almost certainly do all they could to stop her from drawing if they knew. Johanna smiles and opens her book again. "Can I see some of your other drawings, I assume you've got some more?" asks Christy.

Nervously Johanna turns the pages. Christy gasps in astonishment as she sees page after page of beautifully drawn caricatures, mostly of Johnny or the red haired model wearing outfits that Christy guesses Johanna has probably designed herself. She well remembers what a talented artist Johanna was in her schooldays, but assumed she had left all that behind when forced to leave school five years before.

“Wow, that’s Johnny!” chuckles Christy, “What an amazing likeness, I can’t believe it!”

One of the men in the crowd makes an approach. "Excuse me young lady," he says, "I couldn’t help but notice your fantastic drawings, some of the best I've ever seen." Johanna blushes. "I'd like to buy one off you, if I may, perhaps the one you are drawing now of the beach, it's so vivid," he continues. Christy candidly wonders if the man would part with five hundred pounds for one.

"Oh no, I couldn't take any money from you," says Johanna, humbly, "Here, it's yours. Take it." She detaches the page from her journal, and gives it to the man.

"No, I insist," he replies, quickly getting his wallet out and handing Johanna a twenty-pound note. Reluctantly she takes the money from him.

"Thank you so much," she says, a little shyly.

Unbeknown to her the purchaser is Elvis Mansfield. "Are you staying at Happy Daze?" he asks. Johanna nods. Like his employer, Elvis always has his eye out for anything that could make money. He can't wait to show this picture to Louis, convinced he has found himself a child genius. He looks at where Johanna has signed her name 'Johanna Maynard' very neatly in the corner, confident this will make her very easy to track down once Louis is back in Portwynne on Monday.

Christy gets an idea of her own. Get Johanna to draw twenty-four more of these, sell them on the seafront for £20 each, and that would be £500. But that would also be the quickest way of their parents finding out, so forgets she even thought of it.

"I'll leave you alone now," says Christy, happy to let her younger sister have some time to herself.

"What will you say to mum and dad?" asks Johanna, worriedly.

"That you are having a quiet sunbathe on the beach, nothing else," confirms Christy, "but don't be too long, you know what they're like."

Johanna smiles, opens a blank page in her sketchbook and begins to sketch the beach huts again, as Christy makes her way back to Happy Daze.

Meanwhile, no more than ten yards away from her on the sand, Charlotte and Jamie come back to where the others are relaxing in the warm sunshine. Charlotte spots Johanna sitting on the wall and waves at her cheerily. Johanna shyly waves back. Liz turns around to see who Charlotte has spotted, and smiles fondly as she notices who it is. Her parents might be hard work, but the young girl seems friendly enough.

Christy arrives back at the Jolly Roger, to be immediately given the third degree. “Well, where is she, where did she go?” asks Trevor, forcefully.

“She’s down the beach, sitting on a deckchair, enjoying the weather, nothing to worry about,” says Christy.

“On her own?” Trevor starts to panic.

“Yes, on her own, dad, stop fussing, she’s doing no harm, it’ll do her good to have some time to herself.”

“I don’t like the sound of this one bit,” splutters Trevor, knowing he has no control over his youngest daughter while she is out of sight, “In fact, go and get her now Christy, bring her back to us.”

“I will do no such thing,” states Christy, “Johanna will come back in her own time, leave her be for god’s sake.”

Johanna returns an hour later, and another £30 better off, after another holidaymaker insisted on paying her for a drawing.

She decides not to say anything to Christy, instead planning on buying some more pens and another sketch book, as her current one will soon be filled up.

Trevor and Muriel eye her with suspicion, wondering what really happened this afternoon. Seeing Christy glare at them they choose not to probe, but remain deeply suspicious for all that.

Marissa dashes over to Elvis's flat, to spend a precious few hours with him before her night duties. She isn't looking forward to telling tales on her fellow Seasiders and their drug habits, but knows she can't lie to him. They've been a couple for almost three years, getting together during Marissa's first season at Happy Daze. They have had to go to a lot of trouble throughout to ensure Louis doesn't know, both fully aware of his strict rules in place which ban relationships between his staff. No one outside of their families is aware that the two of them are an item, and even they are all sworn to secrecy in case Louis gets to find out.

She lets herself in as usual, in possession of a spare key. Elvis gets up out of his armchair and takes her in his arms, kissing her longingly.

"Mmmm, just what I needed," sighs Marissa, breathlessly, as he kisses her again.

"How long have you got?" asks Elvis.

"Not too long, I'm on dining room duty as usual," she confirms. Elvis pulls a sad face, had hoped for some late afternoon bedroom action. "It's ok, I'll stop over tonight if you like, no one will know," says Marissa. Elvis cheers up straightaway. "About what you asked me before," she continues, "It's true. Half the staff are taking stimulants – not me of course, you won't catch me paying that filthy creep, Bo-Bo."

"I knew it," sighs Elvis, "Louis had an anonymous letter sent to him, warning him about drug use at the leisure park. I guessed Bo-Bo might have been behind it, seeing as his missus works for Colviles."

“Colviles Uppers,” states Marissa, “If you ask me some of the staff are getting hooked on them, Johnny Major for one. What will you tell Louis?”

“I don’t know yet, but if I do say anything I won’t mention you, I promise,” replies Elvis, smiling adoringly.

After another disrupted evening meal, where Trevor’s excuse to get more food was that his gigantic plate of beef curry and rice wasn't nearly big enough and stone cold, a complaint that Barnaby didn't even acknowledge no matter how much he ranted, they all make their way towards Peyton’s Pavilion for another show. This time it's specialty acts on stage.

After last night, Rodney feels it's worth taking his father straight to the Jolly Roger instead of attending the performance, believing that heckling a magician, a fire eater or a knife thrower wouldn't be a wise move.

Having spoken to Liz outside the dining hall, Christy wonders if Johanna and Charlotte should go off together to 'Sonikz Disco', a youngster’s hangout. Liz is happy to agree, as is a delighted Charlotte, and even happier Johanna. To ensure it’s all kept quiet only Christy, Liz and Colin are aware of their true whereabouts, with Trevor, Muriel and the others believing Johanna is in the Family Centre saving tables. Christy is well aware her parents have long discouraged Johanna from going anywhere where people her own age might be, and would make a massive fuss if they knew she was at Sonikz with Charlotte.

The remaining four members of the Chesters family are in the Pavilion, and manage to find seats all on the same row quite near the front. Eleanor, Liz, Colin then Jamie all sat together waiting for the performance to start.

"This should be a good show," says Liz, turning towards Colin, "I hope they don't want volunteers though, don't like the idea of being sawn in two!"

Colin laughs and turns to Jamie. "If the knife thrower wants people on the stage, don't forget to put your hand up to volunteer," he smiles. The blood drains from his young sons face.

"No dad, no one's going to throw knives at me, or cast spells," he says a little shakily. His parents chuckle.

"You'd be alright," says Liz, "It's only magic, and the knife thrower is properly trained. I bet Eleanor wouldn't make such a fuss, would you." Liz turns back to find the seat alongside her empty, and no sign of little Eleanor anywhere.

"Where's she gone," panics Liz.

Colin stands up and looks around, also unable to see her in the slight darkness of the auditorium. "Do you want me to go up the back, to see if she's there? I hope she hasn't gone off to follow Charlotte to the disco, I saw the look on her face when you said she was too young to go," he says, "Stay here Jamie."

Liz looks around worriedly, but thankfully she spots her. "There she is, thank goodness for that," she proclaims, extremely relieved, as Eleanor is seen standing in the corner by the stage talking excitedly to Marissa and Alun.

"I want to be a Seasider, just like you," she tells them, "How do I join? When can I start?"

Alun laughs fondly, quite used to excited youngsters with ambitious dreams. This girl seems a little more determined than most though, he muses.

"Well you have to be a little older," confirms Marissa, kindly, "But if you're not shy of hard work, and enjoy looking out for people, then it might be the job for you, but when you are older."

"But I want to join now, I don't go back school for weeks, I could even start tomorrow!" begs Eleanor.

"Oh, that is very sweet of you, but I have to work in places where you need to be over 18, that won't be any good to you," says Marissa, trying to let this wide eyed girl down gently.

"That doesn't matter, I can do lots of other things, and I don't mind working hard, can't I have a chance, please? I'm available straightaway!" Eleanor implores.

Liz appears at her shoulder. "Eleanor, what are you doing here? I am so sorry if she is mithering you," she says to the two others.

"It's not a problem at all, your daughter would like to be a Seasider, so she says," smiles Alun.

"Oh yes, so I hear," confirms Liz, having heard nothing else all afternoon, "Come back to your seat now Eleanor, and let these two get along with their work."

Eleanor looks at Liz with tears in her eyes. "I want to help too, I can do it, I can help people like Marissa does," she says softly, "Can't I have a chance. Ask Johnny, he's your friend, he'll get me a job, I know he will."

Liz sighs, realising that Eleanor is deadly serious. "Look, when you are a lot older, maybe, but for now please come and sit down," says Liz, leading a reluctant Eleanor away while mouthing 'sorry' to Marissa and Alun.

Over at Sonikz Disco, Charlotte and Johanna are having a very enjoyable time, dancing and gossiping. Johanna knows she looks a little out of place in her child-like outfit, but is still determined to make the most of this new found freedom.

While sat with their glasses of lemonade, Johanna admits to Charlotte about her crush on Johnny, while showing her some of her many drawings. Charlotte is taken completely by surprise. With Johnny being a long standing family friend, she'd never thought of him as anything other than that, but is happy for her new pal. She also can't believe the detail in Johanna's pictures, including the one she drew of Eleanor earlier on.

Like Barnaby and Christy before her, she agrees to keep Johanna's confidence. All too soon though they have to depart, ahead of saving tables in the Family Centre.

Before long the others turn up after seeing the show, Christy and Muriel following close behind after another bingo session. Christy smiles at Johanna knowingly, glad that she was able to have a couple of hours doing something enjoyable, instead of fetching and carrying for their parents.

Trevor and Rodney return from the Jolly Roger. They can see Johanna and Charlotte happily chattering away, which Trevor doesn't like one bit. Johanna spots her dad glaring over at the two of them and makes her excuses, dutifully sitting the other side of her parents. Christy tuts in annoyance, what harm was she doing talking to her new friend, how ridiculous.

The night finishes up almost identically to the one before. Jamie starts to get tired, so Charlotte takes him and Eleanor back to the chalet to allow Colin and Liz some time to themselves. As much as Liz likes Christy, she doesn't want to spend the rest of the evening with her and the other members of the Maynard family. Other than when they were in bed, Liz and Colin have barely had a minute to themselves since they arrived. They politely say goodnight to the others, and head off to the Jolly Roger for an hour.

Colin gets a pint of beer for him, and a large glass of white wine for Liz, as they take a small table in the corner and reflect over the weekends events.

"How are we going to talk Eleanor out of these daft ideas about working here," sighs Liz, "I shouldn't have to keep a non-stop watch on a 12-year-old, but she should know better than to run off without telling us."

"I have no idea what we're going to do, but she really has had her head turned by these 'Seasiders'" says Colin.

"I think she has inherited your performing gene, that's what it is," laughs Liz, "And what do you make of our neighbours the Maynards?"

"Proper Jekyll and Hyde him, mouthpiece," replies Colin, "Nasty piece of work one minute, then perfectly normal the next. Can't make him out, I really can't. His missus is just as clueless I do know that, but the rest of them seem alright I suppose."

"It's nice that Charlotte has made friends with that young girl of theirs," says Liz, "I was a bit worried that there might not have been much here for her, most of the events are for smaller children. There's only that disco place for anyone Charlotte's age otherwise."

"Seems to me that the girls father has made his own mind up though, see how quick she was out of her seat when he turned up," remembers Colin, "Anyway, never mind them, how about you Lizzy, what have you made of this place so far?"

"Well, the food and the entertainment have been excellent, can't be faulted," she confirms, "Pity about the accommodation, and the furniture though."

Colin nods in agreement, already fed up with the loud squeaking of the door, and the even louder creaking of the bed. "Still, apart from that, it's not too bad," he says, leaning over to Liz and kissing her lovingly, "I'm sure we'll have a very nice and quiet week no matter what happens."

Chapter Seven

It's Monday morning. Not long after Marissa departs the flat just before daybreak, Elvis sets off towards South Wales to collect Louis from his mansion.

Two hours later the front gates of Happy Daze open fully to allow Louis' large gold coloured Mercedes, driven by Elvis with Louis sitting in the back seat, up the driveway. Slowly it makes it way around the leisure park, wending its way to a secret secluded spot at the very back, hidden by several large trees and two more tall gates. Behind this is the luxury apartment that is home to Louis when he is in residence.

Standing by the apartment gates waiting for the owner to arrive are Johnny and Marissa, who have a weekly meeting with Louis at this time. Despite it being Johnny's day off he is obliged to fit this in before dashing home to see Olivia and the boys for a few hours. The large gates open to allow the car and the two Seasiders through. Elvis parks up on a small gravel area alongside the apartment.

Louis gets out of the car, greeting his two employees warmly. "Good morning you two," he booms, while smiling fondly.

"Good morning, Louis," they reply in unison. Not many staff are on first name terms with him, but Johnny and Marissa are.

"Shall we go inside? Time for our little catch up," says Louis, opening the front door to the apartment. This weekly debrief is something he considers very important in regards to the smooth running of Happy Daze. Despite having other leisure parks it's this one that has long been his flagship, the one he spends most of his time at hence the specially built accommodation.

Where he expects the guests and staff to stay in very cheap, basic chalets, his own apartment has been spared absolutely nothing in expense, opulent furnishings, and a large collection of rare and priceless Ming vases which are dotted all over the place on shelves, tables and in a grand display cabinet.

Marissa and Elvis exchange a knowing smile as she follows Louis and Johnny inside.

The two Seasiders sit themselves down on a plush leather sofa, while Louis takes an armchair. He sends Elvis off for a wander around the camp, to make sure all is well.

"Ok, what have I missed?" asks Louis. Johnny and Marissa look at one another. Johnny had already told her about being heckled on Saturday night, and who the culprit was. Now is the time to admit this to their boss.

"We had a small amount of bother on Saturday," says Marissa, "Sadly it was all down to one guest."

"Oh no," frowns Louis, "What happened?"

"A man by the name of Mr Maynard, he's known to us, his family come here a lot," replies Marissa, "He made a bit of a scene in the dining hall, wanted extra portions with his main meal, and he was a bit threatening to poor Barnaby Walsh." Louis looks worried, not keen on any trouble between guests and staff. "He got the same large plateful as everyone else, but apparently it wasn't enough, he wanted more," states Marissa.

"You're kidding? Greedy devil, I hope he was told where to go," says Louis.

"Well, I managed to get him to back down, but it caused a bit of a rumpus, which we could have done without," admits Marissa.

"It didn't end there, sadly," says Johnny, "The same man heckled me during my show on Saturday. I couldn't see who it was at the time, found out from some other guests it was the same bloke though."

"He heckled you?" Louis is incredulous.

"I'm afraid so, Alun Williams came to my rescue though," states Johnny.

"Thank goodness for that, we can't have this, keep an eye on him will you," says Louis shaking his head, sorrowfully. A thought suddenly hits him. "Maynard, you say? That's the second time I've heard that surname today. He hasn't got a young daughter by any chance, do you know?" Johnny shakes his head, completely unaware, while Marissa starts to laugh.

"Young daughter? That girl of his is 20 if she's a day, she just looks 12, always wearing kid's clothes, it's quite pitiful really. Why do you ask?"

Louis unlocks his large briefcase and retrieves the drawing Elvis gave to him when he picked him up. Johnny and Marissa look at the drawing in total open mouthed surprise, the vivid recreation of Portwynne Bay, complete with its distinctive beach huts impressing the both of them.

"It would appear Mr Maynards daughter drew this, so Elvis says. Good isn't it!" states Louis, smiling widely.

"She's always scribbling something in a book, I've seen her often," says Marissa, "I had no idea she was producing things like this, wow!"

"I need to go and see Dolly and Val, find out which chalet this young lady is staying in. People will pay good money for stuff like this," proclaims Louis. Marissa suspects there is a good chance Johanna's parents don't know about her endeavours, but if Louis wants to speak to her then she can't rightly prevent him.

"You must know them," says Marissa to Johnny, "We call them 'Wagon Train', there's about ten of them, all the same family, always together, traipsing about the camp, nearly always wind up at the Jolly Roger, whatever the weather." Johnny can't bring them to mind at all, and shakes his head blankly.

"Was there anything else I need to know?" asks Louis.

"We've got Rab McKinley booked for the Midnight Cabaret on Thursday," confirms Marissa.

"Good, good," nods Louis, glad to hear a very popular Scottish performer has been engaged, "We'll have them flocking in for that one, make no mistake." The Midnight Cabaret in the Jolly Roger is the biggest earner of the whole week, with Louis always insisting on big name artists appearing to ensure plenty of cash ends up going over the bar.

"Can't think of anything else I wanted to raise," says Johnny, discreetly looking at his watch, desperately wanting to get away, knowing Olivia is waiting for him to turn up and will moan if he's running late.

"Me neither," says Marissa.

"Ah, well, there was something else I wanted to ask," says Louis, lowering his voice, "I know you are already aware, Johnny, but I'm worried about these rumours about drugs being peddled on the site."

"I already explained to Elvis I don't know anything about this," insists Johnny, wishing these tales would go away.

Marissa knows that Elvis hasn't mentioned her name in all this, but speaks up. "I haven't heard anything either, but if I do," she nods, a little uncomfortable at lying to her boss.

"That'll have to do then I suppose," says Louis, a little disappointed that his two senior Seasiders aren't more forthcoming, "Let's head to reception and find the Maynard child."

Instead of just wandering around the leisure park, casting an eye over business like Louis asked, Elvis takes a direct route towards the Betting Lounge, determined to get to the bottom of what Bo-Bo is up to, with a view to putting a permanent stop to it.

When he gets inside, the lounge is fairly quiet. Old Mr Reynolds is sitting at a table writing out his small bets for the day, two other men are closely studying the form from the newspapers pinned up on the walls, while Bo-Bo is sat behind the counter reading the Sporting Life and drinking a cup of coffee. He looks up to see Elvis, and tries not to scowl.

"Morning, Bo-Bo," says Elvis, trying to not raise any suspicions, leaning on the counter nonchalantly.

"What can I do for you," he replies nervously, not liking Elvis hanging around.

"Have you got last weeks figures, so I can let Louis have a

look at them?" asks Elvis.

"Sure, give me a minute," replies Bo-Bo, heading into the back.

Elvis peers over the counter, but can't see anything untoward. A safe with a kettle and a coffee jar on the top, a box of betting slips, pens, a small radio. Framed photo of Arkle on the wall, several other boxes with files in them. He stands back just as Bo-Bo reappears.

"There you are," he says, handing over the paperwork, "Bad week, not much money around Elvis, none at all, very quiet."

"I see," says Elvis, having a little glance at the fiddled numbers, before putting the papers in his inside jacket pocket. "Thanks for this." He turns to go.

Bo-Bo glares daggers at Elvis as he retreats to the door. He's been a rather too frequent visitor to the betting lounge for someone who hasn't placed so much as one single bet.

Louis, Marissa and Johnny catch up with Elvis, who reports all is well. This allows the two Seasiders to vanish, while Louis and Elvis make their way through the crowds milling around before arriving at a very busy reception hall, where a number of Monday to Friday guests are currently checking in. The two of them let themselves in through the staff door alongside the hatch.

Dolly leaves her sister Val to deal with the queue while she speaks to them. "Hello Louis, hello Elvis," she chirps, "Shall I put the kettle on?"

"Good idea, Dolly," states Louis, taking a seat. "I need a favour from you, I wonder if you could track down the whereabouts of someone staying on the camp," he continues.

Dolly can't believe her ears; the place is crammed full with thousands of holidaymakers. How can she be expected to track down just one!

"Family name of Maynard, I'm after their young daughter," confirms Louis.

Dolly turns around in shock. "Well, that is one family I can soon lead you to, for what it's worth, but their younger daughter isn't young at all. She's 21."

Elvis looks a bit mystified. "Mustn't be her then boss, the girl I saw was all of 12 or 13."

Dolly laughs. "Still at it are they? Dressing the poor girl in kiddies t-shirts, poor thing," she says, "Those dreadful parents of hers have been doing this to her for years, they were the ones who kept altering her year of birth to ensure they only paid childrens rates for her, don't you remember Louis?" The incident rings a bell, but he wouldn't have been able to recall the name. "What do you want with her, anyhow?" asks Dolly, while pouring the tea.

Once again Louis gets the picture Johanna drew of the huts, Portwynne beach, and the people on it, out of his briefcase. "She drew this," he confirms.

Dolly takes the drawing, and looks at it in wonder. "Well, I never did," she states.

"She was sat on the seafront yesterday drawing that, caused quite a stir, very talented girl, and very humble too. I had trouble persuading her to take money for it, but I insisted," says Elvis.

"I'm hoping to find her to get her to draw a few more for me, we could sell them here on the camp, pay her so much per copy and sell them on," states Louis, excitedly, "Where is she likely to be, do you know?"

Dolly knows that the Maynards have a permanent afternoon residency in the Jolly Roger despite the hot weather, and it's likely she will be with them. "Well, I have an idea," says Dolly, "But it's only Johanna you need to speak to really, her parents can be a little difficult, to say the least."

"So I'm led to believe," says Louis, "but it is possible you could bring this girl to see me at the apartment?"

Dolly knows that might just be a challenge too far. "I can try," she says, a little hesitantly, "What time?"

"Well, I've got a few business calls to make this afternoon, so before then? 12 noon?" suggests Louis.

Dolly goes back to the hatch. The queue has died down a little, and Val has everything under control. Two female Seasiders are in the building talking to some of the new arrivals. Dolly beckons one of them over, a young girl called Ruth.

"Ruth, come here, got a job for you," calls Dolly.

"Anything for you," smiles Ruth, a very keen Seasider in her first season at Happy Daze.

"Well, it's not for me as such, it's Mr Peyton who needs a favour," confirms Dolly, before revealing to a horrified Ruth that she needs to track down Johanna Maynard without her parents knowing, and deliver her to Louis's apartment at 12 noon. Ruth is rather too familiar with Trevor, having been on the receiving end of many a leery remark, and as such she can't stand him. Trying to get his daughter away without him knowing will be all but impossible.

Dolly begs her to at least try, knowing whatever Louis wants he usually gets, while explaining about the drawing Elvis had bought. Reluctantly Ruth disappears off in pursuit of her.

She decides to hang around the Jolly Roger, knowing at some point the Maynard clan will be spotted heading that way. Ruth has no idea how she is going to divert Johanna from them without them realising. Luck is on her side. Within five minutes she spots her, along with Charlotte, going inside the camp cafeteria. The two of them had been outside the chalets chatting, same as the previous morning. Christy had appeared and suggested they go off for the day together, pacifying her dim-witted parents by saying 'it'll soon be Saturday, all back to normal then', all the while knowing this won't be true, that Johanna will be out of their mean clutches by the end of the week if she has any say in the matter. Trevor and Muriel reluctantly buy Christy's argument, and a delighted Johanna is happily spending the day with her new friend.

Ruth dashes over into the cafeteria, all the time checking that the rest of the Maynards are nowhere around. By the time she gets to the girls they have both bought an ice cream sundae and are heading for an empty table. Johanna is just getting one of her books out to show Charlotte as Ruth politely interrupts, leading her to nervously put the book away.

"It's ok," says Ruth kindly, "I just wanted to make sure. Is your name Johanna?"

"Yes," she confirms, worried that her parents have sent this Seasider to spy on her. Charlotte also wonders the same.

"It's to do with your drawings," says Ruth, smiling, "Yesterday, a man bought one from you, do you remember?" Johanna nods, wondering what's coming next. "Well, that gentleman works for Louis Peyton, and he has shown him your drawing. Mr Peyton would like to speak to you, if you can spare a few minutes." Ruth can immediately see the fear in Johanna's eyes. "Your friend can come too, but Mr Peyton really would like to see you and your sketch book, just for a short while," she says.

"No, I can't, my parents...." Johanna's voice tails off.

Charlotte speaks up instead. "Her mum and dad don't know about this, and they mustn't find out," she says.

"I know that, and so does Mr Peyton. He is a very kind man, he'll be sympathetic," says Ruth, "Look, why don't you finish your ice cream, I'll let him know I've found you, and then I'll come back and take you both to see him."

Johanna isn't sure, but nods yes.

Ruth disappears again. "It'll be alright you know," says Charlotte kindly, "He probably wants to give you some money as well!"

"I don't want any money, I don't want anything," admits Johanna, "I'd give my pictures away for nothing if I could. But dad and mum would throw my books away if they knew."

"Your sister wouldn't let them, surely, she could have them for safe keeping," says Charlotte.

"She can't keep watch all the time, and I know they'd find a way," Johanna replies, glumly.

Louis is back at the apartment, poring over the paperwork from the betting lounge, while Elvis crosses his fingers hoping that his boss realises the takings are suspiciously low for what had appeared to be a busy six days trading. The weather last week wasn't as warm as this week, and on the number of occasions Elvis dropped in the place was full of punters, all listening intently to the audio commentary provided from a small speaker on the wall. He'd seen plenty of money change hands as well, making these meagre takings even harder to believe.

"Well, Bo-Bo is right about one thing," sighs Louis, "There is no money around. I thought people liked to have a bet, seems I was wrong. I must have Bo-Bo in, see if he has any ideas how to improve matters, and attract more customers." Elvis looks to the heavens, unable to fathom how someone as sharp as Louis can't spot what looks like blatant fraudulent activity.

"I was in there every day he was open, and he wasn't short of customers, not at all," states Elvis, "I'm not sure those figures are right."

"Just because it looked busy, doesn't mean that it was or that people are spending," protests Louis, "Some bet in pennies, or half-pennies, others just go inside to get away from their wives, that I do know."

"I saw pound notes, and plenty of them," confirms Elvis, "Ok, I'll be honest with you, boss, I think Bo-Bo is ripping you off." Louis chortles loudly.

"Don't be ridiculous, he's a solid businessman with a track record for success," states Louis, refusing to believe a word of Elvis's argument, "He got over £100,000 for those rails pitches, including nearly £20,000 for that one at Ascot, so he doesn't need to 'rip me off' as you claim."

"And you saw proof of this? Receipts, invoices?" says Elvis, while trying desperately to plant a seed of doubt in his bosses mind.

"Well, no," says Louis, starting to think, "Any way, if a man says 'here's my hand, here's my heart' then as far as I am concerned that's enough."

"I still think you ought to get the Auditor to pay a mid-season visit," replies Elvis.

"What? Throw good money away? The figures came back clean at the end of last season," states Louis. This wasn't strictly true, as the Auditor had indicated he had numerous concerns over the shops low takings, so much so he had hinted to Louis to close it down as unprofitable.

Elvis shakes his head in exasperation. "Look, have you got his CV still, I guess you have," he says.

"Of course, why?" asks Louis, suspiciously.

"I want to do some digging, I can't shake this gut instinct that he's up to no good," replies Elvis, "And there was something else too, something you have overlooked."

"Really? What's that then?" Louis enquires.

"Where does that bimbo wife of his work, what did she tell you at the dinner party," says Elvis. Louis had held a pre-season dinner party at the apartment, and wives and partners were on the guest list, including Krystal. Louis's face drops, and he starts to feel a little faint.

"Colviles Pharmaceuticals," he says a little quietly, "So not only do you think he's stealing from me, you suspect he's our mystery drug pusher as well."

"There has to be a chance," states Elvis, knowing already this is more than true, "Let me have his CV, and in the meantime I really think you should get that mid-season audit done."

10 minutes later, and after Ruth had seen Trevor and the others from behind going into the Jolly Roger, she collects the girls from the cafeteria and takes them up to Louis's secluded apartment. She presses the intercom on the perimeter gates to announce their arrival.

Elvis lets them all in, and leads them to Louis's study. Louis is sitting behind his large Edwardian oak desk. "Ah, good to see you ladies, please take a seat," he says, cheerfully. Charlotte and Johanna sit down nervously, hardly believing what is happening here, looking around at the grand array of ornaments and vases on display, while Ruth stands protectively behind them. Elvis takes his place, stood behind Louis. Johanna quickly recognises him as the man who gave her £20 for her drawing the previous afternoon.

"Which one of you is Johanna, then?" asks Louis.

"Me," replies Johanna, quietly, leaving Louis unable to understand why a 21-year-old is wearing a childs t-shirt with Daffy Duck on the front.

He continues on. "Now, I know Ruth will have told you why I want to see you," he says to her, "My assistant Elvis here showed me your drawing. It's stunning, I've never seen anything this good before." Johanna blushes. "Have you got anything else, I guess you must have?" asks Louis. Johanna gets even more nervous, knowing there is a very good chance he will spot that her drawings are mostly of Johnny!

"Go on, show him," says Charlotte, softly.

Johanna reaches into her bag and retrieves her latest sketch book. She puts it on Louis's desk. "May I?" he asks, before opening it. Johanna nods. Louis opens the cover, and is immediately dry mouthed with shock, unable to believe what he is seeing. Page after page of superb drawings, caricatures, scenes, incredibly lifelike representations of people and places. "Wow, look at these Elvis," he splutters excitedly, barely able to see the pictures for pound signs.

He stops at a portrait Johanna has drawn of Johnny, the one where he is dancing with the red-haired model Louis has seen on other pages, unaware that the model is who Johanna wishes she was. Charlotte smiles fondly, knowing full well what the drawing depicts. "Well I never, that's Johnny Major isn't it," chortles Louis, "What an amazing likeness. Am I to assume he doesn't know about any of this?" Johanna bows her head, while Charlotte, fully aware of Johanna's fondness for him puts a comforting hand on her arm, and can see her getting a little emotional. Charlotte speaks.

"Don't say anything, please," she implores, "Johanna is really private, and so he mustn't know." Louis has guessed this may be more to do with Johanna's parents finding out rather than any desire to keep Johnny in the dark, knowing that she would definitely show Johnny her pictures if she could.

"How long do these portraits take you?" asks Louis, "Elvis said you drew this one of the beach in no time at all."

"Not long," says Johanna, trying not to cry.

"Could you draw a picture of me?" asks Louis. Johanna looks up at the middle aged, small, dumpy, balding figure of Louis Peyton and knows that this would be an easy task. She nods. He pushes the book back towards her. "Go on then," smiles Louis, "Show me."

Silently, and very nervously, Johanna finds a spare page, gets a black pen out and starts to draw, glancing up now and again as Louis sits smiling behind his desk. Charlotte and Ruth can't believe the ease in which Johanna is delicately stroking the pen over the page, a vivid caricature of Louis Peyton forming within moments. She detaches the page and hands it over.

"There, that's for you," says Johanna, softly. Louis can barely believe his eyes, and immediately reaches for his wallet. "No!" states Johanna, "I can't take money, it's yours, for free."

Louis takes no notice and gets three £20 notes out. "I am not taking no for an answer young lady," says Louis, forcefully. Reluctantly Johanna takes the money and puts it in her purse. Louis leans forward. "You can't hide your talent away, surely your parents would be proud if they saw this work, it's incredible," he says. Johanna starts to tear up again. "How about I speak to them?" asks Louis.

"No!" shouts Johanna in horror, "Sorry, but you don't know my dad, it won't work." Louis is now getting a little exasperated.

"This talent can't be kept hidden though," he says, "It simply can't. That model you draw a lot, are her clothes your ideas or are they out of a magazine?"

"All mine," says Johanna, a trace of a smile for a change, knowing how good her designs would look if they were for real.

"Is that what you do then, work in a sewing factory?" asks Louis, "Is that where you get your ideas from?"

"No, I work on a till at Budget-Buys. I draw in secret only," admits Johanna. Again Louis is shaking his head in disbelief. Why is she wasting her time in such a menial job, when she should be making a fortune fashion designing.

"I don't get it, I just don't get it, a talented girl like you working in a supermarket? Goodness me." Johanna looks at the floor, embarrassed. "Look, I wonder if you will do something for me," asks Louis, "I don't want to disturb your holiday, or spoil time with your friend here, but could you draw, ummm, another ten of these beach pictures. I'll give you money upfront, and a large share of what I can sell them for."

"I can do your drawings, it won't take me very long, but I can't take any more money. And where will you sell them? If you put it them in the shop here my parents will see them," Johanna protests.

"You have my word that I will be discreet," says Louis, not entirely truthfully, knowing most things are bought by people 'window shopping'. "Can you bring them here by, say, 6 o'clock? And here, take this as well please, no arguing," says Louis, handing over another £50, safe in the knowledge his investment will be repaid five times over at least. Again a very reluctant Johanna stashes the notes in her bag, along with her book and pens. "Well, thank you for coming to see me, I'll look forward to seeing you again later," smiles Louis.

Johanna, Charlotte and Ruth make their way out of the apartment. "I can hardly believe what happened there," says Charlotte, "Louis Peyton wants to pay you to draw more pictures! He's a millionaire you know. You'll earn more off him in one day than you would in a month at the supermarket. If your parents are motivated by money, they might not mind after all!"

"My parents motivation, if you can call it that, is control," says Johanna, gloomily, as they make their way back to the centre of the park.

"I'll let you ladies go then," smiles Ruth, "Good luck!" She quickly disappears to begin her next duty of the day.

The next person they see is Barnaby, on his way back from a mid-morning swim. He smiles widely as he sees the girls walking down, and makes his way across to them. "Well, well, well, a very gorgeous sight indeed," he says in his thick Dublin accent. Both Johanna and Charlotte start to blush, not used to such attention. "Where are you two off to?" he asks.

"To the beach, just for a bit," says Charlotte.

"Awww lovely," says Barnaby, "I'd join you's but I'm a bit knackered, need a rest an' all. But I'll see you both later on."

"Ok," blushes Johanna, "Goodbye Barnaby." They continue on their way.

Down at the beach it doesn't take too long for Johanna to draw the pictures Louis asked for. Again her endeavours draw a crowd, several people asking if they can buy one off her. Charlotte is quick to explain that they will be for sale in the Happy Daze souvenir shop on Tuesday morning, knowing fine well Johanna would end up having to draw twice as many to meet demand, making them late.

They make their way back to Louis's apartment, prior to meeting up with their respective families for dinner. Louis looks at the pictures on his desk and grins from ear to ear. "I knew you wouldn't let me down!" he says gleefully, again thinking of how much money he'll be making.

Back in the dining hall Trevor is full of questions, once again he is deeply suspicious as to what Johanna had been up to with Charlotte, and who they had seen or spoken to while out of his sight. Johanna happily lies to him, explaining they had spent the day in the shops and arcades down the front and hadn't seen anyone. He can see Christy glaring across at him as usual, so decides not to ask anything else.

Liz is equally keen to hear what the girls were doing all day. Charlotte is just as untruthful, giving the same explanation Johanna did, that they merely made their way up and down Portwynne front all afternoon.

The same secret agreement as the night before is made, with Johanna and Charlotte going to Sonikz Disco prior to saving seats in the Family Centre, as the others are either heading to Peyton's Pavilion, the bingo or the Jolly Roger again.

Chapter Eight

Elvis decides to have a night in at his flat, determined to get to the bottom of Bo-Bo's shady dealing, all the while waiting for Marissa to finish work for the day, and the sound of her key in the lock. It doesn't take too long before he discovers the true extent of Bo-Bo's deceit.

He puts in a call to the only person he can think of who may be able to shed some light, his cousin Leonard who lives in Cheltenham, less than three miles from the famous racecourse. To start with, Elvis doesn't name the person whose background he says he's looking into on behalf of Louis, but asks him to clarify a few things. Firstly, Bo-Bo's claims about being a successful rails bookmaker, who had sold his pitches for a princely sum.

Leonard laughs loud down the telephone. "You are kidding me," he says in disbelief, "That can't happen. Have you never heard of the 'seniority rule'?" Elvis isn't remotely interested in racing, and is unfamiliar with the terminology.

Leonard is quick to explain that there is such a long waiting list at almost every course in the country for pitches, that if someone vacates one, either willingly because they no longer wish to trade, or unwillingly as bankrupt, the bookmakers behind you move up a pitch, and whoever is top of the waiting list gets the pitch furthest away. Elvis has never heard of this, and clearly Louis hasn't either.

Elvis then asks Leonard if he has heard of either of the referees listed on the CV, one purportedly a racehorse trainer, and the other a bookmaker.

"I've heard of most trainers," replies Leonard, "but that's a new one on me. And I don't recognise the bookies name either, but I'd be hard pushed to remember all of them." Elvis has heard enough, and is grateful for his cousin's information. Before the call ends though, Leonard enquires as to who the CV belongs to. He nearly faints with shock, as he hears the name of Robert Boston.

“Please tell me you’re joking,” splutters Leonard, “Louis Peyton wants his head reading if he’s thinking of employing that shyster. And if you know where he lives, then feel free to tell me, I know at least six people who are after him for substantial gambling debts.”

He then goes on to explain how Bo-Bo was well known on the racing scene, but as a useless punter, and definitely not as a bookmaker. Elvis isn’t surprised in the slightest, but doesn’t know how to break the news to Louis that he has managed to rumble Bo-Bo with just one phone call.

Over at Sonikz Disco, Charlotte and Johanna are once again enjoying the loud pop music, as many others their age are up dancing and or sitting around tables chatting. As usual Johanna feels self-conscious in her t-shirt and shorts, wishing she had a summer dress on like Charlotte, but on the other hand it’s nice to have another few hours enjoyment away from her parents. After having a quick dance, they return to their table to find Barnaby sitting there.

"Hello ladies, you don't mind if I join ya?" he asks.

"No, that's fine," smiles Charlotte, shyly.

"I'm not stopping long," he confirms, "No beer in here, but I like the music, better than the rubbish Busbys Canyon churn out."

Johanna feels the need to speak up. "I'm really sorry my dad gives you such a hard time," she says, feeling ashamed at Trevor’s appalling behaviour towards him every day.

"Nah, it's ok," says Barnaby, "I'm only a lowly paid skivvy like he told me, the abuse goes with the job."

"Well it shouldn't have to," says Johanna. Barnaby smiles at her fondly, making her blush. He can't quite decide who he fancies the most out of Charlotte and Johanna. Charlotte looks more naturally pretty at first glance of course, but he also thinks that despite the scraped back pony tail and make-up-less face that Johanna is equally pretty. He would happily take either of them out, but the thought of Trevor chasing after him for his trouble is more than a little off putting. He also thinks Colin might not approve of him asking Charlotte for a date either. Oh well, best just enjoy their company for now, he decides.

Despite saying he wasn't going to stay, Barnaby has enjoyed chatting to the girls that much the time has flown by, long past the 8.30pm that Johanna and Charlotte were supposed to be in the Family Centre by, waiting for their families to return from the Pavilion, the bingo and the Jolly Roger.

As the others enter the Family Centre, Christy is the first to notice the two of them are missing, as she comes back from the bingo with Muriel. Liz, Colin, Eleanor and Jamie are not far behind looking for Charlotte. Christy turns around to see the Chesters family standing there and is mightily relieved. "I'll go and get them," she whispers to Liz, correctly guessing that they are still at the disco but not wanting her mother to know.

"Ok, no problem," says Liz, fully understanding that Muriel isn't to be made aware of her youngest daughter's true whereabouts. "Shall we find a table Mrs Maynard?" asks Liz, leading Muriel away.

"Where's Johanna, thought she was at the theatre with you?" asks Muriel suspiciously.

"Ah, they've just gone to the cafeteria, Christy is making sure they're alright," says Liz, still leading Muriel towards the tables, glad to see Eunice, Neil, Rodney, Sandra and the twins already there.

Just as Christy is making her way up towards the disco, Trevor is staggering drunkenly out of the Jolly Roger on his own, having wanting to finish his umpteenth pint of beer before going to the Family Centre. He spots her, and immediately starts to follow. Where is she off to? Nothing up here for her, what the heck is going on?

Christy goes through the double doors of Sonikz Disco, totally unaware she is currently being stalked by her own father. Trevor can feel the anger rising inside, assuming that Johanna will be found in there. Unable to control his rage he barges through the doors, slamming them open aggressively.

He can barely believe his eyes when he sees Christy laughing and smiling with the three people around the table nearest the disco floor. Within ten seconds he launches himself at Barnaby, hands around his throat. "What the hell are you doing with my daughter, you thick Irish navvy, leave her alone," he bellows, nastily, as Barnaby is desperately attempting to get out of his violent, vice like choke-grip.

Two Seasiders quickly dash across, grab hold of Trevor and manage to drag him off. Johanna immediately bursts into tears, while a horrified Charlotte comforts her.

"What the hell do you think you're doing, dad," shouts Christy, as several hundred youngsters stare.

"He has no right talking to my daughter, and what the hell are they doing in here with him anyway, this place is out of bounds as you well know, Johanna, how many more times," spits Trevor.

A stunned Barnaby scrambles to his feet, as the taller of the two Seasiders, known as Big Barry, frogmarches Trevor to the door, slinging him out.

"Are you alright?" Christy asks Barnaby, with concern, "I am so sorry, I had no idea he'd followed me."

"It's ok, just makes me want to stand up to the big bully even more now. It's wrong how he treats Johanna, she's lovely," he says. Christy smiles fondly, while thinking how kind of this boy to put Johanna's feelings ahead of any distress he might be in after this unprovoked assault.

"Yes, well, I don't approve either, but it won't be for much longer," she says quietly. Christy sits at the table, looking at her distraught sister.

"We were only talking," says Charlotte.

"I know that, you weren't doing anything wrong at all," confirms Christy. Barnaby sits back down with the three others, refusing to be scared off by Trevor. "Look, you three stay here, no need to come back with me, I'll sort everything out I promise. If you want to stay in our chalet instead, Johanna, then that's fine," says Christy.

Johanna shakes her head. "They won't let me stay with you and Neil, I know they won't," she says, glumly.

"It's not up to them," says Christy, throwing her chalet key across the table towards her, "I'll leave you lovely youngsters to it! And don't worry about anything, ok?"

Back at the Family Centre everyone is in good spirits. Trevor decides to play dumb, assuming everyone will think he's just wandered back from the Jolly Roger, and that when Christy and the girls come back they will say nothing. Christy returns alone five minutes later, and she spares no time in telling Trevor exactly what she thinks of him.

"You are a total disgrace, how flaming well dare you."

"What's going on?" asks Muriel, a little bemused, "And where's Johanna?"

"She's still at Sonikz Disco, same as she has been all night with Charlotte, having a very nice time, until this prat starting throwing his weight around," says Christy, "Decided to attack that young Irish waiter didn't you."

"What is Johanna doing at a disco?" shouts an incredulous Muriel, not caring that Trevor might have assaulted someone. Trevor is on his feet in a rage.

"That filthy Irish pig had no right to be speaking to Johanna, she shouldn't even be in there, she knows the rules," he says, nastily. Liz and Colin turn around from their table wondering what is going on. "Your daughter is as much to blame, corrupting our Johanna," shouts Trevor.

"I beg your pardon?" snaps Colin, "Now listen here you...." Liz calms him down.

"Don't rise to him, he isn't worth it," she says.

"Dad. You are a complete joke, and nothing less" states Christy, "They are just three normal youngsters having a night out.

You had no right to storm in like that."

"I had every right," booms Trevor, "I'm not letting that filthy Irish pig get his hands on Johanna."

"It wasn't like that, you stupid git, it's three youngsters chatting, listening to pop music, doing what people their age do, what is your problem," seethes Christy. She turns to Colin and Liz. "I've told them to stay there as long as they want to."

"That's fine with us," smiles Liz, as they turn back to find Eleanor missing again. This time she's collared Johnny to tell him about her intention to be employed as a Seasider.

Liz groans. "Not again," she says.

"Leave her to it," chuckles Colin, "If anyone is able to talk her out of this daft fantasy, it'll be Johnny."

Within 5 minutes he's leading her by the hand back to them. "This little lady wants to be a Seasider!" says Johnny, "Wants to know if I can get her a job here!"

"Ah yes," says Liz, a little embarrassed that Eleanor wants to bother anyone she can find wearing a light blue blazer with her big ideas. "I'm sorry, Johnny," she says, "Come and sit down Eleanor, stop disturbing Johnny while he's busy."

"Well, if he's that busy I can help him!" insists Eleanor, "It's easy, I know it is, please let me try."

"Well, we are fully staffed right now," says Johnny, kindly, "but in a few years when you are older, you might like to apply."

Liz breathes a sigh of relief, hoping that the message might finally get through. No such luck.

"I don't want to wait that long, and you can never have too many Seasiders. I'd work for free as well, call it a trial run!" smiles Eleanor, excitedly.

"Stop mithering," sighs Liz, "I'm so sorry Johnny."

"Oh it's alright Liz, nothing wrong with being keen," he grins.

Meanwhile, after more dancing and chat, Charlotte, Johanna and Barnaby make their way back to their respective accommodation. Barnaby has half an idea to invite the other two back to his chalet, to wind the night down with cups of instant coffee and powdered milk. After being attacked by Trevor once already, the thought is quickly banished. He does point out which chalet is his, with an open invite to call round for coffee anytime. Charlotte and Johanna head back to Primrose Block to wait up for the others.

After a short while everyone else, aside from Trevor and Muriel, arrive. Christy had given her parents one last chance to come back to the chalet and apologise to Johanna. Selfishly, they prefer their beer and state they will only return when they feel like it.

Having only seen lights on in the Chesters' chalet both Liz and Christy go inside, knowing that Charlotte and Johanna would be there together. Liz is the first with questions.

"What is this boy like then, the Irish lad?"

"His name is Barnaby, and he's really kind, polite and that," replies Charlotte, "He likes the same music we do, we were only talking."

"I know you were, I was just wondering that's all," says Liz.

Colin takes Jamie off to his bedroom, while Christy has her say. "I won't let dad, or anyone, pick on you like that again, it stops now."

"It won't work," says Johanna, "You know what they're like."

"Not any more, you can stay with us, I'll lend you a nightdress, I've got a spare, come on let's go," says Christy, kindly. Johanna gives Charlotte a fond hug before leaving the chalet.

Once they leave, Liz sits down on the bed beside her. "It's nice you're getting on with Johanna, her sister tells me she's 21 and hasn't got any friends at home," she says.

"That's because everyone knows who her dad is, and run the other way, but he doesn't scare me," says Charlotte, "It was horrible when he was strangling Barnaby, good job those Seasiders were there, they dragged him away and threw him out."

"There you go, Eleanor," says Liz, "It's not always as

wonderful as you seem to think, being a Seasider."

"Don't care," says Eleanor, getting into her nightwear, "I still want to be one, I'm going to ask Johnny again when I see him next." Liz looks at Eleanor in disappointment as nothing seems to be getting through, that at 12 she's any number of years too young to be considered for this line of work.

"Right, I will leave you to it, put the light out soon please, good night," says Liz, making her way to her own bedroom.

Liz gets into bed alongside Colin, the bedframe making it's unforgiving creaking sound as she does. This is nothing in comparison, however, with the noisy commotion going on outside on the landing, as a drunken Trevor and Muriel are frantically beating down Neil and Christy's door.

Rodney appears out of his own chalet. "Pack this in dad, you're scaring the twins, and disturbing everyone else," he hisses.

"Stop this now Trevor," begs Eunice, wondering how long before others will be outside complaining.

"Get Johanna out here now!" shouts Trevor, hammering on the next door along. Christy and Neil come to the door.

"Clear off dad, she's staying with us," states Christy.

"Go back to your own chalet, sleep it off Trevor, that'll be best," says Neil, "We can talk again in the morning." They close the door in his face.

Rodney comes over, quickly ushering his parents back inside their own chalet, quickly closing the door behind them. Trevor punches the wall in frustration, not liking his control of Johanna being taken away one bit.

Chapter Nine

Marissa sneaks into Happy Daze through a hole in the perimeter fence, which backs onto the staff chalet line. It's 6.30 in the morning, and generally the only danger of being spotted at this time is by wildlife, as the exhausted Seasiders and other workers are usually safely still in bed at this time. Her good fortune decides to run out.

Barnaby, on his way back from an early morning jog around the leisure park, can barely believe his eyes seeing Marissa squeeze through what is a well-known, and well used, secret entrance for anyone who has been out late-night revelling. He stands outside his door chuckling, as she almost gets stuck. Eventually she climbs through to the other side, if a little ungainly. Looking up, she wants the floor to swallow her after being seen.

"Where've you been?" laughs Barnaby, finding it odd that Marissa is on her own and not with others, returning from an all-night session. She also has what looks like an overnight bag with her.

"Umm, I couldn't sleep, went for a walk," she lies, unconvincingly.

"Yeah, right," chuckles Barnaby, "Where've you really been?" Marissa shuffles nervously. "Oh, I see," says Barnaby, "Who's the lucky fella then?" Marissa looks at the floor.

"No-one you know," she says, bustling her way past towards her own chalet.

While talking in bed, Trevor and Muriel decide that only way that they'll regain any sort of control over Johanna is to play things by the book until they are safely back home again, go with whatever the others say, even if they don't really want to. After issuing an apology to her that they don't completely mean, she is persuaded to return back to their chalet to spend the day with them and the rest of the family. Johanna is a little unhappy, having thoroughly enjoyed spending time with Charlotte.

Liz is not too disappointed to hear about this though, hoping that Charlotte will be the one who will finally drill home to her younger sister that she will not be quitting school to become a Seasider anytime soon.

Elvis marches purposefully up to the front door of Louis's apartment, barely able to wait to tell his boss about his findings. He gets an unpleasant shock as he makes his way to the study. Bo-Bo is sat across from Louis.

"So, as I say boss, there is no money around at all, very little indeed," lies Bo-Bo, turning around to see Elvis standing in the doorway.

"I'll come back in a bit, if you want," says Elvis.

"Nonsense, come in Elvis," states Louis, leading Elvis to wonder what exactly he had already said to Bo-Bo before he got there. He stands behind Louis, as usual. "Bo-Bo was just explaining the poor takings, it's exactly as he says, slow trade," confirms deluded Louis. Elvis decides now is not the time to reveal his suspicions, preferring to wait until Bo-Bo is safely out of the way. "And he believes if any drugs are on the site, he knows who's responsible."

"Yes, that Barnaby Walsh, you know what these youngsters are like, always up to no good," states Bo-Bo, "If you send him packing back to Ireland, then job done I'd say."

Elvis is disgusted at how low Bo-Bo is prepared to stoop to cover his own back, fully aware that clean living fitness-freak Barnaby is the last person who'd have anything to do with drugs. He's now having to bite his tongue, barely able to keep quiet, just waiting now for this dishonest toad to clear off so he can put Louis well and truly in the picture.

"Was there anything else, Louis?" says Bo-Bo, keen to get away and set the betting lounge up for another blatantly dishonest days trading. He also knows there is a chance several members of staff will be wanting Uppers from him before he opens.

"No, nothing else, and I will speak to the Irish boy, don't you worry, leave it with me," states Louis, as Bo-Bo gets up to go, while throwing a nervous look at Elvis. "Oh, yes, there was one more thing, just remembered, I'm getting Bryn Sanders down for a mid-season audit," says Louis, as an afterthought. Not what Bo-Bo wants to hear, his doctored paperwork being inspected when he hasn't had proper time to cover his tracks.

"Really? No need for that is there, Louis? Expensive things, audits," says Bo-Bo, hoping that neither Louis nor Elvis can see the sweat breaking out on his brow.

"It won't do any harm," confirms Louis.

"Ok, if you say so," replies a rather shaken Bo-Bo, wondering what the hell he is going to do to cover up his deceit in a short space of time.

Once Bo-Bo has safely departed the apartment it's time for Elvis to pass on the information Leonard happily gave up. He takes a seat across from Louis. "Well, I have very bad news for you, boss," he confirms, "Seems my suspicions were correct – and didn't you notice how panicked he looked just then when you mentioned about Bryn coming down?"

Louis sighs, knowing he is not going to like what he hears next. "Go on then, let me have it," he says, unhappily.

"Well, this CV is nothing more than a tissue of lies, I'm so sorry boss," says Elvis, seeing Louis going very pale, while wondering just how big a fool he's being made of. Elvis spares nothing, telling Louis the information he found out, about Bo-Bo's shady past, his gambling debts, and that he invented the story about selling his pitches, while explaining how it couldn't possibly happen and why. "And if you think young Barnaby is behind the drugs thing, then I'm sorry boss, you couldn't be more wrong," states Elvis, "If you charged an entrance fee to use the swimming pool and the gym, he'd be your best customer by a mile."

"I know that already," replies Louis, "Never suspected him for a second. Looks like we've got Bo-Bo bang to rights, on the face of it. That said we may need more solid proof, not that I doubt your cousin of course."

"What more proof do you need?" says Elvis, "Shall I get Len to come down here to speak to you, he's only in Cheltenham, could be here in an hour and a half?"

"No, no need for that, I'm sure it's all true, but we still need to trip Bo-Bo up somehow. Let me have a think," says Louis.

The Maynards are making their way through the centre of the camp, ahead of a morning in the arcades on the front. They pass right by a large souvenir shop. To Johanna's horror one of her drawings is on display right in the middle of the window, with a large sign above it stating 'NEW IN - PORTRAITS OF PORTWYNNE'. She can't believe that Louis Peyton has immediately betrayed her like this.

Christy has quickly spotted it as well, and looks at her open mouthed. Seeing the fear on Johanna's face, she knows straightaway she had no idea about this. Trevor has also noticed the drawing, but is blissfully unaware who the artist is, not bothering to look close enough at the name signed neatly in the corner.

"What the bloody hell is that thing?" he says, jabbing his thumb in the direction of the picture, "Who in their right mind would want that on their wall, piece of rubbish."

Christy can see through the shop window at least two people at the till with copies in their hand, while wondering how this could have possibly happened. Luckily, she manages to get a quiet word with Johanna. "Dad, I'm just going in here to get a bottle of pop," says Christy, "Come with me Johanna."

Trevor doesn't question this, and the two of them go into the cafeteria.

"Well, what's going on?" asks Christy.

"The man who bought my picture the other day, he works for Louis Peyton and showed it to him. Yesterday I had to go and see Mr Peyton and he asked me to draw ten more the same, he gave me some money for it," admits Johanna, who goes onto explain how she was tracked down and that her and Charlotte were taken to Louis's apartment, where he made his request, and how they had managed to sneak back there once the pictures were done. "He promised he'd be discreet, I had no idea he was tricking me," says Johanna sadly.

Christy isn't daft, knowing fine well that Louis Peyton would see Johanna as a money making machine, and not caring about the hard time she would get if Trevor and Muriel knew what was going on. They re-join their unaware parents and the others and head down to Portwynne promenade.

10 minutes later the Chesters make their own way past the same shop. Charlotte can't believe her eyes when she sees Johanna’s drawing in the window. "On my god," she says out loud.

"What's the matter?" asks Liz, wondering what has caused this sudden outburst. Charlotte sees no choice but to come clean.

"If I tell you, it must be kept a secret," she says.

"I don't understand," says a mystified Liz.

"See that drawing there, in the window, well Johanna drew that," admits Charlotte, "But don't say anything, her mum and dad don’t know."

Liz and Colin go up to the window to have a closer look. "Did she really draw this, it's very good," smiles Colin.

"She draws in secret, her parents would throw her books away if they knew," says Charlotte, sadly.

"So, what you are saying is Johanna Maynard drew this picture, but her parents don't know anything about it?" says Liz, a little surprised.

Charlotte tells them about how Louis Peyton had found out, and asked her to draw some more. They go inside to see if the others are on display. The five left are displayed prominently on a stand in the middle of the shop, as another holidaymaker takes one down and heads for the till.

"Well I never," chuckles Liz, "Could she draw us one, do you think?"

"I'm sure she would, but you know what her dad’s like," says Charlotte, "He made her leave school at 16 instead of going to Art College."

"I don't believe it, she's so gifted," says Liz, "Her parents should be proud!"

"This is Trevor Maynard we're talking about, ignorant oaf," states Colin.

"Well, that's true enough. What a shame though, poor Johanna," says Liz, turning to go.

Once again their number is one light, as Eleanor has disappeared.

A large display of replica Seasider-wear, especially for kids to dress up in with a large 'Seasider In Training' logo printed on them so no-one cold feasibly pass themselves off as a real one, has immediately caught her eye. "Mum, look at these," she smiles excitedly, looking at the replica polo shirt and Seasiders light blue blazer, along with pairs of white shorts, skirts and blouses.

Liz silently curses Louis Peyton under her breath. "I wish you would forget all these daft ideas, you know."

"Please mum, oh go on dad. Let me have these," pleads Eleanor, "Please."

Unsurprisingly, Colin quickly caves in to his youngest daughter. "Oh go on then," he sighs, "One of everything, in age 12."

To pacify Jamie, before he comes out with 'what about me', a football with a Manchester United badge on it is also purchased. They too head down to the promenade.

Despite the resort being full of holidaymakers it isn't long before the Chesters' catch up with Trevor, Muriel and Johanna in one of the many arcades on the front. The rest of the Maynard family have headed for the beach, while Trevor is busily feeding a fruit machine with 5 pence pieces, with Muriel looking over his shoulder, and Johanna standing behind them looking bored.

Charlotte thinks nothing of approaching them, wanting to see Johanna and hopefully getting her away, knowing she will need some private time to be able to fulfil Louis's latest order. Trevor half looks over his shoulder.

"What do you want, piss off," he says, threateningly.

Charlotte doesn't care, and won't be intimidated by this big bully. "I wanted to see if Johanna wanted to come to the coffee shop with me, it's only just down the front, we won't be far." Johanna brightens up immediately.

"No," states Trevor, while hammering the buttons on an unforgiving machine, that is eating coins at a rate of knots. He looks over his shoulder again. "You still here?" He spots Colin, Liz and the others peering through the front door, remembers his pledge to play things cool, and quickly backs down. "Oh whatever, go on, clear off then, but we'll be out looking for you in a bit though," he states.

Johanna and Charlotte leave the arcade happily, and Liz smiles as she sees them both approaching. She lowers her voice a little. "Charlotte told me about your drawings, but it's alright, I won't breathe a word."

"They're excellent," confirms Colin, "Can't understand why your parents wouldn't be proud."

"I don't understand either, but my dad would think nothing of throwing my books away if he knew," says Johanna, sadly, "He saw my drawing in the shop window and said it was a piece of rubbish!"

Liz shakes her head in despair. "Anyway, where are you two off to?"

"Johanna needs to draw some more pictures for Mr Peyton, we'll go in that coffee shop down there," confirms Charlotte. Trevor comes out of the arcade.

"Give me some more money, Johanna, I've lost it all," he shouts, not acknowledging anyone else. Reluctantly she hands over £5, knowing he will soon lose that as well. He disappears back inside without another word.

Charlotte and Johanna go on their way, while the others head across to the beach.

Once safely hidden away in the coffee shop, Johanna quickly gets her sketch book and pens out, to create more portraits as Louis had asked. "Mum and dad said sorry to me this morning," she says, as starts the first one, "Dad didn't apologise to Barnaby though, didn't say anything at all when he saw him at breakfast."

"He should have said sorry at the very least, that was terrible what he did to him," replies Charlotte, watching Johanna in awe, "It's amazing how you can draw these pictures, brilliant. How do you do it?"

"It's easy," smiles Johanna, in her element, creating an identical scene to the ones before, "I look at something and then like a camera I take a mental photo, and after that I draw what I can see in my head."

Charlotte smiles broadly. "That is such a gift to have, I don't know anyone else who can do this," she says.

"I will need your help though, Charlotte," replies Johanna, "I won't be able to get away from those two for long enough to get to Mr Peyton today, so could you take them for me? I'll give you some of the money."

"Of course I'll help you, but I'm not taking your money," states Charlotte.

"I can't believe Mr Peyton told lies about being discreet with my pictures," says Johanna, feeling a little upset.

"Neither can I, but he's a businessman, he makes money, and the only way to do that is by putting your pictures where everyone can see them," Charlotte replies, "It's wrong of him though." This gives Charlotte an idea, which she keeps to herself.

Just as Johanna is finishing her 6th picture in rapid succession, Charlotte sees Muriel peeping through the window. "Quick, give them to me, your mum and dad are outside," she says, carefully putting them into her bag.

Johanna manages to stash her book and pens away in time before her mother strides up to the table, demanding her return. Having refused to allow Charlotte to spend the afternoon with them, Charlotte instead crosses the road to the beach looking for Colin, Liz and her younger siblings.

Back at Happy Daze, Louis decides to make a surprise visit to the betting lounge, hoping to catch Bo-Bo off guard. He's already been on the telephone to the Auditors office, arranging a visit, and has also put in a call to Portwynne job centre, hastily requesting a vacancy card for a Betting Lounge manager and cashier to be put up, having already decided that the trust has completely gone, and that proof or not he will be relieving Bo-Bo of his position before the week is out.

When he arrives, the place is full. At least thirty men, craning their ears to hear the commentary of the latest greyhound race from Hackney. A man who is having a fortnights stay, and had been losing a substantial amount day after day, is at the counter. Bo-Bo had been creaming this mans losings off with alarming regularity, confident that his pattern of backing a string of outsiders at a tenner a time would never bear fruit.

Bo-Bo nearly faints with the shock as the man moves away from the counter, revealing Louis's presence. He tries to keep calm. "Hello boss, to what do I owe the pleasure," he says, shakily.

"Just seeing how things are ticking over," replies Louis, "Busy for a change, I see."

"Yes, ummm big meeting at Haydock this afternoon," lies Bo-Bo, knowing fine well he'd be this busy if the only thing to bet on was two spiders crawling up a wall. Another punter brandishing a five-pound note puts a bet on.

"Can I come round the back, I'm taking your counter up," says Louis. Bo-Bo is less than keen, but unlocks the side door to allow his employer in.

Louis looks around, not immediately seeing anything untoward, until his eye is drawn to a plastic box under the counter. It's stuffed full of money, but totally separate to the till drawer he can see half open, as Bo-Bo takes more bets. "What's that?" asks Louis, pointing at the box containing what his dishonest manager had been putting on one side.

"Erm, it's the banking, I'll be paying it in before I get here tomorrow," he lies. Louis doesn't totally believe him, but has no proof it's anything else. He looks around again, but with the drugs safely hidden behind the false wall at the back of the safe, there isn't anything else for Louis to find.

"Right, ok then," he says, "I'll leave you to it." He goes back into the lounge, as a steady stream of customers are queuing up, happy to part with their money.

At 6pm, in line with the agreement, Charlotte heads up to Louis's apartment. She now only has 5 new pictures on her after Liz asked to hang on to one, with the promise of treating Johanna to 'something nice' in return. Elvis is stood by the gates waiting.

"Johanna can't come tonight, she's stuck with her mum and dad, can't get away," admits Charlotte.

"No bother," replies Elvis, "What have you got."

"Only five. Johanna is really sorry, but she has had no proper time to herself at all."

"I see, well, that is something, please give her this," says Elvis, "Her share of the profit and an advance for these." He hands over £80, holding back a further £20 due to only having five more to sell. The first ten, including the one in the window, sold out before lunchtime.

Now is the time for Charlotte to reveal her plan. "Johanna says she might not be able to draw any more, says that Mr Peyton has played a trick on her, putting her drawing in the window where everyone can see it," she says, mischievously, "Her dad saw it, but doesn't know it's Johanna's drawing. He said it was rubbish, but that isn't the point."

"I realise," says Elvis, a little sheepishly, "I will ask Louis to be more discreet, but make sure she brings us some more tomorrow, these are going like hot cakes."

"Ok, but please don't put them in the window, Johanna wont draw any more if you do." Charlotte knows this is a lie, that she never said anything of the sort about stopping production, but feels it's only fair Johanna has some protection. If her parents knew for a minute what was going on they would quite quickly put a stop to it, and spend what money she'd earned on beer and fish suppers.

Chapter Ten

Tuesday night is the one night where getting to the Family Centre extremely early is necessary to guarantee anywhere to sit. 'Happy Families Night' is widely advertised about the camp, with the highlight being the 'Happy Families Competition', where first prize is a free fortnights holiday at Happy Daze, and £100 in vouchers to be spent in the shops and bars around the park.

It's such a big night that Louis Peyton himself attends, as one of the judges. He's already there sat behind a table on the edge of the dance floor, closely guarded by Elvis. He has Johnny and Marissa either side of him also as judges. It's taking all of Elvis's concentration to keep his mind on Louis, with the faint aroma of Marissa's perfume, that he bought her for her birthday, wafting around, exciting him greatly.

The competition itself is very straightforward; four members of any family, with at least one adult and one child amongst them, are interviewed by Seasider Alun, with the most worthy, or most interesting family being named the winner. In the early days of running this popular competition Louis found himself being bought in by sob stories, with families coming out of all sorts of hard luck tales, true or otherwise, in an attempt to win.

More recently, and in light of many letters of complaint about cheats using underhand tactics, he's a little more careful. Anyone mentioning illness, burnt down houses, or lost jobs doesn't win, while anyone mentioning good deeds, charity or achievements, however, is a strong candidate for the much sought after prizes.

Colin makes a suggestion that Liz and the children take part, however having seen Johnny as one of the judges the idea is quickly abandoned, knowing that if they didn't win Johnny would feel bad, and if they did, it might cause cries of 'fix', if it got out that Johnny knows them personally. Also, Eleanor has insisted on wearing her new 'Seasider in Training' blazer, blouse and skirt, despite Liz's pleas for her not to.

Charlotte tells the others that the tall gentleman stood behind Louis Peyton is the one who bought Johanna's painting on Sunday afternoon.

Rodney, Sandra and the twins are entering the contest however, with Trevor telling them in no uncertain terms to do all they can to win the free holiday and "£100 in beer tokens for me and your mum."

On what is a very busy week for at Happy Daze, 23 different families have lined up to take part. Alun is already rolling his eyes, knowing it will take forever to have enough words with everyone, to ensure an equal chance for them all to win. Dave Busby & Busbys Canyon strike up a Fanfare as Alun takes to the floor.

"Good evening ladies and gentlemen, boys and girls. Tonight as you all know it's 'Happy Families Night' here in the Family Centre, and many of you I know are looking forward to our special competition," he says to the assembled crowd, "so without further ado, let me introduce to you our judges this evening. Our chief Seasiders Marissa Black and Johnny Major, along with the main man himself, the owner of this wonderful leisure park Mr Louis Peyton."

The crowd applaud enthusiastically, as all three of them wave back cheerily.

The competition begins with Alun inviting the first family up. Nothing spectacular about them, just an ordinary family here for a good time. No sob story, no good deeds to report, and nothing particularly interesting to say. Alun knows that if this is replicated a further 22 times, it'll be a very long night indeed.

The next few families are no better than the first one, with one families sole achievement being their young son recently gaining his 100 metre swimming badge. Alun manages to remain cheerful and polite throughout, using all of his Seasider charm to make sure interest in the competition is kept and that people don't start wandering off to the bar, the cafeteria or the Jolly Roger with boredom. One of those weeks, he muses. It's not much fun on the judges table either, with Johnny doing his best to stay awake, despite taking three Uppers earlier on. 'How the heck are we going to pick a deserving winner out of this lot?' he thinks, 'bloody impossible, all as plain as one another.'

Rodney, Sandra, Karl and Mikey take their turn. Trevor and Muriel jump to their feet shouting support a little too enthusiastically, to the annoyance of everyone else, including their four family members on the floor.

"Now who do we have here?" asks Alun. Although he already knows the identity of the family in front of him, he has to pretend otherwise.

"My name is Rodney Maynard, this is my wife Sandra, and our twin boys Mikey and Karl," confirms Rodney.

"Lovely," says Alun, "And what would you like to tell us about yourselves."

"Well, my son Mikey has recently had a trial at Birmingham City Football Club, and now plays for their Under 9s team as a striker."

"Very nice," says Alun, as yet another banal fact is trawled out, "Anything else?"

"My wife Sandra here does a lot of fundraising for charity, her parents are members of the Salvation Army, so Sandra bakes cakes and knits dolls for them to sell. Raised £150 at their Easter fete." Alun smiles at this, but can't believe any member of the Maynard family could have a religious side to them, despite Rodney being perfectly truthful. His in-laws are senior members of their local branch of the Salvation Army, and Sandra's baking and knitted toys are big money-makers.

"Anything else you'd like to tell us?" asks Alun, again.

"Well, I just wanted to say a massive thank you to Mr Peyton for giving ordinary families like us, with not much money, a chance to have a week away, with top class catering and entertainment. I can't believe he's not been honoured by the Queen, as one of this countries most foremost businessmen." A few people applaud in agreement, but there are plenty of groans at this blatant attempt to catch Louis Peyton's attention and win the prizes.

Louis is quietly delighted at this praise, but having heard a surname of Maynard knows they must be related to Johanna, and in turn her troublesome father. There is no doubt however that they are the pick of the families so far. Trevor and Muriel are sitting smugly.

"Got it in the bag," says Trevor confidently, "Good idea of yours that Muriel, about mentioning the Queen."

"Yes, that should nail it for us," she smiles.

Several more families take their turn, all no more interesting than the earlier entrants, making it clear that Rodney and his family are streets ahead of the competition.

There's two families left. A nondescript blonde haired woman with her three mixed race children take to the floor. "And who have we here?" asks Alun once again.

"My name is Maxine Evans, and my children are Louise, Rachel and Danny," she smiles.

"And what would you like to tell us about yourselves," says Alun.

"Well, it's not so much me, but my husband actually," replies Maxine, while pointing towards a tall West Indian gentleman sat near the back, "He runs sports teams for underprivileged children in our area. There is a lot of poverty where we live, but Desmond helps those who can't afford equipment, to play cricket in the summer and football in the wintertime. We fund raise to get balls, bats, and pads and so on."

"Very nice," says Alun, knowing this will be music to Louis's ears.

"However," continues Maxine, "just 3 weeks before the Cricket Season started in April, we had a burglary. Someone broke into our council lock up, and took all our equipment."

Alun tries not to groan, seeing all this ladies hard work undone by a sob story, in the knowledge that Louis will not be impressed by that one bit. If only she hadn't mentioned it, he thinks.

She hasn't quite finished her tale though. "Well, we won't be beaten by bullies, so we all clubbed together, had several sponsored events, and thanks to our local newspaper we received a donation from our local county cricket team." Maxine gets out a piece of newspaper showing her husband collecting a cheque from a well-known cricketer. "We managed to replace the equipment with a couple of days to spare. My wonderful husband does all this for free, out of a passion for helping those with not much. He works full time as a bus driver too, so this is all done in his spare time. We all help out, even the kids."

Alun smiles widely, happy she pulled it back. This is the best story heard so far by a long way he thinks, as she walks off. The last family have nothing better to offer, and the competition is brought to a swift close.

"Thank you to all the families who have entered tonight, the standard was very high," lies Alun, knowing fine well the Evans family have this sewn up, "Now, while the judges make their final deliberations, let's have some music from our resident band Dave Busby and Busbys Canyon!"

Alun is glad to depart the floor for a while, grabbing a much needed glass of water.

Trevor is glaring angrily at the Evans' table, seeing his 'beer tokens' go up in smoke. "Bloody typical," he moans. No one else, aside from Muriel, is remotely bothered that they won't win, not even Rodney and Sandra, more than happy to see someone else more deserving take the prize.

On the judges table though, things aren't so cut and dried. Louis knows he's making a small fortune from Johanna's paintings, and is worried the supply will completely dry up, given her unhappiness at seeing them in the window of the shop, as Elvis had informed him. By making her relatives the winner, that'll mend the bridges he thinks.

Johnny and Marissa are without doubt though. "Only one

winner there," states Johnny, "Them ones two from the end. It's marvellous he does all that for poor kids, while holding down a full time job."

"And they didn't let the thieves beat them," says Marissa, "We can't give it to anyone else."

"There were others who were quite good," says Louis sheepishly, "The family with the young swimming champion, and that other lot who fund raise for the Sally Army, just as worthy." Marissa can't believe her ears, but the light soon dawns.

"Is this to do with young Johanna who draws the pictures?" she asks, "Are you planning on giving her brother the winnings to keep her happy?"

Louis glares at Marissa, unhappy that any of his employees should see straight through him with such ease.

"I'm only suggesting," he insists, "The family you mention are not the only ones, that's all."

Johnny is also mystified, unable to fathom why Louis is looking elsewhere for this weeks winner. Unfortunately, though, Louis has the final say, and choosing greed over popular opinion decides that the Maynards are to be the winners. Marissa is horrified, and Johnny is totally baffled. Both value their employment more than anything else, so choose to say nothing in the light of this shameful decision.

Alun takes to the floor again to announce the winning family, accompanied by another fanfare. He looks at the card in his hand with the victor's surname on, and is astonished to see it reads anything other than Evans. For a moment it crosses his mind to lie, but also concerned for his job over his opinion reads the words verbatim.

"Thank you everyone," he says, a little uneasily, "The judges have deliberated and their final decision is made. The winner of this weeks 'Happy Families Competition' is...." He can barely get the words out, knowing this to be an injustice of the highest order, "The MAYNARDS!" A stunned Rodney thinks he is hearing things, while

Trevor and Muriel are punching the air in unexpected delight.

The rest of the family, although pleased, are thoroughly ashamed. This decision is not well received elsewhere either, the boos and catcalls from all around the Family Centre are audible. Everyone else knows Rodney and Sandra were not the moral winners, and are unable to understand how the judges came to this outcome.

Rodney goes up to Alun to collect the envelope containing the prizes, but is more than a little embarrassed and can barely look him in the eye. "Congratulations," says Alun, not meaning it for a minute, "Have you a few words for us?"

"I have actually," says Rodney a little quietly, "I can't accept this, we should not have won. I'd like to give that other family over there the prizes instead, if that is possible." A loud cheer goes up at this noble gesture, as Rodney strides over to the Evans's table, handing over the envelope and warmly shaking Desmond Evans by the hand. Maxine is filling up with tears, and gets up to give Rodney a hug.

Predictably this is not going down well with Trevor and Muriel, who selfishly still want the winnings for themselves. Trevor is out of his seat spoiling for an argument.

"Sit down dad, for god's sake," says an exasperated Christy, knowing fine well Rodney has done the right thing.

"They have stolen our prizes, we're the winners," he shouts, striding towards where Rodney and the Evans family are happily chatting. Alun and Johnny can see the trouble coming, and are in pursuit, while Louis has his head in his hands, knowing he's the orchestrator of all this. Muriel is chasing across as well. The Seasiders manage to get their hands on Trevor just as he's swinging a punch at Desmond Evans.

"Get him out of here," splutters Louis to Elvis. Elvis dashes across the dance floor to help Alun and Johnny eject him from the Family Centre. The only other member of the Maynards who follows him out of the building is Muriel. They glare angrily at Elvis,

Alun and Johnny, but make no further fuss. They go off the Jolly Roger to lick their wounds.

The rest of the family are sitting at their table in complete shock and embarrassment. Liz and Colin, sat two tables away, turn around. "I feel so sorry for you," says Liz with concern, knowing that the rest of the family are totally blameless and are being let down by Trevor yet again.

Charlotte goes over to comfort Johanna, upset at her family being made fools of in front of Johnny for the umpteenth time. Busbys Canyon start playing some loud, up-tempo numbers to try and lighten the mood, as Louis wanders over to where the remaining Maynards are sitting. Christy can't believe he won't do anything other than make things a million times worse than they already are.

"I just wanted to say I am sorry, but I genuinely believed you were the best on the night," he says, trying to make the best of the situation.

"No you didn't," spits Christy, "You don't have to hide anything from us, we all know you are up to, ripping off my sister, it's only my thick headed parents who aren't aware."

"No he isn't, that's not true," protests Johanna, "I like drawing, if Mr Peyton wants my pictures then he can have them, I don't even want any money for them."

"You made Rodney the winner on purpose to please Johanna, we're not stupid," states Christy, "He did the right thing in letting the other family have the prizes, as they should have won all along."

"I don't agree," says Louis, stubbornly determined to stick to his lies, "I was very impressed, and thought you deserved to win." Christy shakes her head. "Also, I am very sorry Johanna," he continues, "I have let you down somewhat, but like I told you already, your drawings should not be hidden away. If only your parents could be made to see this. I will leave you good people to the rest of your night."

With that he swiftly leaves the Family Centre, shadowed by Elvis.

A little while later on, in bed, are Elvis and Marissa, with Marissa chancing her arm for a third night in succession, too loved up to contemplate her rickety falling down chalet with its draughty windows, preferring the strong arms of her secret love, while confident enough she won't be spotted like she was earlier on.

"I got caught sneaking back in this morning," she admits, "Barnaby Walsh saw me, I couldn't believe it."

"What did you tell him?" asks Elvis, concerned, fearful of Louis finding out, and that being the end of their relationship.

"That I was seeing no-one he knew," replies Marissa, snuggling up tight to him, "I hate all this secrecy, Elvis."

"So do I, but what can we do," he says, kissing her softly, "You know what will happen, he'll pull rank."

"He might not, if he sees how much we love each other," gushes Marissa, hopefully. Elvis isn't so sure, knowing Louis's strong stance on relations between his staff. Marissa, on the other hand, knows something that means their secret may not be a secret for too much longer.

Also in bed, Liz whispers to Colin her many concerns about their holiday so far. "I want to go home, enough is enough," she moans, "A chalet that is falling apart, our daughter wanting to leave school to work here as a Seasider, frightful neighbours, the list goes on."

"It's not all bad," whispers Colin, "Jamie is enjoying himself, made friends with the twins."

"He doesn't have to be here to play football all day, he's just as happy in our back garden, as you well know," counters Liz.

"It's been nice to see Johnny, which was why we came in the first place, to see him," replies Colin, "The beer is cheap, the food plentiful and the entertainment at the theatre has been top notch.

So not all bad at all Lizzy, I'm sure we'll make it to next Saturday."

"Not sure I will," moans Liz, cuddling up to Colin, as the bed makes it customary loud squeak.

"Thought you were looking forward to that 'Grown Ups Sports Day' tomorrow, and the talent show later on," says Colin softly, referring to two events they had seen in the events programme.

"Well yes, I suppose so," whispers Liz, "But surely you can understand why I'm a little fed up."

Colin kisses her lovingly. "Don't worry Lizzy, everything will work out just fine," he says, while remembering this is not the first time he's had to put his beloved wife's mind at rest.

Chapter Eleven

It's not only Liz who is getting another restless night's sleep. Over in his staff chalet, Barnaby is also unable to rest easy. Tuesday was his day off, aside from serving at breakfast time. He spent most of the day hiding away in his chalet, afraid of being seen by Trevor, not knowing if he would try to attack him again, if seeing him away from the dining hall.

The only time he ventured out after his breakfast shift was for his regular morning trip to the indoor pool, and for his dinner. All the while though he was looking over his shoulder, in case he was being followed or chased. He still can't get Johanna or Charlotte out of his mind, attracted to both of them immensely. What should he do? Forget about both of them? 'If only it was that easy,' he thinks, while turning over, desperately trying to get some rest ahead of another full days work.

Louis is also lying awake, troubled at the thought of the previous days mither. The realisation that someone he thought he trusted is stealing his money, and possibly dealing drugs to his staff, also, his new money-maker, Johanna's drawings, possibly coming to a grinding halt thanks to stupidly putting them where her nuisance parents could see them, and to top it all the fracas in the Family Centre.

What is bothering him more than anything is not having concrete proof Bo-Bo is up to no good, that he currently has only assumption and second hand information to go on. And with the Seasiders stonewalling every time he raises the issues of drugs, it's becoming a massive frustration. Louis has already decided to give Bo-Bo his cards in any case, but knows he may be making more trouble than it's worth if he can't find due cause to fire him. What to do.

As he lies quietly, inspiration strikes. It's 4.30 in the morning, but that doesn't stop Louis immediately getting on the telephone to

Elvis with his idea.

Elvis and Marissa are soundly dozing in the flat when the shrill ring of the telephone goes off by his bedside, causing them both to wake with a jolt. He guesses in an instance it's Louis, and groans when he sees the time of day. What the hell is going on?

"Hello?" he mutters sleepily.

"Elvis? It's me. I've got it!" states Louis.

"Who is it," mutters Marissa, yawning.

Elvis covers the receiver. "It's Louis, shush," he whispers, before replying, annoyed at his employer for being disturbed, "What? Got what?"

"I've thought of how we can smoke Bo-Bo out, how we can get certain proof he definitely is our mystery drug dealer," says Louis, with barely concealed excitement.

"Ok, how," says Elvis, quietly wishing this could wait until he got to the apartment at a better hour.

"Bring Barnaby Walsh to see me, before he's due on work, tell him he's got the morning off," says Louis, "I've got a plan." He doesn't expand on his idea, but insists that Barnaby is brought to the apartment, that he will be the perfect plant to catch out Bo-Bo for once and for all.

Elvis is happy to do as his boss asks, but has to get to Barnabys chalet at ½ past six, after Marissas information that this diligent member of staff always arrives at the dining hall extra early, usually after his morning jog around the park. Barnaby is up and about, just back from completing his run, having a quick cup of coffee in his chalet before heading out for his shift. He nearly jumps out of his skin when he hears a loud knock on the door, petrified that it's Trevor looking for him.

Slowly, Barnaby opens the door, and doesn't know whether to be relieved or alarmed to see Elvis standing there. Elvis is quick to tell him that he's not in any sort of trouble, that Louis has a job for him that will give him a shift off. A mystified Barnaby makes his way to Louis's apartment two hours later. Apart from tracking down Barnaby, Louis also has an extra early morning task for Elvis.

Over in Primrose Block, just as Trevor, Muriel, Eunice and Johanna are about to head down for breakfast, they receive a visitor at the chalet door. It's Elvis, there on Louis's instruction.

"What the hell do you want," splutters Trevor, realising this is the man who threw him out of the Family Centre the night before.

"I have a letter for you, from Louis Peyton," confirms Elvis, "I suggest you read it very carefully and note the contents." Trevor opens the envelope, and can barely believe what he sees.

'Dear Mr Maynard,

In light of last nights incident, and other misdemeanours brought to my attention, you and your wife are now prohibited from entering the following premises at Happy Daze, Portwynne, with immediate effect:

Family Centre
Peytons Pavilion
Sonikz Disco

This banning order is indefinite. Please be advised that the restrictions do not affect any other members of your family, who are welcome to come and go as they please. My staff are fully aware of the situation, and you and your wife will not be granted access to any of the above buildings.

I trust there will be no further issues, and that this instruction will be heeded.

Yours faithfully,

L Peyton Esq'

“He can't do this!" shouts a furious Trevor, "I pay to stay here, so I'll go where the hell I want to. Look at this Muriel. This is outrageous!"

"As sole proprietor of this leisure park, Mr Peyton can act as he sees fit," says Elvis.

It's all Johanna can do not to burst out laughing and say 'serves you right'. Reluctantly Trevor and Muriel decide to take their punishment, knowing at least they can get their beer in the Jolly Roger, and Muriel can still play her bingo.

Johanna asks if she can go off with Charlotte again, with something in mind. Having been kept awake, as normal, by loud snores from her parents rattling the thin walls, she spent most of the night drawing some more beach pictures for Louis, with an idea to try and deliver them early, allowing her a day off. The initial instinct is for her parents to disallow her going off again, but mindful of the trouble they are already in they reluctantly agree to her request, and she heads next-door.

Barnaby is sat across from Louis in the study, wondering what exactly he wants with him, given that Elvis had said he wasn’t in trouble. “I have a very important mission for you,” confirms Louis, “But before I tell you what it is, I need you to be honest with me. I assure you I will not repeat anything you tell me.”

“Sure, boss,” says Barnaby, “What did you want to know?”

“I’ve heard that some of my staff might be taking drugs, supplied by someone else on my payroll,” says Louis, “Do you know anything about this?”

Of course Barnaby is fully aware of who is taking drugs, and where they are coming from, but as someone who enjoys keeping fit has nothing to do with such things, quietly minding his own business. Despite Louis asking him to be honest, he isn’t sure how much he should reveal, knowing that many of his colleagues depend on Uppers just to get from one day to another. “I know a little bit,” he says quietly.

"Go on, tell me what you know, all in confidence," implores Louis.

Barnaby sighs, hoping that Louis is as good as his word. "Rob Boston gets the tablets, but I don't know from where," confirms Barnaby. He doesn't know about Krystal, has never met her.

"That's fine, I just needed my suspicions confirmed," nods Louis, "And do you know what these drugs are, or who takes them."

"They are called 'Colviles Uppers', I think they are a stimulant of some sort, stops burn-out," says Barnaby, "But I couldn't tell you who takes them exactly, I certainly don't in any case, don't touch the stuff."

"I know you don't, which is why I want you to help me get the evidence I need to get rid of this parasite for good," says Louis, stopping short of mentioning the money laundering also going on.

Louis asks Barnaby to approach Bo-Bo, on the premise of wanting a small supply of Uppers for himself. Barnaby laughs out loud. "No way in a million years will he believe that," he says, knowing fine well of his own clean-living reputation.

"You have to try for me, until I've got those tablets in my hands I have nothing," states Louis, "At least try, think of anything you can to get them. I'll pay you handsomely for this, I promise."

"Ok, but I can't see it working, he'll sniff a rat, I'm certain," says Barnaby.

"I want rid of him, and need you to help me do that," insists Louis.

Having no choice in the matter, Barnaby leaves the apartment to go to the Betting Lounge. Just as he walks towards the apartment gates he sees Johanna and Charlotte, and can't help but smile. "Well, fancy seeing you here," he beams, fondly.

"We could say the same," replies Charlotte.

"Louis has given me a job to do, but what are you doing here?" asks Barnaby.

"I've drawn some more pictures, for Mr Peyton to sell, like I told you about," says Johanna.

"Oh, very good then, I won't keep you in that case, see you later," he says, making his way past them. Suddenly he gets the perfect idea. "Where are you two off to after this?" he asks.

"Going for breakfast, then I'm taking my little sister swimming," says Charlotte.

"I'm going down the arcades with Christy," confirms Johanna.

"Could one of you spare the time to help me with this job for Mr Peyton?" enquires Barnaby. He quickly explains what is expected of him, but thinks he'll be a little more convincing if he has a 'girlfriend' in tow. Johanna knows she won't get away with not turning up for breakfast, and Charlotte isn't keen on the idea either, but gives in.

With the drawings safely dropped off with a delighted Louis, Johanna heads back to the dining hall with excuses from Charlotte, while Charlotte and Barnaby go off to the Betting Lounge.

"What do you actually need me to do?" asks Charlotte.

"Nothing especially, just make it look like we are 'together'," replies Barnaby as they head up the stairs to the first floor. The lounge is closed, and with no light seen through the frosted glass door they both know that Bo-Bo is yet to arrive. They hover in the doorway of the Games Room nearby, keeping a look out.

Within ten minutes he appears, and spots the two youngsters. Barnaby acts quickly to look convincing, that Charlotte really is his girlfriend, by kissing her full on the lips, hoping she doesn't scream or recoil in horror as Bo-Bo looks across at them, then averts his gaze, disinterestedly.

Charlotte isn't happy, but plays along. As soon as they hear the door of the Betting Lounge locked behind him, she quickly pulls away. "I'm sorry, ok," says Barnaby.

An embarrassed Charlotte is glad only the Betting Lounge manager saw them, as she has no romantic designs on Barnaby whatsoever. Time to put the rest of the plan into action.

"Wait here, I won't be long," he says.

Barnaby knocks on the door of the Betting Lounge. It's not unusual for Seasiders, or other staff, to turn up wanting Uppers before opening time, so Bo-Bo isn't too concerned as he answers the door, expecting a regular customer. "What do you want?" he asks, astonished to see Barnaby standing there.

"Look, this is a bit awkward," replies Barnaby, glancing over at Charlotte, "Can I come in?"

"I suppose so," says Bo-Bo, a little unsure, but letting him inside. He quickly locks the door behind him. "Well, what can I do for you?" he says.

"I'm after some Uppers, I was told you have some for sale?" states Barnaby. Bo-Bo can't believe his ears.

"I have no idea what you're on about, mate," he fibs.

"Yes you do, Johnny Major told me you have some," says Barnaby, also untruthfully, but correctly guessing that if anyone is taking these pills, Johnny is.

"Did he now," replies Bo-Bo, "And what would a strapping young lad like you want with Uppers, every time I see you you're either jogging or coming out of the gym?"

"Umm, that is the problem, see my girlfriend out there, well, I'm that knackered afterwards, I'm struggling to ummm perform, she's getting a little cross with me," says Barnaby, shuffling awkwardly. Bo-Bo laughs out loud.

"Ok, you win, mate, but you tell Johnny from me to keep his gob shut, I don't want too many more knowing about this. Twenty quid for six, and only take one if you need to perform!"

A relieved Barnaby is happy enough to part with the money that Louis had already told him would be repaid many times over, once the evidence was presented. "I hope your girlfriend is grateful," says Bo-Bo, leading Barnaby back to the door, quickly hustling him outside, and swiftly locking the door again.

"Well?" asks Charlotte.

"I've got them," says Barnaby, breathing heavily with nerves.

"What did you tell him?" asks Charlotte.

"Ummm, nothing, just that I was feeling a bit run down, and I knew he had drugs to help," he replies.

"So you didn't need me at all then?" says Charlotte, feeling a little fed up, and taken advantage of.

"Ok, I told him we were having bedroom problems, you know, if you get me," states Barnaby, looking at the floor. Charlotte is horrified.

"Wonderful," she says, upset.

"Look, I had to think of something didn't I," insists Barnaby, "and I've got what Louis wanted."

Chapter Twelve

Charlotte and Barnaby quickly part ways outside, so she can catch up with the rest of her family in the dining hall and he can make tracks back to Louis's apartment.

Louis can barely believe the ease with which this matter can now be resolved, while happily paying Barnaby £100 for his time. "I knew you would come up trumps," exclaims Louis, while counting out the money, "What did you tell him, by the way?"

"It's not important," replies Barnaby, a little sheepishly, knowing it is likely Charlotte will never forgive him.

A quick telephone call to Colviles later and the truth is soon unravelled. Using the serial number on the box, this batch is traced back to a bogus order, supposedly shipped to a pharmacy on the outskirts of Portwynne, who themselves go on to claim they haven't ordered Uppers for almost six months. Further digging in regards to this totally fraudulent behaviour leads straight to Colviles Head of Sales, who quickly implicates the Financial Director, and his PA Krystal Boston.

To save his own skin he decides honesty is the best policy, explaining how Krystal was the mule, and how her husband was selling the tablets on at Happy Daze. Krystal is fired by the Managing Director on the spot, and the other two rogues are suspended in lieu of a full enquiry. Between the Managing Director of Colviles and Louis Peyton, they decide a word with the police wouldn't go amiss.

Charlotte gets back to the dining hall just as the rest of her family members are leaving. "Where did you get to?" enquires Liz, not totally believing Johanna's story of Charlotte going off to get some postcards to send home.

"I just wanted to get a few bits and pieces, before it got too busy," she lies. Colin and Liz wonder where she really got to, but can't tell that she's lying.

As planned Charlotte and Eleanor go off to spend the morning at the large indoor swimming complex at the front of the park. Colin has taken Jamie off for some football coaching, along with Rodney and the twins. Liz tells the girls to 'get on with it', while deciding to wait in the poolside coffee bar, preferring to read a magazine while the other two go off to swim.

Charlotte comes out of the changing room first to find Barnaby just getting out of the pool. He is the last person she wants to see, after their awkward encounter earlier on. Barnaby on the other hand, his eyes nearly fall out of his head at the pretty sight in front of him in her pink swimsuit. He can't help but approach her again, smiling widely, hoping to be forgiven.

"Wow, you look gorgeous," he says, "I can see you're getting a tan now as well, it really suits you."

Charlotte blushes, while thinking 'I wish he wouldn't say that, I don't even fancy him'. As much as she has enjoyed his company in the main these past few days, this kindly Irish boy is not Charlotte's idea of boyfriend material at all.

Eleanor appears behind them, and sees her sister being chatted up. Having already failed in getting a job, or even an application form out of any of the Seasiders she has so far mithered, perhaps it's not time to give up hope just yet.

"So, what are you up to later on?" Barnaby asks Charlotte.

"Well, I know my mum wants to take part in the 'Grown Ups Sports Day' later, so we'll be on the sports field," replies Charlotte, "Johanna will probably be there as well." She can see Barnaby tensing up slightly. "Look, I don't think her dad will attack you again, he's been banned from nearly everywhere on the camp, so we've heard," she confirms.

"I'm not surprised, he's nothing but a big bully," says Barnaby, spotting Eleanor looking over at them. "I best get dried off, perhaps I'll see you later, and I really am sorry for before," he says.

"It's ok, you only did what you had to," says Charlotte, keen to get away. Barnaby takes the hint, and heads towards the doors.

He doesn't get far, as sneaky Eleanor blocks his path. "Are you going out with my sister? Is she your girlfriend?" she asks, michievously.

"No, but between you and me I would like to ask her for a date, but don't let on to anyone," confirms Barnaby, despite knowing he's probably blown any chance he had, "She's very nice."

"If you can get me a job application form to work here as a Seasider, I can organise a date with her, do we have a deal?" replies Eleanor, through narrowed eyes.

Barnaby laughs. "You're not old enough to work here as a Seasider or anything, don't talk daft," he says.

"I mean it. I'm going to be a Seasider. Or would you like me to tell my dad I saw you and Charlotte kissing, and then he'll chase after you, like Johanna's dad did!" says Eleanor, naughtily.

Barnaby's throat goes dry. How the hell did she know about that, surely Charlotte didn't tell her? In a split second though he realises that Eleanor is just telling tales to get her own way.

"So, if I get you a form, you will get me a date with your sister, and you won't go running off telling lies to your parents, is that right?" says Barnaby, barely believing his ears.

"Got it in one," smiles Eleanor, proudly.

"I suppose I'll have to see what I can do then," he sighs, looking over his shoulder admiringly at Charlotte sat down with her legs dangling in the pool, while unable to understand why he is being held to ransom by a young girl.

Marissa is in the cafeteria, grabbing a quick coffee on a busy morning in-between stewarding the ladies darts competition, before taking charge of a Pub Quiz and onto the 'Grown Ups Sports Day'. She's known for over a fortnight that she is pregnant, but petrified of telling Elvis. In all the time they've been together marriage or kids have never been on the agenda, and she doesn't know how or if she can bring herself to tell him. If she decides to go through with it, letting Louis know she won't be returning to Happy Daze is also a scary proposition.

"Penny for 'em?" says Elvis, looking down at her. Marissa nearly jumps out of her skin.

"Oh, not worth a penny," she says.

"I'm just having a wander around, Louis wants me out of the way for some reason," he goes on, "Any chance of you dropping round later on?"

"Yes, of course, can I stop over again?" asks Marissa.

"No need to ask," smiles Elvis, adoringly.

Marissa knows she should be honest, and tell him he's going to be a father. Perhaps I'll tell him tonight, she thinks.

After an enjoyable morning at the pool, Charlotte, Eleanor and Liz head over to the sports field for the 'Grown Ups Sports Day', a weekly chance for parents, and other adults, to have a go at various events, such as tug of war and a penalty shootout competition. There is a massive crowd gathered on the sports field, with it being a very sunny day once again.

Stubbornly, Trevor and Muriel have no interest in attending. Rather than enjoying an afternoon in the sunshine with the rest of their family, they are holed up in the Jolly Roger, but everyone else is there, with Christy, Neil and Rodney all keen to take part, as Liz also joins them. Sandra is busy keeping her eye on the twins as they kick a football about nearby along with Jamie, while Colin insists "I'm too old for all this, I'll just watch if it's all the same." Charlotte and Johanna sit together chatting happily, however Liz has given Charlotte specific instructions to keep a keen eye on her younger sister, who is wearing her 'Seasider In Training' polo shirt and shorts, in case she takes it upon herself to get under the feet of the real Seasiders, knowing plenty of their number will be around.

The first tug of war is being assembled by Johnny and Big Barry, although they can see that the two sides are a little lop-sided. Johnny calls across to Marissa, who he can see chatting with some members of the crowd. “Oy, Marissa, join that side will you, level it up a bit.” Marissa looks nervously across, not wanting to take part at all for obvious reasons.

“Ummm, I can’t, swollen ankle, struggling to put weight on it,” she says, untruthfully. Johnny scowls a little, not keen on being part of the tug of war himself, but now having no choice in the matter.

A lovely afternoon spent in very high spirits, Johanna has her book out sketching the assorted goings on, having already drawn several more beach pictures to take to Louis for selling on tomorrow, very confident that her selfish parents won’t desert their beer for an afternoons entertainment in the sunshine.

Across the field Barnaby, having quickly looked around to ensure Trevor wasn’t there, makes his way over to where they are sat, looking forward to a nice relaxing time, enjoying the warm weather. He glances nervously at Colin, knowing he too would be unhappy if he knew what he had involved his daughter in this morning.

The large crowd on the sports field cheer loudly as the first tug of war gets under way, everyone there very much enjoying the afternoons event.

Over in the Jolly Roger, it's another story. Only Trevor and Muriel are in there, one of the very few places they are currently welcome, with everyone else outside enjoying the hot summer weather. Currently the staff are outnumbering them two-to-one. One bar manager, two bar staff, and one glass collector are more than a little fed up.

An agreement made with Louis Peyton, pinned up behind the bar, indicates that if business is very slow, or the pub is completely empty on any weekday afternoon, the staff reserve the right to close the doors until 7pm, but won’t be paid if they do. On a day like today the staff are not bothered about losing a few pounds in their pay packets. But unless they can persuade the

Maynards to leave, the bar will most likely have to stay open for as long as they want it to, to the aggravation of the staff who would prefer to be outside. Asking them to leave because business doesn't warrant being the bar being open won't wash with Trevor, they already know this.

To add to their annoyance, Trevor and Muriel are making the £5 given to them by Rodney last as long as possible, only slowly drinking their beer. Bar manager Hayley is scowling in their direction. "Bloody nuisance them pair," she mutters, "I wish they would clear off."

Glass collector Jed is equally as unforgiving, totally unbothered about missing a couple of hour's wages. He is Seasider Ruth's older brother, and would rather be on the Sports Field watching her at work, instead of hanging around waiting for the Maynards to drain their glasses. "Who wants to be inside in on a day like this, it's stupid."

Eventually, Trevor ambles his way to the bar for two more pints of beer. Hayley has had enough. "We're closing sir, having problems with the electrics," she lies, "Pumps aren't working."

"You what?" splutters a disbelieving Trevor, "We'll have bottled beer instead, it's all the same to us."

"The problem is affecting the coolers too, I would be breaking the law if I was serving beer below a certain temperature," says Hayley, the lies coming a little easier than she thought they would.

"I'm a sparky, let me have a look," says Trevor, who was once an electrician in the days he actually had a job. He tries to get behind the end of the bar. Jed defiantly blocks his way.

"Staff only, sir, I can't let you past," he states, "I'm sorry. We need to wait for the camp maintenance guys, and they might be some time. So for now, the bar is closed."

"Bloody liberty," shouts Trevor, "My wife and I want more beer, and it's your duty to find us some."

"I am sorry," confirms Jed, "but you will not get any in here."

Trevor knows that as they are banned from the Family Centre, and the Pavilion, they won't be getting their liquor anywhere on the camp right now.

"Look, I'm not bothered about the beer being warm, just get us two bottles, go on," he pleads.

"That would be against the law, as I already told you. If it gave you an upset stomach, we'd all be in trouble," insists Hayley, hoping the message gets through. It does. The thought of being ill doesn't appeal, so the pair of them slunk their miserable way out of the Jolly Roger, allowing a relieved Hayley to lock up behind them.

Liz, Christy, Neil and Rodney are up waiting to take part in another tug of war. Everyone else is standing up, ready to cheer them all on. Johnny, bringing Eleanor back with him after she had again hunted him down, comes across to where Charlotte and Johanna are. Johanna quickly puts her sketch book away, still not keen on him seeing her portraits.

"Got someone for you," chuckles Johnny.

"Stop mithering people, Eleanor," says Charlotte, "You know what mum said."

"I'm not doing any harm, I only wanted to help," says Eleanor, determined, "I want to be a Seasider! Why won't anyone listen to me!"

"I hear you, one day in the future maybe. Well, I need to get along, see you all later," smiles Johnny. He looks across and sees Trevor, with Muriel scurrying behind him, as they make their way across the sports field. Already in a foul mood after being made to depart the pub against his wishes, when he sees Johnny talking to Johanna and Charlotte this gets Trevor in an almighty rage. Barnaby also quickly makes himself scarce amongst the large crowd.

"What is that flaming dancing pouffe doing talking to Johanna, I knew it was a mistake letting her out of our sight," complains Trevor, loudly, while marching purposefully up to them, all ideas of playing things by the book quickly forgotten.

Johnny has seen him coming and hastily runs away in the other direction. The others look on in horror as a very scared Johanna wonders what is going to happen to her next. "Right, Johanna, what did we tell you, about who you can and can't speak to, come on, we're going back the chalet, you clearly can't be trusted," bellows Trevor, grabbing a very upset Johanna by the arm, dragging her away.

"Oy, what are you doing," shouts Charlotte, "You can't do that."

"Leave her alone Trevor, for goodness sake," shouts Eunice, unhappy at seeing her granddaughter being humiliated like this.

"You can all shut up, the lot of ya," snarls Trevor nastily, dragging Johanna away with Muriel in close pursuit.

Charlotte bursts into tears, feeling totally helpless. "Why are they like this, Johanna is the sweetest person ever, this is awful," she cries. Colin is on hand to put a comforting arm around her.

From the middle of the sports field Christy has spotted the fracas and is frantically running after her parents, no intention of letting them get away with this. Unable to get out of her father's firm grip, a destroyed Johanna is sobbing her heart out while seeing no choice but to comply. Just as Trevor thinks they've managed to get away, a very determined Christy flies at him from behind, making him let go.

"Go to my chalet, quickly, have you still got my spare key?" she shouts at Johanna, who nods and then runs away as her sister requested.

"Come back!" shouts Muriel, "Come back this minute!" Johanna takes no notice and keeps on running, while a winded Trevor, full of beer, tries to get to his feet.

"How could you," spits Christy, "Why did you do that? What for? Make a complete show of her, and the rest of us, you are pure evil."

"She wants teaching a lesson, she knows she shouldn't be speaking to that dancing fairy, or that Irish git, I know he's here somewhere an' all, we've told her enough times" snarls Trevor.

Back on the field, no one can believe what they've just witnessed.

"I'm going after her," says a defiant Charlotte. Colin, now joined by Liz, isn't so sure.

"Her sister is sorting it out," he says.

"Don't worry about it, no need for you to get involved," says Liz.

"No, mum, I can't leave her, I just can't," insists Charlotte, and runs away across the field in the direction of where the others disappeared.

The commotion allows Eleanor to go off again. She stands by Ruth proudly, pretending she is a proper Seasider. Ruth is trying to referee a penalty shootout, and doesn't need Eleanor hanging around, but is too polite tell her to go away.

"You two are disgraceful, you can't treat a 21-year-old like that," says Christy, getting emotional.

"We'll do what we want, she's our daughter," shouts Trevor, as Charlotte also appears.

"How could you do that to her," she says, tearfully, "And where's she gone to?"

"She's back at ours, it's alright," says Christy, as Charlotte quickly makes her way to comfort her friend.

"Why can't you all mind your own flaming business," spits Trevor, not liking his control of Johanna being taken away.

"Because you can't do this to her, it's wrong, I'm so sick of this," states Christy, also striding off in the direction of Primrose Block.

Charlotte bangs on Christy's door. "It's me. Charlotte. Let me in," she says, loudly, "I'm on my own." Johanna opens the door slowly to let her inside. She collapses in sobs, and Charlotte comforts her.

"Why did they do that, in front of Johnny as well, I just wanted to die," wails Johanna.

"It's alright now, they won't get you here, me and Christy will make sure of that." Christy arrives.

"Right, you are definitely staying here with us for the rest of the week, even if they apologise. That is it, final. Things are completely changing as of now." She looks out of the window, waiting for the rest of her family to return.

Trevor and Muriel come back first, but don't even bother coming round to Christy and Neil's chalet. When the others finally appear, Christy heads outside straightaway. "Rodney? We need to tell those pair now, right this minute, that things are changing big style," she states forcefully. Her brother Rodney also realises the time has come to give their parents a dose of the truth.

As the other members of the Maynard family go into their respective chalets, Christy knocks on Trevor's door, not even knowing if her father will open it. He does, slowly. As his two eldest children enter the chalet he sits beside Muriel, looking miserable.

"Right," says Rodney, "This wasn't supposed to happen just yet, but your behaviour has forced us to speak to you earlier."

"What you did this afternoon was despicable, and you know it," says Christy, getting tearful, "and believe me, it won't be happening again. Johanna isn't some little girl that you need to discipline, she's a grown woman, who should be having her own life, not acting as your skivvy."

"And not only that, from now on, dad," continues Rodney, "your gravy train just stopped rolling. If you want things, you pay for them yourself, I am not handing a penny more of my hard earned over to you two, enough is enough."

"Now you listen to me," shouts Trevor.

"No!" Christy shouts back, "We've had enough, we have all had enough. Johanna is no longer doing your bidding, so get used to that."

"And I am spending my money on Sandra and the kids instead of you," confirms Rodney.

Christy flounces past into the back bedroom to retrieve Johanna's clothes. The drawer where they are is quickly located, with Christy incredulous at the sorry state of them. Cartoon t-shirts, kids shorts, only one pair of jeans. Not a single dress or skirt to be seen. Christy shakes her head, sorrowfully. "I'll get that £500, even if I have to rob a bank for it," she mutters, while putting Johanna's meagre belongings into a carrier bag.

When she returns to the front room, she finds Rodney has been replaced by Eunice, who is currently clouting Trevor over the head with her hand. "You're not too old for one of these," states Eunice, while issuing another whack, "Don't you ever EVER do that to my granddaughter again, do you understand, utterly shameful the pair of you."

Christy smirks at the sight of her father cowering from his own mother, before departing.

Chapter Thirteen

Krystal Boston is doing everything she can to make her husband Bo-Bo aware of the huge heap of trouble they are both in. Trying to call him at Happy Daze failed, as Dolly Mason refused to transfer her calls or pass on her messages, well aware that the police are already on their way to arrest him.

Turning up at the Leisure Park is also out of the question, as with her massive shock of bleach-blonde hair, and her 40 inch chest, she is instantly recognisable, and would not be admitted by the security guard on the gate, who is already looking out for her, on instruction from Louis, should she dare to appear. Instead, she is sobbing loudly with her head in her hands, awaiting the inevitable knock on the door, only a matter of time before the police turn up wanting answers.

As such, Bo-Bo is unwittingly still going about his business, fleecing his punters and Louis as usual. He locks the door just after 5pm, same as normal, after another profitable day for himself. As he splits the takings between him and the shop there is a knock on the door. "Who is it?" he shouts up.

"It's me, Johnny," comes the reply. Bo-Bo lets his best customer in, and quickly locks the door behind him.

"I want a word with you, Johnny," says Bo-Bo, "How many people have you told about my little side-line?"

"No-one," says Johnny, truthfully, only speaking about Uppers in front of others who already knew.

"Are you sure about that," says Bo-Bo, heading behind the counter, "Had that Irish waiter here this morning wanting gear, said he'd heard about it from you." Johnny wonders how this could have happened, and assumes he must have overheard a rumour.

"I didn't say anything directly, he's probably overheard me somewhere, sorry Bo-Bo, I'll make sure it doesn't happen again. Can I have another dozen?"

"Yes, here you go, forty quid, mate," says Bo-Bo, getting two boxes out.

"Thanks Bo-Bo, you are a lifesaver," says Johnny, handing over the money, "I'll leave you to it, probably see you in a day or two." He goes to the door, which Bo-Bo swiftly locks behind him.

He's barely back behind the counter when the door goes again. Assuming it's Johnny coming back having forgotten something, or that it will be another regular customer, he doesn't even think to ask who's there this time, as he usually would. Two policemen are stood outside, to his utter disbelief.

"Robert Boston?" asks one of them.

"Yes," says Bo-Bo, trying to remain calm.

"Can we come in, have a quick chat with you?" says the other one. Silently, he lets them both in. The first one goes straight behind the counter, taking a look around. As Bo-Bo was still counting out the day's takings, the safe is wide open. The policeman looks inside, spots what looks like a crudely made false wall, which he quickly manages to dislogdge, revealing two dozen hidden boxes of Colviles Uppers.

"Well, well, well," he says, holding up a couple, "What have we here?"

Bo-Bo is swiftly arrested on suspicion of embezzlement, and the illegal possession and distribution of prescription drugs. The second policeman handcuffs him, and he is quickly escorted off the premises.

Elvis, stood outside the betting lounge, and now fully aware why Louis wanted him out of the way for a couple of hours while speaking to the police and Colviles, is given full responsibility to safely lock up, as the first policeman bags up the tablets as evidence. Krystal has also received her visit, finding herself arrested for theft, and the distribution of stolen property.

Word gets back to Louis, who is glad he can get a proper night's sleep at last.

To avoid having to face Trevor and Muriel so soon after

humiliating her, Christy and Neil decide they will take Johanna, along with Charlotte, for dinner outside of the camp, in one of the seafront restaurants. Johanna is quick to tell them that she wants to pay for this special treat, as she has banked more money off Louis than she has been able to spend, with having to keep her gains to herself without her parents being aware.

In exchange, Christy gives Johanna one of her dresses to wear. It's a little bit too big for Johanna's sparrow like frame, but a whole lot better than her usual outfits.

They settle in a small pizza restaurant with a beautiful sea view, and Christy gets Johanna to admit the scale of the treatment she had been receiving at the hands of their parents, while feeling extremely guilty that neither her or anyone else did anything much to stop it until now.

Tearfully, Johanna explains how miserable her life is. Long hours at the supermarket, followed by chores at home. No social life, early nights in bed with her sketch books. Her day off spent fetching and carrying for Trevor and Muriel, dragging their shopping home on the bus, making her accountable for everything she spends, while handing over every remaining penny of her wages.

A truly pitiful existence, all designed to make sure their lazy parents don't have to do anything around the house, or get a job.

Charlotte feels more than a little sad as well, while thinking of her own happy life. Liz busily running the house, nights out with her friends, nice clothes, happy and settled at college.

Christy states forcefully that Johanna can stay with her and Neil in their little terrace when they get back home, and that she will take her down the local polytechnic to register for an art course at night school. "Things are going to change from now on," she says. Johanna protests that once her dad and mum find out they will do everything to stop Christy's intentions. "No way," says Christy, "I should have done this long ago, and I will do everything I can to make things better for you."

Back at the leisure park, the rest of the Chesters family are having their dinner in the dining hall as normal. Eleanor is giving Barnaby the evil-eye, hoping he's been as good as his word and got her an application form. He's deliberately avoided their table, sending a different waiter to see to them, to purposely keep out of her way. Eleanor decides to hunt him down for herself.

"I need the toilet, mum," she lies, getting up from the table.

"Ok," says Liz, while making her way through an oversized platter of Chicken and Chips.

Eleanor hijacks Barnaby on the way. "Well? Have you got it?" she hisses, "My dad is only over there you know, it won't take me a minute to tell him what I saw."

"What you didn't see, you mean," says Barnaby, "And no I haven't yet, but I will. Tomorrow morning, I will go to Reception and ask for one."

"You'd better," says Eleanor, knowing how naughty she is being, happy to tell lies to get her own way and attempt to join the staff as a Seasider.

Christy, Neil, Johanna and Charlotte return to Happy Daze, where Christy goes off to play her nightly session of bingo, while the others go to Peyton's Pavilion for the talent show.

She strides into the bingo hall, heads to the straight to the bar and gets a large glass of wine. "I'm more than ready for this", she thinks, looking across, seeing her Mother sat at their usual table. She takes her chardonnay, and sits as far away as possible from her on purpose, no way does she want anything to do with Muriel, that disgraceful treatment of Johanna in front of Johnny and several hundred onlookers is the final straw.

"Oy, you," shouts Muriel loudly, making everyone turn around and stare. Christy glares. "Fine way to treat your own mother, sitting miles away from me, shameful," Muriel continues to rant.

"No more shameful than dressing your 21-year-old daughter

in Disney t-shirts, treating her like a slave and then dragging her away from something she was enjoying, I am done with you, you are despicable," shouts Christy, unhappy at the Maynard family washing being hung out in public once again.

She sits back down, arranging her small pile of bingo tickets, taking no notice as Muriel can still be heard cursing loudly. Christy has tears in her eyes, thinking back to the afternoon's events. I'll get that £500 quid if it kills me when I get home, get a loan, get a credit card, anything, she silently promises, I will help my little sister.

The bingo games go normally. Christy doesn't win anything, although she hears Muriel claim a line, for a few pounds. Christy's tickets don't seem to be yielding any excitement at all, another fruitless session she muses, oh well, should be used to this by now.

All too soon it gets to the very last game of the night. The bingo caller announces from the stage. "We come to our very last house of the night, ladies and gentlemen, 'Peyton's Big Jackpot Flyer', big money this folks, so make sure you shout loud when you claim, it's me you have to stop not the person sat next to you," he laughs. "Our prize money for the Big Jackpot Flyer this evening. One Line for £100, Two Lines on the same ticket please for £200, your Full House for the Big Jackpot Flyer tonight is FIVE HUNDRED POUNDS!!!" A small whoop is heard around the lounge, the many players hugely excited at the thought of winning this massive prize money.

"£500," says Christy to herself, "Johanna's money, what are the chances. No flaming chance."

The game commences. The first line is won very quickly by a man sat two tables away from her, making his claim in a loud booming voice, in line with the caller's instructions. Christy looks down at her own tickets, gloomily. "Nowhere near," she thinks, sadly.

The game goes on. Two lines is claimed by a woman on the same table as the man who won previously, the two of them beaming excitedly at their unexpected double-good fortune.

Christy starts to put her jacket on, and drains her wine glass. "I want 6 numbers to win, no chance, waste of time," she mutters to herself. The caller continues the game. Slowly but surely 6 numbers become 5, 4, 3, 2 and 1 to go – Christy's heart starts pounding loudly. "I can win this, oh my god, come on 88, please, 88, come on!" Three more numbers are called, with no sign of number 88. Christy is trembling, surely it's going to come. The caller carries on.

"On its own, the number 4."

"HOUSSSSSSSSSSSSSSSE" screams a familiar sounding voice from the back of the room. Christy closes her eyes, gutted at being so close to winning the big money. She turns around in horror to see Muriel gleefully waving her winning ticket in the air, standing on her feet doing a happy dance. Christy almost bursts into tears, furious that her selfish mother has just pocketed £500 that will probably never see the light of day.

She gets ready to go, wanting to get to back to Neil, Johanna and the others, who by now are back in the Family Centre.

Just as she pushes her losing tickets away in heart-breaking disappointment, she hears something that her ears don't quite believe, as Muriel's ticket is checked. "47 did you say?" queries the bingo caller, "That's not gone. 47 has NOT gone, so that is a FALSE CALL everyone, a FALSE CALL. That ticket is now void," meaning even if 47 came out afterwards, Muriel would not be allowed to claim the win off the same ticket again.

The caller has to raise his voice loudly over the chatter and hubbub to make himself heard, as people were already quickly heading for the exit, thinking this particular session was over.

"Back to your seats ladies and gents, that claim was not valid, we are still playing for the full house."

Christy turns around again to see a furious Muriel shouting, stamping her feet, and waving her fist at the caller. "That number HAS gone, don't you lie to me you little shit, it has!!!! 47 HAS

GONE!! I know it has!!! Give me my money now!!!!"

"No it hasn't," smiles Christy, checking her own bingo ticket, seeing 47 unmarked.

Many others are also quick to tell Muriel she's made a mistake, most of them shouting "Sit down, stupid woman, it's a false call," as they scramble on the floor and in the bins for their spent tickets.

The caller waits a couple of minutes for everyone to be ready again before carrying on. Christy holds her breath as the caller continues, suspecting that within a few numbers it'll be someone else's turn to win, not her. "Eyes down again folks, your last number was on its own the number 4. And your next number is. All the 8's...."

"Yesssssss!! House!!!! Yesssssss!!!!" Christy squeals, while shaking with the shock, not believing the number came out, or the high pitch shriek that followed it. She sits nervously as the checker reads her 15 numbers out, hoping she hasn't made the same blunder as her mother did, marking a number off that hadn't been called.

"That claim is correct," confirms the bingo caller, "and that house was called in 61 numbers, many congratulations to our Big Jackpot winner, that's ya lot for this evening, your next session of bingo is at 7pm tomorrow night." Christy is dry mouthed with shock as the other players in the bingo hall, apart from Muriel who is currently knocking into people clumsily as she makes her ungainly way over to Christy's table in a jealous rage, cheer and applaud. The staff bring a bulging envelope with twenty five £20 notes inside, asking Christy to sign for the winnings first, and then counting it out in front of her before putting it back in the envelope and handing it over, as her hands tremble uncontrollably. I won, she thinks, I bloody well won, Johanna's money! I did it!

Muriel parks up alongside Christy. "Well done Christy," she says, pretending to be delighted, when all the time greedily wanting a share. "Surely you can see I was the moral winner there, so I think you should give me at least half, I am your mother after all."

"You've got a nerve," says Christy, "You won't see a penny piece of this, and neither will me or Neil for that matter. This is for Johanna, to get her away from you and Dad, and give her a proper life, not the shameful one she has with you."

"I beg your pardon," seethes Muriel, trying to make a grab for Christy's handbag, and the envelope of money hidden safely inside it.

"You heard me," replies Christy. "I've had enough of you."

With that she gets up, striding quickly towards the double doors leading out of the bingo lounge, making the short trip across the way to the Family Centre, where she had previously arranged to meet up with the rest of the family after the show. No way would Muriel dare to attempt to follow her in there, relieved as she can see Seasiders Alun and Big Barry on the door.

"Evening, Mrs Hassall," says Alun, cheerfully.

"Hi Alun," says Christy swiftly disappearing inside. The two Seasiders spot Muriel Maynard puffing and panting behind her, and quickly stand guard in front of the doors.

"You can't come in here love," states Barry forcefully, knowing that allowing her to breach the banning order would effectively cost him his job.

"Let me past! My son, daughters, and grandchildren are all in there," she protests loudly.

"You and your husband are prohibited from entering these premises, Mrs Maynard, as you already know, by order of Louis Peyton," confirms Alun. Defeated, she turns back around to head to the one other place they are not banned from, the Jolly Roger.

Meanwhile, Christy looks over and can see the rest of her family, aside from Trevor, sitting by a family sized table laughing and joking with Colin and Liz. Johanna is deep in conversation with Charlotte and Eleanor over a copy of a pop music magazine, and her nephews are swapping football stickers with Jamie and couple of other youngsters.

"Did you win?" asks Neil, getting up to fetch Christy a drink.

"Hang on a minute," says Colin, reaching for his wallet, not allowing Christy to answer, "I'll get this - actually get a full bottle of that wine, you said your good lady drinks it, and so does mine, they can share it between them."

"Thank you so much, Mr Chesters," smiles Christy a little guiltily, knowing that the drinks should be on her. No, the money is all going to Johanna, final decision.

She waits until Neil returns, after squeezing in-between Liz and Johanna. Liz pours Christy a large glassful of chardonnay, and tops up her own. "Well then, have you won?" asks Liz, kindly.

"Yes, I did," confirms Christy, quietly, "actually," she raises her voice a little, "I have something to say." She gets the envelope of money out and turns to Johanna. "This is for you, all of it for you," confirms Christy, tearfully, "Go on, take it."

"I can't take this, it's your winnings," says Johanna, shaking her head, not noticing the amount written on the front in black biro, politely pushing the envelope away.

"I mean it, it's all yours," insists Christy. Johanna looks at the envelope in astonishment. How much is this? She reads the front of the envelope, and goes light headed with shock.

"£500. No, no, take it back, it's yours, I can’t have this," states Johanna, getting a little emotional at the thought of her sister handing her this fortune of money. The others around the table can't believe what they are seeing.

"This is for you," insists Christy again, "To get you out of that hell hole, away from those slave drivers, a proper life. When we get back home, yeah, we'll help you. You can live with us while you get sorted, me and Neil will help you find a flat and some furniture, and this £500 is yours for all that. So take it, please."

Even Liz is getting a little emotional, overwhelmed by the generosity being shown, guessing that Neil and Christy are far from well off themselves and that £500 would be a massive help to them, Neil is smiling also at his wifes kindness to her younger sister, what an amazing thing to do.

"I can't believe it," cries Johanna, flinging her arms around Christy.

"You deserve it, putting up with those pair for all these years," says Christy, "But all that stops now."

"Tell you what," pipes up her grandma Eunice, "I'll match that. I've a bit put away, and you know I've got a good pension, so I'll give you £500 as well. You may as well have it now, it'll only end up with that useless father of yours if I die. I'll go down the bank to draw it out first thing Monday. Why didn't I think of this before?"

"Thank you Nana, but I can't take your money, none of it," she protests. Christy tells Johanna what she had been doing back home.

"Look, you didn't know, no one did, but for the last two years I was putting money away in a savings bank, just for you," she says to her, "Ok, there were times it had money in it, times when I had to borrow from it, but anyway, the goal was to save £500 and as soon as I had, sign the account over to you."

Johanna doesn't understand. "You were doing what?" she asks, shocked.

"No one more than me and Neil have been horrified at the treatment you have had to suffer from mum and dad, I was fed up, I had to try and do something," replies Christy, "Anyhow, shamefully, I had to take the holiday money out of it, had no choice, but there's £75 left. What we can do is perhaps take £75 out of this money, so you will still have £500 when we get back home, and I can take you shopping, get you some proper clothes, some make up. What do you say?"

Johanna can feel tears welling up. Her sister has always looked out for her, but this is kindness beyond anything she's had in her whole life. "Yes, ok, I would like that," nods Johanna, "Can't keep wearing your clothes!" As nice as Christy's summer dress looks on her, it's two sizes too big.

"That's sorted then, we'll go into town on the bus, and get

you all glammed up," she says.

Christy picks up her drink. As she is taking a large mouthful she can hear Dave Busby and Busbys Canyon playing a slow tune, and can see Johnny and some of the other Seasiders dancing with other guests. Predictably Johnny is enjoying his dance with a stunning brunette. Christy makes a promise to Johanna. "See that woman Johnny is dancing with," she says. Johanna looks up a little unhappily, being overlooked by Johnny is getting a habit she thinks. "Well, tomorrow night," states Christy, "that'll be you. I promise."

Johanna shakes her head. "He only dances with the pretty ones, that's obvious," says Johanna, sadly.

"You have my solemn word," confirms Christy, "You will get your dance with Johnny." She squeezes Johanna's hand fondly.

At Portwynne police station, both Bo-Bo and Krystal are released on bail after being charged with their various offences. There was no point in contesting the evidence, finally their scams and dishonest lifestyle are coming to an end. More bad news is waiting on their doorstep as the taxi that took them from the police station drops them off at home. Via information Elvis passed on to his cousin Leonard, two men that Bo-Bo left huge gambling debts with are waiting for him, and don't look like leaving until they get their money!

Chapter Fourteen

Marissa is getting up, after another blissful night in Elvis's arms, ready to creep back through the hole in the fence at Happy Daze as usual. She still hasn't had the courage to admit to him about being pregnant, worried he won't be happy, and that she'd be left to cope on her own. Not telling him is eating her up a bit, knowing she can't keep up the pretence for much longer. 'I'll tell him later,' she thinks, while putting her clothes on.

Elvis looks up at her from under the sheets adoringly. Marissa still isn't entirely sure whether his loyalty to her will ever match his loyalty to Louis.

Having had to put up with a squeaking door and bed, and no intimacy from Colin all week long, Liz is at the end of her tether by Thursday morning.

"I'm going over to that Reception place, see if they can send a man with an oil can to sort out the door, and ask if we can have a replacement bedframe," she states. Colin isn't too disappointed to hear her mention about a new bed, fed up of not being able to make love to her thanks to the too loud noise of the creaky bed frame.

"We've only got two more days though," says Charlotte, "Surely you can manage for that long." Colin throws Liz a knowing look.

"No, best get it sorted, I'll go down after we've had breakfast," she confirms.

Dolly and Val Mason are hard at work in Reception as usual, Dolly sorting out the latest correspondence and new bookings, while Val is busy processing invoices. The telephone at Dollys elbow rings. "Happy Daze, Portwynne, Dolly speaking."

"Morning Dolly," comes the unmistakable booming voice of Louis Peyton.

"Oh, morning Louis," smiles Dolly, "How are you?"

"A bit troubled," he admits, "I need a couple of favours from you. Firstly, can you arrange for someone track down Mr Maynard senior and tell him I'm rescinding his ban from the Family Centre, not really fair to keep him away from his family. He is still banned from the other buildings though." Louis has already given instructions to Elvis to keep his eye on Trevor Maynard, ensuring no repeat of Tuesday night.

"Ok, no problem with that, I'll get someone on to it," states Dolly, looking up to see Liz standing at the reception hatch. Dolly smiles at her fondly, but knows she needs to conclude her call with the boss first. "Was there anything else Louis?" she asks, while trying to get away to see to Liz.

"Yes, I bring bad news. Rab McKinley can't do the Midnight Cabaret tonight." Dolly frowns. Rab is a very popular all round entertainer, and a mainstay of the Thursday Midnight Cabaret in the Jolly Roger.

"Oh, that's a pity, what happened there then?" she asks.

"He fell off the stage at Shooting Starzz last night, it's put him in traction," states Louis. Shooting Starzz is another leisure park in the Peyton's chain.

"Good heavens, no," says Dolly sympathetically, shaking her head, "Who's coming in his place then?"

"Ah, well, that's the problem, I don't know who I can get," sighs Louis, "Too short notice, you see. I don't want to have to cancel the Midnight Cabaret, but who can I get at this late hour. Will you look in some of those agent brochures you've got, try anyone, absolutely anyone you can think of." Dolly knows she's got little chance of getting anyone in at the last minute. With Happy Daze being on the west coast of Wales, it's a bit far for most acts to get to. She covers the receiver.

"I won't be a minute," she says to Liz before returning to the call, "I'll see what I can do, see if I can rustle something up."

Inspiration strikes in a split second as Dolly remembers who the blonde lady at the hatch is married to, that they have a ready-made Midnight Cabaret star staying on the camp. She nearly drops the receiver on the floor with excitement. "Actually Louis, I might have solved that problem for you already, can I call you back in a minute?"

"Yes of course Dolly, let me know what you come up with," says Louis. The call ends.

Just as Dolly comes to the hatch, Barnaby appears alongside Liz. Given the reason for him being there, he can barely believe who he sees and gets very nervous indeed. Dolly looks at him. "What can I do for you Barnaby?" she asks, wanting to get rid of him before dealing with Liz.

"Ummm can I have a job application form," he quickly gabbles, not daring to look at Liz.

"Yes, of course, who for?" replies Dolly, getting a ledger out, wanting to make a note of the recipient's name in line with company policy.

Barnaby is almost stumped, never even thinking that Dolly would need to know the person's name. He quickly thinks on his feet. "Ummm my cousin Seamus, from Limerick," he lies.

"Seamus what," says Dolly, not looking up.

"Ummm, Walsh, same as me," says Barnaby. He quickly glances at Liz, nervously, while trying not to make Dolly suspicious.

"There you go then," says Dolly handing over the form, "What does your cousin do?"

"Ummm, he wants a waiter's job, like mine," he says, "For next year."

"Ok, no worries, was that all?"

"Yes, thank you," says Barnaby, quickly disappearing.

"Right, Liz, sorry about that," says Dolly, smiling.

Liz is a little annoyed at Dollys forward and informal manner again. She doesn't know me, what is wrong with calling me 'Mrs Chesters' she thinks.

"I was about to say what can I do for you, but it might be

what your husband can do for me!" continues Dolly.

Liz is a bit surprised. What the heck does she mean? "I don't follow?" says Liz, a little mystified.

"That was Louis Peyton on the phone," confirms Dolly, "Our Midnight Cabaret performer has let us down, indisposed. How would it be if we asked your husband to perform in his place?"

Liz is flabbergasted. So much for a relaxed family break. "I don't know, I'd have to ask him I suppose," she says.

"Oh would you?" says Dolly, "He really would be getting us out of a hole."

"Well, we can pop back down in a bit if you like, he'll give you a decision then, I guess you need to know pretty soon?" asks Liz.

"Yes, as soon as possible really, I do hope Colin will agree," says Dolly, crossing her fingers hopefully.

"Well, ok then, I'll ask him. Now, the reason I'm here," says Liz, "Our front door is squeaking something terrible, could you send someone up with a can of oil?"

"Yes, I'll get Malc the Maintenance up to you, what number chalet was it again?"

"114, Primrose Block," says Liz, "And something else as well. Ummm, our bed. That is also squeaking, but I'm not sure oil would solve that. Can we have a replacement bedframe? The double bed we've got makes a truly dreadful racket."

Dolly looks at Liz little quizzically. "A new bedframe?"

"Yes, ummm, my husband is a terribly light sleeper, every time we move it creaks very loudly, and it wakes him up, you see," says Liz, not altogether truthfully of course. If they want Colin to appear tonight, then the very least they can do is replace our bed.

"Well, I can see what we can do about that, but most of the beds squeak I think, it might not make any difference," says Dolly, scratching her head.

"Well, if you can see about sorting that for us, I'll send my husband down here to negotiate terms for the Cabaret," states Liz.

Dolly smiles.

"That's a deal then, Liz!" she says.

Half an hour later Liz and Colin return to the Reception hall, while the others make tracks for the shops and arcades on the seafront. Dolly gets up to see to them, smiling widely. "Well, the good news is I've sorted you a new bed, Malc will get two of his boys to swap it for the old one at the same time as oiling your front door."

"That's good then, I have already taken the bedclothes off the other one ready," confirms Liz.

"I understand you might have some work to put my way," chuckles Colin.

"Oh, we certainly have," smiles Dolly, "Our Midnight Cabaret artist has let us down at the last minute, I wonder if you would consider taking his place?"

"Hmmm, I don't know about that. It's been quite a while. No one will know who I am!" says Colin.

"Rubbish, you're still a household name and a massive draw," replies Dolly, "It would be two 45 minute spots, for the usual Peytons fee of £500. What do you say?"

Colin and Liz can't believe their ears. £500 for an hour and half's work? Liz looks at Colin, wondering what he's thinking. He looks back at her. "What do you reckon?" he says.

"If you want to do it, then why not," replies Liz, smiling.

"Ok, I'll do it then," confirms Colin.

"Oh that is fabulous, Colin, you've really saved our bacon, I'll ring Louis straightaway, he'll be thrilled," confirms a very relieved Dolly.

At the local Magistrates court both Bo-Bo and Krystal await their fate. It's not all bad news, as Colviles have agreed to drop their complaint against Krystal, fully aware that she isn't the brightest spark and she was merely doing her deceitful husbands bidding.

She's cleared, and free to go.

Bo-Bo is not getting off quite so lightly though, his charges of embezzlement against 'Peytons Leisure Parks' and the illegal distribution of stolen prescription drugs are upheld, and referred to Crown Court. As he sits in the dock, now sporting a black eye and a split lip that he claims were the outcome of a clumsy fall, he's allowed out on conditional bail until the case is heard in a month's time.

Word of his arrest is spreading like wildfire around the horrified staff at Happy Daze. Thursday is pay-day, and many who stock up weekly on Uppers are frantically wondering what the heck they are going to do without them.

Christy and Johanna make their way to the bus stop, on their way into Portwynne town centre. Johanna has the full £500 on her, not trusting it to be left behind, concerned that her parents might find some way of getting into Christy and Neil's chalet to rummage around her things while she's out. Before they left, and unbeknown to Johanna, Christy made her way to the payphone at the end of Primrose Block to make an extra special arrangement, a surprise treat for Johanna at the end of their shopping trip.

After three hours of choosing a whole new wardrobe, and buying make up and other items, it's time for Christy's final surprise. "Now you know you said I could do anything I want with you, because you do trust me, right?" states Christy.

"Yes, of course, and I meant it," replies Johanna, wondering what her sister has in mind.

"Come with me," says Christy cheerfully, taking Johanna by the arm while heading for an expensive looking hairdressers.

"What are we doing?" asks a shocked Johanna, not used to such places. Christy leans across and speaks to the woman on the desk.

"Appointment for Maynard," she says. This is quickly confirmed and the two of them go through to the large salon.

"Ok then, what can we do for you," asks kindly stylist Natalie, looking a bit quizzically at Johanna with her mousy, straight, dry looking locks scraped back in a ponytail. Christy takes the lead by grabbing the scrunchy out of Johanna's hair, letting it fall down way past her shoulders. Johanna is too stunned to speak at her sister's forward behaviour.

Instead, Christy continues on. "Make my beautiful sister into a raving, curly haired redhead," she beams. Johanna's jaw drops. "Go on, show her," says Christy, imploring Johanna to reveal to the stylist her drawings, aware that the sketch book containing Johanna's self-portraits depicting her as a flame haired supermodel will be close at hand. Johanna can't believe it, but nervously gets her book out, showing Natalie one of her drawings.

"Hang the expense," states Christy, "Give this amazing lady the best hair makeover anyone has ever seen." Natalie is always up for a challenge, but this one beats absolutely everything.

"Well?" she asks Johanna, not wanting to commit to anything without her full agreement. Johanna looks at Christy and remembers her solemn promise to have Johnny dance with her, something that could never happen in her present state. She nods.

"Let's go for it."

A couple of hours later, which allows Johanna to complete some more drawings for Louis, and after a bright red dye has been successfully applied along with a spiral perm, the transformation is complete. Johanna looks absolutely stunning, and a lot more like her 21 years, if not older. Her green eyes sparkle amongst the mane of shiny red curls. Christy can barely believe the person looking back at her is the same one she has seen over and over again in Johanna's sketch book. A spitting image.

To finish her new look, Johanna applies some bright red lipstick, dark eye liner, and mascara. Christy sheds tears of happiness. "Oh my god, you look absolutely incredible, this really is the real you, just like those pictures you drew of yourself. This is totally amazing."

"Mum and dad will kill me," says Johanna, although thrilled with her new look is also extremely wary.

"Who cares what they think," replies Christy, "I'll be behind you every step of the way, have no fear," while she gleefully settles the expensive salon bill, and the two of them get the bus back to Happy Daze.

On their return, they leave their many shopping bags in Christy and Neil's chalet, while Johanna changes into one of her new outfits, a very flattering silver mini-dress. They head straight over to the Jolly Roger, knowing fine well that Trevor and Muriel will be in there as usual. Best get this over and done with, both Johanna and Christy agree.

One thing that Johanna has quickly noticed, as they make their way, is that men have started to stare at her, and smile in adoration. Feeling very confident, she smiles back at them, while quietly hoping she has the same effect on Johnny later on.

With the Betting Lounge having no manager, Louis asks Elvis to take care of matters while he interviews for new staff. Not entirely sure what he's doing, and armed with only a ready-reckoner and a pocket calculator, he attempts to serve the punters and settle the many bets being made.

After a couple of hours, and with lots of money changing hands, Elvis sub-totals the till. The amount he sees, even after only a small amount of trading, puts some of those measly looking takes Bo-Bo reported well and truly in the shade. It also makes him a little sad, wondering exactly how much money Louis had lost to this thief this past 18 months.

As the rest of the Maynards have now totally ostracised Trevor and Muriel, it's only the two of them in the Jolly Roger, one of those rare occasions they haven't had to push two tables together as they are on their completely on their own; even Eunice has gone off without them. They look up to see Christy walking over with someone they don't immediately recognise.

Within seconds though, they realise the unfamiliar redhead with her is Johanna. Trevor explodes. "What the flaming hell do you call that get-up," he shouts.

Both Christy and Johanna are more than ready to stand up to him. "It's the real me, if you must know," states Johanna.

"You look a complete mess, like a clown," screeches Muriel, on her feet in a flash, "Get that muck off your face, and tie your hair back for gods sake. And as for that tawdry piece of rag you're draped in, ugh. Take it off!" Both Trevor and Muriel use their rage to hide their true feelings of panic, not used to such lack of control over their youngest daughter.

"She'll be doing no such thing," insists Christy, "You should be proud of how beautiful she looks."

Muriel shakes her head. "She looks like something the cat dragged in, a common tart, the neighbourhood slapper," she says nastily, "Well, make the most of this Johanna, we'll have you back to normal in no time when we get home."

"You are kidding? Like I ever looked any sort of normal!" states Johanna.

"She's still staying in our chalet, she won't be coming back to you," confirms Christy.

"Now listen here," shouts Trevor, "You've done enough damage for one day, Johanna stays with us."

"Not anymore," says Johanna, "And when we get home I'm moving in with Christy and Neil, until I get my own place." This time the look of panic on their parents' faces is very clear to see, the stark realisation that their cushy lifestyle really is coming to an end. "From now on, you can make your own tea, do your own ironing, and pay your own bills."

With that, Johanna and Christy turn around and make for the exit while Trevor and Muriel look at one another in disbelieving shock.

The two girls make their way over to the outdoor swimming pool area, where the others are already gathered. The Chesters family are also there. Mikey and Karl, along with Jamie, are in the kid's fun pool splashing each other violently.

"Jamie! Calm down will you," shouts Liz, concerned that everyone on the side will end up getting splashed as well. She looks up to see Christy coming across. But who is that with her? Again it only takes a second or two to realise. Broad smiles all around at Johanna's striking new look.

Her brother Rodney is off his sun lounger in a flash, giving her a big hug. "You look gorgeous," he states proudly. Johanna beams, then squeals, as she gets splashed by her over enthusiastic nephews and their friend. "Pack that in," shouts Rodney.

"Yes, that's enough," says Liz, "Time you were getting out."

Charlotte is next up to hug her new best friend, barely believing the pictures in Johanna's sketch book have come to life. Christy is smiling proudly, fully aware that her selfish parents made sure Johanna had no friends her own age, and safe in the knowledge that her friendship with Charlotte will go far beyond their week in Portwynne.

Chapter Fifteen

Elvis gets to the end of a very busy day, quietly glad once the last race has finished, so he can close the shop and find out exactly how much they have taken. Cashing up the till fully, counting the money, working out how much has been paid out. The figures he can see in front of him are far in excess of anything he has seen while Bo-Bo ran things.

Elvis knows that from now on, this part of Louis's enterprise will definitely make a small fortune. A soft knock on the door disturbs him. Elvis is surprised to see Marissa standing there, having made no arrangement to see her while both on duty. "Well, this is a lovely surprise," he grins, letting her in. He doesn't spare a moment of this unexpected visit, quickly taking her in his arms, kissing her. Looking at her, he can see that her blue eyes are filling up with tears. "What's the matter," he asks, not understanding.

"I have something to tell you," she says, tears falling down her face. She takes a deep breath, bracing herself. "Oh god," she says, between sobs, "I'm pregnant, Elvis, I'm so sorry." Elvis can't believe his ears.

"What? You can't be," he replies, "We've always been careful, oh no."

"I know, so I'm not sure what went wrong, but there it is," sobs Marissa.

Elvis cradles her close, knowing he can't alter this life changing event. 'I'm going to be a dad,' he thinks, barely able to get his head around the fact.

"I need to tell Louis that I'll be leaving at the end of the season," she says, "but he doesn't need to know you're involved, none of his business if I have a boyfriend."

"No, we'll be honest with him," decides Elvis, "We'll face this together, everything."

"I better go," sighs Marissa, "I'm due in the Family Centre in ten minutes."

"Don't overdo things," replies Elvis, with concern.

"I'll be fine, and I feel a bit better for telling you, was scared about how you'd react," she says.

"It's the best news ever," grins Elvis, hugging her lovingly, rather liking the idea, despite never considering it previously.

Eleanor is almost beside herself with excitement, unable to wait to see Barnaby and get her hands her little piece of treasure, the job application form. There is another side to this of course, the fact she had promised him a date with Charlotte. As they sit in the chalet waiting for everyone else to be ready for dinner, it's time for crafty Eleanor to get to work.

"Wonder if that Irish boy will be serving tonight," she says, mischievously.

"So what," replies Charlotte, reading a magazine, not remotely interested.

"I think he really likes you, you know," says Eleanor.

"So what if he does, I'm not interested in him," confirms Charlotte, not even looking up.

"Oh I think you are, I saw you two the other day at the swimming pool," smiles Eleanor, "I thought he was asking you out."

"No he wasn't, and the answer would have been no in any case, I'm not interested, like I just said."

Eleanor starts to panic a little, but continues on. "What harm would it do, if he did ask you," she states.

"Why do you keep going on, has he been saying something to you?" asks Charlotte, worriedly.

"Possibly," replies Eleanor, sneakily.

"Oh no, what did he say?" says Charlotte, a little annoyed.

"That he really likes you, and he wants to ask you out. You will say yes when he does won't you," says Eleanor, hopefully.

"No I will not," replies Charlotte, "I don't like him in that way."

Eleanor starts to panic a bit more. "You must say yes, you have to!" she gabbles quickly.

"Why must I. What is going on?" demands Charlotte.

"Don't say anything to mum and dad, please," pleads Eleanor, looking up to make sure Liz and Colin haven't come out of the bathroom and bedroom respectively.

"Well?" demands Charlotte.

"He promised to get me an application form to be a Seasider, and I promised I would get you to go out with him in return," says Eleanor, while not bothering her with the lies she was prepared to tell if she didn't get her own way.

"What the hell did you do that for, and mum is right, all these stupid ideas about working here, let them go, it won't happen," seethes Charlotte, deeply unhappy at Eleanor's meddling.

"I don't care what you say, it will happen," says Eleanor defiantly, "But please go out with him, even for one day, please."

Charlotte can see that Eleanor is deadly serious and sighs. "Look alright then, but I'm not keen on this one bit, and I don't like keeping secrets from mum and dad," she says, looking up and seeing Liz along with a freshly bathed Jamie, with Colin right behind them after a quick nap.

"What are you two whispering about?" asks Liz.

"Nothing mum," replies Eleanor innocently. Liz isn't totally convinced but doesn't probe further.

Once in the dining room Eleanor is desperate to seek out Barnaby. Seeing him appear from out of the kitchens with two large platters gives her the opportunity. Using the same excuse as yesterday, she gets up from the table. Liz is a little more suspicious today, having took no notice the day before. 'What is she up to?' thinks Liz. Seeing Eleanor go immediately in the direction of the ladies puts her mind at rest for now. When she reappears she goes straight up to Barnaby, busily serving at a different table. When he turns around he nearly jumps out of his skin to see Eleanor standing there. "Well? Do you have it?" she asks.

Barnaby sighs. "Here you go," he says, discreetly passing her the form, which she quickly puts into her small handbag.

"Thank you, now if you ask my sister out, I guarantee she will say yes," says Eleanor, walking away, trying not to skip with excitement.

Over her shoulder Barnaby sees something that quickly

makes him forget all about Charlotte, as he sees Christy, Neil, and a beautiful redhead in a stunning mini-dress, which he immediately realises is Johanna. They are asking Seasider Ruth if they can have a different table from normal, in case Trevor and Muriel turn up. His chin nearly hits the floor in astonishment, can barely believe the total transformation. Once they are seated he quickly makes his way over, keen to take their order before any other member of the waiting staff does. Instead of his usual 'What'll it be', as he opens his mouth to speak, the words "You look absolutely gorgeous," come out.

Johanna goes the same shade as her newly coloured hair and lipstick. Barnaby stops short of asking her for a date, believing she would say no, and that the others would wonder why he hadn't bothered asking her before, while silently cursing not having the courage prior to her makeover, being far too scared of Trevor. "Ok," he smiles, "What'll it be?"

A different waiter has already seen to the Chesters, but still fancying his chances with Charlotte, Barnaby finally makes his approach. "We've already ordered," confirms Liz, as he appears at their table.

"It's ok, I know you have," says Barnaby, who can see a mischievous look on Eleanor's face, "But what I wanted to know is if Charlotte fancied coming to Sonikz with me later. Would you join me?"

"Erm, I don't know," says Charlotte, knowing full well why he's asking, and automatically expecting her to say yes, thanks to her devious younger sister. Colin glares at Barnaby, not too impressed that some random waiter is brazen enough to ask Charlotte for a date in front of him and everyone else.

Liz is a little more forgiving. "Why not, Charlotte, what harm would it do?"

Charlotte feels a little cornered, but is still cross at his behaviour towards her the other day. She sees no choice in the matter for all that. "Well, ok then, but I can't stay for long," she says, knowing she will have to take Eleanor and Jamie back to the chalet once Colin and Liz go over to the Jolly Roger for the Midnight

Cabaret.

"Great!" smiles Barnaby, "I finish my shift at 7, I'll see you in Sonikz about quarter past?"

"Ok, I'll be there," says Charlotte. A delighted Barnaby goes back to his work, while Eleanor breathes a huge sigh of relief.

After dinner, Johanna goes to Louis's apartment as normal. Elvis is waiting by the gate with his eyes out on stalks, hardly believing this is Johanna in front of him. "Good god alive," he splutters, "What a difference, how did this happen?"

"It was all down to my sister," grins Johanna, confidently, as Elvis is looking as admiringly at her, as almost every single other man she'd seen since her makeover.

"Well, I never," smiles Elvis, as Johanna hands over the latest batch of drawings, "Ummm, did you want to see Louis, now you're here?" Elvis is in no hurry to let Johanna go anywhere.

"No, thank you, if it's all the same," says Johanna, wanting to get back to Christy and the others.

"That's a shame," replies a very disappointed Elvis, "I'm sure he would be thrilled to see the 'new you', as it were."

"It's the 'same old' me, just slightly different packaging," laughs Johanna, quietly pleased with herself, not used to coming out with jokes like that.

Elvis laughs loudly. "Ok then, but you don't mind me telling him I assume?"

"If you like. Actually, would he be free tomorrow afternoon, if I came here then?" enquires Johanna.

"Louis will always make time for you, have no concerns there," smiles Elvis.

In a show of solidarity for Johanna, all of the Maynard family, aside from Trevor and Muriel, sit at a totally different table than usual in the Family Centre. Christy decides that her luck won't stretch to another day, so abandons the bingo hall to join the rest of the clan. She looks admiringly at her younger sister, with her new dress and her flame red hair, excitedly waiting for Johnny to make his way over, making all of Johanna's daydreams come true.

Johnny and Alun are backstage, in conference over the problems they are having now their supply of Uppers has dried up. "I've got three left," says Alun, "Didn't have one today, trying to make them last, and I feel completely knackered already."

Johnny, even more dependent, shares his concerns. "I'm down to my last half dozen, might have to go without tomorrow, like you, need to make them last."

"Who the hell dobbed him in to Louis though, if I could only get my hands on them," moans Alun, "If only he or she knew how many of us are going to burn out without any Uppers to fall back on."

"I know, I'm dreading the rest of the season, I'll be back to how I was at the beginning," confirms Johnny, who had taken his tablets today and feels wide awake for now, but dreading the certain lethargy heading his way.

Trevor and Muriel sheepishly make their way over to their normal table, fully aware they are all but disowned by their own family, seeing their previously easy lifestyle with Johanna doing their bidding quickly disappearing into thin air. They had decided before coming down to the Family Centre that the only chance they have of getting Johanna back is by being as nice as possible, lulling her into a false sense of security. "That'll do it, I know it will," says deluded Muriel.

Within five minutes Trevor is wandering over to the rest of the clan, in this final attempt to re-build bridges. "Go away dad, you're not welcome here," hisses Christy.

"Now, now, hear me out," replies Trevor, "Look, Johanna, your mum and I are very sorry we said those things to you, you look lovely, I mean it."

"Too late," states Johanna, "Do as Christy says and clear off, I don't want to know."

It's all Trevor can do not to shout his youngest daughter down like he normally would, but shows some restraint for once. "Don't do this to your mother, she's as upset as I am," he begs.

"It's far too late for that," states Johanna, "You've made my whole life hell, now at last, thanks to Christy, I can start to have a proper life. Go away." Trevor slunks off, unhappily.

The Chesters family, minus Charlotte, arrive, and wave cheerily at the larger gathering of the Maynards as they go by. "Doesn't she look so much better," says Liz, "Such a pretty girl." Colin goes to get them all drinks from the bar as Liz finds a table. Ahead of his cabaret performance Colin ensures no slip ups, so sticks to water instead of beer.

Liz wonders if her husband is nervous or not, it being a couple of years since he'd done anything other than after dinner speaking, which is slightly different to the regular stand up he used to do, but decides not to ask him.

Dave Busby takes to the stage as usual, along with the rest of Busbys Canyon. The first number they strike up is the theme tune to one of Colin's old shows, as an advert for the surprise Midnight Cabaret, which embarrasses him a bit, but was entirely deliberate with Louis Peyton insisting as much publicity as possible was needed due to the last minute change of act. "Did any of you recognise that, then?" states Dave Busby to everyone watching, "The theme tune to that fantastic TV show 'Make 'em Laugh', yes? Well, in case you didn't know, we have one of the stars of the show in our special Thursday Midnight Cabaret at the Jolly Roger later on, I hope as many of you as you can will come and see the brilliantly funny Colin Chesters, what a fabulous night of entertainment it promises to be."

Everyone cheers and applauds, enthusiastically. Colin is squirming a little, never comfortable with any sort of praise. Liz smiles widely, extremely proud that her husband can still illicit such a reaction despite being out of the public eye for a couple of years.

The longer the night goes on, the more Trevor drinks. He glares over at the others, but decides to heed the instruction of keeping away. Eventually he sees something that tips him right over the edge. Johnny makes his way cheerily across to where the other Maynards are sitting.

"How is everyone this evening, having a good time?" he asks. Johanna is almost trembling, barely daring to hope her dreams are about to be realised. Johnny is looking straight at her for the first time ever. "Shall we dance?" he asks. Johanna is on her feet in a flash.

Trevor has seen Johnny making his way towards their table and completely loses it. No way is he getting his hands on Johanna. Luckily Elvis has had his eyes trained on the table where Trevor and Muriel are sitting, under Louis Peytons instruction. He grabs hold of Trevor just as it looks like he is going to get his hands on Johnny, and make a scene. "Get off me," protests Trevor loudly, as Elvis forcefully holds him back, while Johnny and Johanna are dancing closely unaware.

Alun has seen Elvis snuff out the potential trouble, and heads backstage quickly to ring Louis, letting him know that Trevor Maynard had once again attempted to disrupt events. Elvis forces Trevor back into his seat, to the astonishment of both him and Muriel. Meanwhile, in front of them, Johnny is spinning Johanna around the floor gracefully, with Johanna feeling like she is walking on air, everything she had daydreamed about for months finally coming true.

Alun makes contact with Louis Peyton, currently in his study at the apartment, quick to tell him that Trevor Maynard was about to cause more mayhem had it not been for Elvis. "Get Mr Maynard on this phone now," shouts Louis, while looking up at his newly framed portrait that Johanna had drawn. As requested Alun puts down the receiver and goes back into the Family Centre heading straight for Trevor, who is being forced into staying where he is by Elvis.

"I need to borrow you for a few moments, Mr Maynard, please come this way," states Alun. A mystified Trevor gets up and follows Alun backstage unsure what is going on. Alun hands him the receiver.

"Hello?" says Trevor, a little shakily.

"Louis Peyton here, Mr Maynard, I gather you were trying to make trouble again?" he booms down the phone.

"Erm, I think there's been a misunderstanding, Mr Peyton," splutters Trevor.

"There has been no misunderstanding, Mr Maynard, I am told if it wasn't for Elvis you would have destroyed the happiest thing that has ever happened to your delightful youngest daughter," confirms Louis.

Trevor can't believe his ears. "I didn't want that dancing fairy getting his hands on her, that's all," he replies, sheepishly, while not understanding how Louis Peyton could possibly know Johanna.

"If what I have heard is true you make a habit of interfering with Johanna's life," says Louis, "Anyhow, I need to inform you of this. You and your wife have 24 hours to leave my camp for good. The rest of your family can complete their holiday as normal, and are welcome back any time, but you and your wife are now barred from Happy Daze, and all of Peyton's Leisure Parks, on a permanent basis. So far this week you have threatened my staff, tried to hit another guest, made spurious complaints about anything to get extras you are not entitled to, and now this. Enough is enough."

"You can't do that?" shouts an exasperated Trevor, "We all came together, how's everyone going to get home, my mother is 85!"

"I will ensure that complimentary transport is laid on to get everyone else back to Birmingham, but you two need to leave at the soonest opportunity, and that is final," insists Louis.

Trevor hands the receiver back to Alun, head bowed, unable to believe Louis Payton has just handed them a life ban from his leisure parks.

The night continues on for the others in good spirits, Johanna feeling a little giddy from the bottle of wine she is quickly putting away, and the precious memory of her special dance with Johnny. She looks on as other girls get their turn, but instead of feeling jealous as normal, she's glad that others have got the chance she had, being twirled around by this handsome entertainer.

Charlotte and Barnaby appear. "Here you go Mr Chesters," smiles Barnaby, "Delivered back safely." Charlotte smiles at Barnaby fondly, as the date had not been too bad after all, and he had been truly apologetic for pouncing on her for effect on Tuesday. She's in no hurry for a repeat though, one night has been plenty.

"Can I get you something to drink?" asks Colin, happy that Barnaby has been a perfect gentleman.

"Thank you, a beer would be nice," replies Barnaby, pleased to have a few more moments in Charlotte's company.

Half an hour later it's time for Charlotte to get ready to take Eleanor and Jamie back to the chalet, to allow Colin and Liz to make their way to the Jolly Roger ahead of the Midnight Cabaret. Barnaby is quick to offer to walk them all back. Charlotte gives her dad a big hug and kiss for luck, a little disappointed to not be able to see his gig for herself but aware she is not quite old enough to be in the Jolly Roger at this time of night, and also of her responsibility to make sure her younger siblings are taken care of. Jamie and Eleanor also give him a big hug, before leaving along with Barnaby. Colin and Liz depart the Family Centre hand-in-hand.

Rodney and Sandra opt to go back to the chalet with the twins, as both Mikey and Karl are almost falling asleep at the table. Trevor and Muriel have already left unnoticed, no longer in the mood for anything after Louis Peyton dropped his bombshell.

"We're going to get a table in the Jolly Roger," Christy says to Johanna, "Are you coming with us?"

Johanna looks over to where Johnny is standing, laughing and joking with Marissa and Ruth. "I'll just finish my wine first," she says, "Don't know if I want to go to the cabaret or not, I'm feeling a bit tired, it's been a long day, I might just go back to the chalet and go to bed."

"Ok then, well, we'll either see you or not," says Christy, as her and Neil get up and go.

Chapter Sixteen

Johanna pours out the last of her wine, and takes a slow sip. Looking up she gets a shock as Johnny as appears at her table.

"On your own?" he asks.

"Yes, the others have gone back to the chalet, or to the Jolly Roger," Johanna confirms.

"Oh, are you heading to the cabaret as well, then?" enquires Johnny, "Going to be a good 'un."

"No, I don't think so, I'm a bit tired," she says.

"That's a shame, you'll miss a fantastic performer," replies Johnny, taking a seat across from her. He gets an idea. "Look, I'm knocking off now, and going over to the Jolly Roger," he says, "Come with me, as my guest, go on, say yes."

Johanna can't believe her ears. "Me?" she asks, in surprise.

"Yes, you, why not," smiles Johnny, fondly.

Johanna's heart feels like it's going to burst. "Ok then, yes," she smiles back.

"Great, let me finish off here, and I'll be right back," he says, quickly disappearing. Johanna still can't believe it, but does all she can to not get carried away. It's not a date, she thinks, just an hour in his company, nothing else.

After five minutes Johnny returns, in a normal jacket as opposed to his light blue Seasiders one. "You ready, then?" he asks. Johanna gets to her feet a little unsteadily due the wine, Johnny taking her hand to allow her to balance herself. Feeling a little brave, she looks at him intently. He smiles kindly back at her, but lets go of her hand as soon as she is safely on her feet, keen not to give Johanna any ideas. She's just a consort, company at Colin's gig, nothing else.

They leave the Family Centre together, Johanna glancing across at Johnny proudly. He's with me, she thinks. Might be just for a short while, but he's with me.

They just about manage to get a very small table in an

already tightly packed Jolly Roger. No one notices them there especially, Johanna looks around unable to spot either Christy or Neil anywhere through the crowds of people. They are sitting down the front with Liz, who saw them come into the bar and invited them to sit with her at an especially reserved table right by the stage. An extra seat was kept by just in case Johanna decided to join them. They all assume she must have gone back to the chalet when they don't see her.

Colin is waiting nervously in the artist's room, having a last minute cigarette. He always used to get a little nervous prior to any gig, but this is worse than he can ever remember. Should've had a beer while I had the chance, he muses, oh well too late for that now.

By the bar Elvis is on the phone to Louis Peyton. Louis has given strict instruction that the line be left open so he can hear the show for himself while sat in his study.

The lights in the Jolly Roger dim, and a recorded fanfare plays. Liz is smiling from ear to ear, nervously awaiting her beloved husband's appearance. Seasider Big Barry takes the stage to make the introduction. "Good evening ladies and gentleman, it's the highlight of our week here in the Jolly Roger, our Thursday Midnight Cabaret, and what a performer we have for you this week. Star of those fabulous television shows 'Make 'em Laugh' and 'Joking Aside', please put your hands together for the one and only COLIN CHESTERS!!!"

Everyone in the bar is cheering and applauding enthusiastically, as Colin makes his way onto the small stage. Liz is glowing with pride at the reception, humbled that everyone remembers her husband fondly from his long gone television days.

Despite being incredibly nervous, he's soon well into his stride. A mixture of his well-remembered gags, along with some new ones that Liz hasn't heard before. The whole of the crowd packed into the Jolly Roger are rocking with laughter, as Colin cracks joke after joke. Elvis is holding the phone receiver high in the air to ensure Louis can hear above the laughter. He must be able to, as Elvis can hear loud guffaws emanating from the other end of the line.

At the back of the room Johnny and Johanna are also enjoying the show immensely, as Colin continues his routine.

After the first 45-minute spot he has a short break to allow him and everyone else to get a drink. He comes straight over to Liz, where two pints of beer are waiting for him. He kisses her lovingly. "Thanks Lizzy, I'm ready for this," he says, picking up the first pint.

"I got you that one, Neil got the other," confirms Liz.

"Oh, right, cheers Neil," smiles Colin raising his glass at Neil and Christy.

"My pleasure, you deserve that mate," says Neil.

"Well, was I any good?" replies Colin. He heard the laughter, the applause, the cheering, but like most performers doesn't dare believe it unless someone says.

Liz beams with delight. "You were incredible; I am so proud of you."

"Liz is right," confirms Christy, also smiling, "You should still be on the telly, you're so much better than the rubbish on there."

Over at the bar Elvis is talking to Louis down the phone. "What did you think boss, he's still got it," chuckles Elvis.

"You can say that again," booms Louis, while sipping on a large glass of brandy, "Absolutely incredible. The very best. I'm going to make him an offer, permanent residency at Happy Daze, and out of season him and Johnny Major in a stage show on a nationwide tour. It'll make me fortunes, Elvis, packed out houses guaranteed, I can see it now, it'll be an absolute smash! Can't fail!"

Colin looks around at the people who are crammed into the Jolly Roger, many trying to get served at a heaving bar area. "Is your sister not here then?" he asks Christy.

"She wasn't sure if she was coming or not," says Christy also looking around. Neither of them can see her sitting at a small table right near the back with Johnny, while he's drinking a beer and she is enjoying a further large glass of wine.

Elvis makes his way across to Colin's table, whispering busily in his ear. Liz looks quizzically, wondering what Louis Peyton's assistant wants with him. Colin nods, and gets to his feet. "I won't be a minute," he says, heading towards the bar with Elvis leading the way. "Hello?" says Colin down the phone.

"Hello there, Colin," replies Louis Peyton, in his unmistakable rich Welsh baritone, "Fabulous show so far, brilliant, top class. I can't tell you how much I enjoyed it."

"Thank you Mr Peyton, that's very kind of you," says Colin, a little humbled.

Louis is straight to the point. "I want to make you an offer. Permanent weekly residency in the Jolly Roger, £500 per gig same as tonight, and the possibility of more work in the close season, what do you say?" Colin is shocked, can't quite believe the generous offer being made to him totally out of the blue, earning more per week than one of his after dinner engagements currently pays.

"That's very nice of you," says Colin, a little shakily. He looks over towards Liz, while wondering about the practicalities of returning back here week after week, an overnight stay. He can see his pretty wife smiling and laughing along with Neil and Christy, and decides in a heartbeat he can't accept. The thought of being apart from her even one night a week doesn't appeal, he loves her far too much and they are already comfortably off.

Louis can sense the hesitation in Colin's voice and immediately ups the ante. "Did I say £500 per gig? Silly me, £750 I mean, all expenses paid, your wife and family could come too if they want to, all paid for." Louis knows that with packed out shows, and brisk bar trade he would still be making a large profit on the night, even after Colin's fee for performing.

Colin gulps, the money on offer for his services is incredible, too much in effect he thinks. 'Blimey, he really wants me,' he muses. Again he glances over at Liz, while Louis holds his breath. Surely he can't say no. "Thank you for your very generous offer Mr

Peyton, but I will have to think about it, and speak to my wife of course."

Louis's heart sinks a little, knowing fine well there is a good chance he'll refuse if Liz was to be consulted. One of the reasons Louis Peyton never married was because 'women interfere too much'. "A thousand pounds! One-thousand-pounds per gig, 2 one hour slots, say yes, job for life," gabbles Louis in one final attempt to get Colin to agree on the spot.

Colin knows that Louis is offering him daft money in a panic. He knows he should be biting his hand off, and putting pen to paper immediately, but as a devoted family man, no matter how much the fee, he has to speak to Liz first. He takes a deep breath, standing up to Louis's forceful offer. "I have to consult Lizzy, but I will seriously think about this," says Colin.

Louis is a little disappointed, has quickly noticed that throwing money at him isn't making any difference at all. "Ok, I understand," he says, "But please let the answer be yes, it's too good an opportunity, you must see this, Colin."

"Thank you. It's a very generous offer, Mr Peyton, like I said, but I have to speak to Lizzy," confirms Colin, defiantly, "I'll let you know once I've made a decision." Once again he looks over at Liz, not knowing what she's going to say once she hears Louis Peyton is offering him silly money for a weekly repeat. He hands the receiver back to Elvis and heads back to the table.

"What was that about?" asks Liz, as Colin drinks up his first pint, before taking a large gulp of the second one. He's not sure how much he should be revealing in front of Neil and Christy, but decides he trusts them enough to say nothing.

"That was Louis Peyton on the phone, wants to offer me more gigs," he admits, "£1000 a time, weekly residency here."

"How much?" splutters Liz, thinking her ears are playing tricks.

"He started at £500, but kept raising the fee, so £1000 per gig was where we left it," confirms Colin. Liz shakes her head in disbelief.

"So, let's get this right, Louis Peyton wants to pay you £1000 per week to do a gig like this one?" says Liz, "He's not expecting you to do what Johnny does as well? Work as a 'Seasider'?" She panics slightly, not liking the idea of Colin being away for months on end, and unsure how Eleanor would take the news.

"No, he never said that, and I wouldn't be interested in any case," he says, "Just a weekly gig in here. £1000. I can't believe it."

"Blimey, that's not bad," says Neil, wondering how difficult this stand-up comedy lark actually is, while thinking about his paltry earnings at the steelworks.

Colin suddenly realises the folly of being offered an almost obscene amount of money. "I'm going to tell him no," he says, "It's very kind of him, but no." He puts his arm around Liz, devotedly. "All the money in the world wouldn't tempt me, this one off is enough," he confirms, kissing Liz on the side of her head.

Liz smiles fondly. "You don't have to say no, not on my part, at least think about it," she says, not sure whether Colin means no or not, that he feels obliged to say no because of her and the children.

"I don't want it Lizzy, ridiculous money in any case, he could get someone else for a fraction of the price, there are plenty of other funny-men out there," states Colin.

At that moment Big Barry appears, asking Colin to take the stage for his second spot. He asks Barry if he can finish his drink first.

Elvis and Louis are still on the phone. "Do everything you can to persuade Colin to say yes," says a panicked Louis, concerned that Liz will talk Colin out of the job.

"I'll try, but he is a big family man, I know that," states Elvis.

"They can come too, I told him that, talk him into saying yes," implores Louis, "whatever it takes," as Elvis sees Colin take the stage to loud cheers. He holds the receiver towards the stage again, allowing his boss to hear the second spot.

The second half is as well received as the first one, as the standing room only crowd tightly packed into the Jolly Roger are once again convulsed with laughter. Colin has never been a 'blue' comedian, preferring family friendly jokes, but as the crowd is solely of over 18s he does add a couple of suggestive gags which go down very well indeed, if taking Liz a little by surprise. It's a one off she muses, and a room full of adults. Not really him though she thinks.

By the end of his act the large crowd in the Jolly Roger are on their feet cheering, applauding, whistling. Colin can't believe the reaction. Elvis, meanwhile, is busily feeding this information down the line to Louis, who is now struggling to hear above the raucous show of appreciation as Colin leaves the stage, going into the artists room for a few moments to calm down. Barry appears around the door with Colin's fee, £500 in an envelope that he signs in receipt of. Barry cheekily asks for an additional autograph at the same time for himself!

Liz is sitting proudly at the table waiting for Colin to reappear again. While she does so, elderly Mr Reynolds taps Liz on the shoulder. "I thought he said he wasn't performing," he says.

"He wasn't supposed to be," admits Liz, not bothering to go over the circumstances that brought the gig about.

"Well he was bloody brilliant," says Mr Reynolds, "We've been coming here since the camp opened, 20 years, and this has been the best night ever." Liz smiles at the old gentleman kindly.

"Thank you so much," she says.

Mr Reynolds toddles off with his wife just as Colin comes back out. He stops for a moment to have a quick word with the two of them, shaking the old man's hand before coming back to the others. Neil and Christy get up to go, to allow Liz and Colin to have a few undisturbed minutes together.

"That was fantastic, really enjoyable, but we must get off. See you in the morning," smiles Christy.

"Ok, see you then," smiles Liz, as the two of them make their way.

Colin gazes at Liz adoringly. "Well, how was the second half," he asks, still a little unsure.

"You were amazing, no wonder Louis Peyton wants to pay you all that money!" smiles Liz. Colin kisses her.

"I'm turning Mr Peyton's offer down," he confirms, "You and the kids mean more to me than that." Liz smiles as they kiss again.

"It would be alright with me, if you did want to," says Liz softly.

"No. I don't want the hassle of traveling down here every week, and traveling back again. Yes, the money is amazing, but we're comfortably off, we've no worries," replies Colin, looking at Liz intently, "I love you Lizzy. He could offer me a million pounds and I'd still say no, that's how much you mean to me." He kisses her again, before they finish their drinks and leave the Jolly Roger.

Johnny and Johanna have already made their way out of the bar, along with many others, all heading back towards their accommodation. "Where are you staying? I'll walk you back there," states Johnny, "Can't have you walking back on your own."

"I'll be fine," replies Johanna, "Just walk me half way, that'll be alright, honest." Approximately halfway between the Jolly Roger and Primrose Block, Johanna stops. "I'll be alright now from here, thank you for tonight, I really enjoyed myself," she says.

Johnny looks at her. It's semi darkness, and here he is with a pretty young girl, one who definitely wants him, he thinks, and he's getting no affection at home from wife Olivia. Johnny makes the most of the moment and leans in to kiss her. Unsurprisingly Johanna makes no resistance, even though she knows she is no more than an ego boost for him, but determined to enjoy the moment as a one off. Johnny knows exactly what he's doing, but would give anything for it to be Olivia instead.

Liz and Colin make their way from the Jolly Roger, arms around each other, wandering slowly in the direction of Primrose Block. "Money for old rope that, if I'm being honest," muses Colin, knowing the £500 he pocketed for that one off Midnight Cabaret has paid for their week away, even if it wasn't expected.

"Well, seeing as that other guy let them down it was a good job you were here!" smiles Liz, "You're still the best joke teller ever, no one better than you!" She kisses him on the cheek.

"Get off, Lizzy," replies Colin, while smiling back at her fondly.

“It's true I tell you - oh look at that over there," says Liz, dropping her voice a little as she can see a couple canoodling in the moonlight. "We used to do that, do you remember."

Colin is sure the man he can see in silhouette looks familiar, as does the girl. The penny drops. "That looks like Johnny, it can't be." Liz squints into the darkness.

"Good god, it is as well, and that's Johanna with him, oh Johnny you stupid devil," tuts Liz, not happy that he's leading on a young girl while still married to Olivia.

"Leave 'em to it, none of our business," says Colin, turning away. Johanna looks over Johnny’s shoulder just as he is getting a little more carried away, nibbling at her neck. She sees Liz and Colin, knows fine well they've been spotted, and can only pray that her near neighbours keep quiet. She says nothing to Johnny, wanting to carry on enjoying his attention while she has the opportunity, the only time in her life any man has been this close to her. She might be a little drunk from the wine, but is realistic to know that he doesn't have any real feelings for her, and never will. She doesn't resist his kisses though, as their illicit clinch carries on.

After a short while Johanna starts to get ideas, wondering if he wants this to escalate into something more, as Johnny seems to be in no hurry to let her go. Not entirely sure what she's doing, she rubs herself suggestively up against him as he carries on kissing her deeply. Johanna quickly realises her moves are having the desired effect. Johnny can feel himself getting aroused and snaps back into reality. He stops their intimate moment immediately, slightly pushing Johanna away. He knows she is new to all this, correctly guessing she’s never been with a man before. I can’t do this to her, I can't be her first, must stop.

"It's time we weren't here, time to go," he says to her quietly.

Johanna isn't giving up that easily. He wants me, she thinks, he actually wants to sleep with me. She kisses him passionately again, like he hadn't spoken. Again he pushes her away gently.

"I mean it, time to go," he repeats, "You're a great girl, you'll make someone a lovely girlfriend. But when all is said and done I'm a married man." Johanna looks on sadly, hearing his words. He's feeling guilty about his wife, only natural I suppose she thinks.

Defeated, she kisses him one last time. "Goodnight Johnny," she says breathlessly before scurrying towards Primrose Block.

Colin and Liz arrive back at their chalet, and for once they don't have to worry about a squeaky front door waking up their sleeping daughters. They creep inside, hearing soft snores from both Eleanor and Charlotte. Liz puts her head around Jamie's door briefly, making sure he too is asleep. He is. They get into their replacement bed. Liz bounces slightly on the thin mattress, testing it for creaks. A little noise, but nothing like the loud resonating squeaks of the previous one. At last the two of them can contentedly make love to one another without worrying that everyone else can hear what they're doing.

A lovely end to what has been an incredible day.

Chapter Seventeen

Friday morning, and for once the sunshine has disappeared and rain is pouring down. That doesn't prevent Colin and Liz having a spring in their step, on a high after a successful gig and a very romantic night in bed afterwards.

Prior to them getting up Eleanor is already wide awake, and very neatly filling in her precious application form. She's a bit stumped when it asks for 'Qualifications', suspecting that 'Cycle Proficiency' or 'Grade 9 Piano' wouldn't do as an answer. The rest of the form is fairly straightforward to complete, although she doesn't realise that listing her dad as a reference isn't the correct way of going about applying for a job however.

Just as they are all about to head out for breakfast, Johanna knocks on the door. Liz answers. Johanna looks at her a bit fearful, wondering if she had said anything to Charlotte about what she'd seen the night before. Liz is sympathetic, more cross with Johnny for taking advantage.

"Can I see Charlotte?" asks Johanna, nervously.

"Sure," says Liz, not saying another word.

"Hi, you alright?" asks Charlotte, coming to the door.

"Yes," says Johanna, knowing immediately that Liz has said nothing to her as of yet, "What are you doing after breakfast, fancy a walk down the front, Christy has got a brolly we can use," states Johanna.

"Sounds good to me," smiles Charlotte, "Actually - mum - is it alright for me to go off with Johanna now, instead of hanging around here." Charlotte is in no hurry to face Barnaby at the dining hall.

"I suppose so," sighs Liz, "Off you go then."

Charlotte and Johanna decide to give breakfast a swerve and head down to the coffee shop on the front instead.

Johnny is lying in bed, barely bothered about getting up. He hardly slept a wink, feeling incredibly guilty of overstepping the mark with Johanna. He glances across at a photograph of Olivia and the children he has on a small table beside, barely being able look at it properly, knowing their marriage would most likely be well and truly over if she ever found out he'd been getting close to another woman, and how near he had been to being totally unfaithful. He decides he must carry on as if nothing happened, as he gets up.

He takes the small box from under his bed, and swallows the last of his Uppers, the only thing that is currently getting him through the day. Not knowing what he is going to do now he's run out.

Eleanor, meanwhile, is trying to think of a way of being able to deliver her completed form to Reception without anyone else knowing. Already aware that her step-mother Liz is fed up of her wandering off all the time, as a result she is constantly watched like a hawk no matter where they are. Must try and find a way she thinks, while making her way with Colin, Liz and Jamie to the dining hall.

In the coffee shop, Johanna decides telling the truth is the best policy, and begins to confide in Charlotte about what happened. "I saw your dad's show in the Jolly Roger last night," she begins, "I went with Johnny, he invited me to go with him." Charlotte is opened mouthed with shock.

"How did that happen? And isn't he married?" she says.

"I wasn't going to go to the Jolly Roger, I was going to come back to Primrose Block. Christy and Neil had already gone, and I was on my own when he approached me," admits Johanna.

"Then what happened?" asks Charlotte.

"He asked me if I was going to the cabaret, and I said no. Then he asked me if I would go to the show with him, as his guest," continues Johanna, "so I agreed. I know I shouldn't have, but I was a little bit drunk."

"Oh my god, what happened then?" enquires Charlotte.

Johanna takes a deep breath. "We watched the show together, no one noticed us, we were sat at the back - your dad is brilliant by the way, really funny."

"Thank you," smiles Charlotte proudly, "And was that it?"

"No," says Johanna quietly, "He offered to walk me back to the chalet, I said no, just half way would do, didn't want anyone to see us together."

"Ok, and then what?" Charlotte can feel herself panicking, wondering what else could have possibly happened.

"We stopped half way, and I thought that would be it, but - oh god - he made a pass at me," says Johanna, tears starting to fall.

"Oh no, he did what, you mean, he kissed you or something?" asks Charlotte. Johanna nods.

"I've been so foolish, should have told him to stop, I couldn't help it."

"Hey, it's ok, that was totally wrong of Johnny to have done that to you, none of this is your fault," says Charlotte, sympathetically, "Ummm, was that it?"

"Just about, although I think he might have wanted more, if you understand me," says Johanna, a little embarrassed.

"You're joking? You mean he asked you back to his chalet?" says Charlotte in shock.

"No, he didn't, I thought he was going to though, things were happening, but he said we had to stop because he was married," replies Johanna, "I ran the rest of the way back to the chalet."

"Perhaps that was for the best, I mean, he was taking advantage of you," says Charlotte.

"One more thing," continues Johanna, "Your mum and dad saw us, I know they did. God knows what they must think of me now."

"They're not daft, they'll know it was all Johnny's doing, don't be worried about that at all, they won't say anything, they didn't say anything to me did they," says Charlotte, "Does Christy know?"

"I didn't tell her, thought she would chase after Johnny same as dad would," says Johanna, "No need for her to know."

Back in the dining room, Barnaby is serving breakfasts. He's a bit disappointed that Charlotte isn't there, had thought of chancing his arm by asking for another date. Oh well, he muses as he clears some empty plates off a nearby table.

"We need to go to that Reception place after, so they can contact Louis Peyton and tell him I'm declining his offer," says Colin.

"Yes, we do," agrees Liz, "You've not had second thoughts then?"

"No, not at all, I'm turning him down," confirms Colin.

Eleanor gets an idea. "Shall I go to Reception and ask what time Mr Peyton will be available?" she asks.

"What on earth for?" asks Liz, suspiciously.

"Just trying to be helpful, getting dad an appointment," she lies.

"What harm will it do, Lizzy," says Colin, knowing how over protective she had been over Eleanor lately.

"Oh well, go on then, but straight there and straight back, and no bothering any Seasiders on the way, understand?" says Liz. A smiling Eleanor quickly dashes off.

Charlotte and Johanna continue their chat at the coffee shop, with Charlotte trying to change the subject by telling her about Barnaby and their date, that it was nice, but she doesn't want him as a boyfriend. Partly because she doesn't fancy him, and partly because they will be going back home tomorrow. It isn't long before the conversation turns back to Johnny however.

"I will have to see Johnny at some point, tell him how I won't go blabbing to his wife, and that I forgive him," says Johanna.

"Would it not be best to keep out of his way?" says

Charlotte.

"And how am I going to do that, he'll be in the Family Centre later on, can't avoid him there," states Johanna. She remembers something from her previous visit to Happy Daze where she was following him around. "I know, he'll be in the cafeteria for his lunch, he always goes there, I used to see him in there, he gets there at 12 o clock every day," says Johanna, although still upset over what happened still wants to see him desperately.

"He might not like you following him around, he might get cross," says Charlotte warily.

"I have to speak to him, I must," insists Johanna.

Eleanor arrives at the Reception Hall, but for once it's deserted. She looks around this unfamiliar building, not sure where she should go to next.

Dolly Mason appears at the hatch. "Can I help you, young lady?" she asks, cheerily. Eleanor walks over.

"Yes, well firstly my dad is Colin Chesters, and he needs an appointment to speak to Mr Peyton," she confirms.

"I see, well he doesn't need an appointment, Louis can always be reached by telephone at any time during the day, tell your dad to call in at whenever he wants, I do know that Louis is expecting to speak to him about the job offer," replies Dolly, having already had him on the telephone instructing her to do all she can to make sure Colin agrees.

"He's going to say no, by the way," says Eleanor, a little naughtily, knowing fine well it isn't her business to reveal this.

"Really? Well, I would rather hear that from him, all the same," replies Dolly, "Was there anything else?"

"Yes, can I give you this and make sure Mr Peyton gets it straightaway, I can start as soon as he wants me to," says Eleanor, proudly handing over her completed form.

"I beg your pardon?" says Dolly, mystified.

"You heard me," states Eleanor, "I'm going to be a

Seasider. So let him have this form please, so he knows all about me, and that I'm available to start right now."

It's all Dolly can do not to laugh out loud. Seeing the determination on Eleanor's face, she decides humouring her may be a better option. "I see, well I'm not sure we need any more Seasiders at the moment, but I could ask him all the same," says Dolly, "Umm, how did you get this form? I don't remember your name appearing on the list," she says, looking down at her ledger.

"Does it matter?" says Eleanor, not wanting to get Barnaby in any trouble.

"Well, I suppose not," says Dolly, knowing this is all a complete waste of time.

"Oh, and you mustn't say anything to my mum and dad, I only want to tell them when Mr Peyton gives me a job," says Eleanor, smiling.

"Ok then, I won't breathe a word in that case," says Dolly, quietly.

"I must go, mum told me not to hang around, but I will come back later, give you time to speak to Mr Peyton first," states Eleanor, heading back towards the door. Dolly looks on shaking her head, while laughing to herself.

Eleanor arrives back at the dining hall, just as her bowl of cereal arrives. "You don't need an appointment, dad, the lady says to go at any time," says Eleanor, innocently.

"I knew that's what she would say, I honestly don't know why you needed to bother them, unless you were up to something else?" replies Liz, deeply suspicious.

"Nothing mum, honest," smiles Eleanor.

Louis is in a good mood, having managed to secure the services of a new manager and cashier for the betting lounge, and having them start work for him on Saturday, meaning only one more day for Elvis to be in sole control. Having seen the figures from yesterday, Louis knows before long anything that Bo-Bo mugged him for will quickly be recouped when the betting lounge is being run correctly.

Breakfast completed, the Chesters go to the Reception. Dolly is already at the hatch waiting for them. "Hello Colin, Liz, hello kids," she chirps, "I've just had Louis on the telephone, wonders if he can see all of you in person. He's here, in his apartment at the back of the park." Liz and Colin look a bit confused.

"What apartment?" asks Liz, just as Seasider Ruth comes through the doors, sent by Louis.

"It's ok, I'll show you the way," she smiles.

Ruth leads them through the gates as Liz and Colin look at the Apartment in wonder, with Liz remembering that Charlotte had said something about this place, that she and Johanna came here when he spoke to them about the pictures. They are invited into Louis's large study, as he comes out from behind his desk smiling widely.

"Colin, good for you to come and see me," he says, shaking him warmly by the hand, "And you too Mrs Chesters, and your delightful children." He goes to sit back down at his desk. "Now, hear me out before saying anything," states Louis, forcefully, as the others also sit down. "I trust you have thought long and hard about the offer I made you, and it still holds firm. £1000 per week, permanent residency in the Jolly Roger, as our special Thursday Midnight Cabaret. Your lovely wife, and your children, are welcome here too, all at my own expense. I'll ensure you get a first class chalet, and anything else you require, money no object, what do you say?" asks Louis hopefully.

"Thank you, Mr Peyton," says Colin, "I have talked it through with my wife, and have decided to decline your very generous offer." Louis's face drops. "I'm a big family man, and I know you say they're welcome too, but once the children are back at school it won't be practical for me to be this far away from home, so I'm sorry, but I can't accept."

Louis is a little upset, of the belief that Liz has interfered and talked him out of saying yes. "What will it take for me to change your mind, name your price, your own terms, anything, and I will guarantee you work out of season too, you and Johnny Major, I want to put a stage show together, it'll be a massive hit!" Louis is determined to not let Colin get away.

"This is all very kind of you, but I still can't accept," says Colin, "I'm a family man at the end of the day, like I said, and we are quite comfortably off already, I have no monetary need for work." He holds Liz's hand affectionately.

"Please consider some more," begs Louis, "This is an amazing opportunity, you must see this. There isn't any comic better than you, no one at all."

"Thank you, but I'm sorry Mr Peyton, the answer is still no," says Colin, a little annoyed that his refusal is clearly not getting through, "and I won't be changing my mind. Sorry."

"I don't know what to say, I'm very, very disappointed Colin," says Louis, shaking his head solemnly, "Very disappointed indeed. You should still be on TV in my opinion."

"That's very nice of you to say so, but I'm extremely happy with my life as it is right now, I wouldn't change a single thing," replies Colin, smiling lovingly at Liz.

"Are you absolutely sure?" asks Louis, making one final desperate attempt.

"Absolutely, but thank you very much, I was very flattered," admits Colin.

"Oh well, that's that then, such a shame," says Louis, as Colin reaches over to shake his hand again. "There was one final thing," Louis continues. He reaches into his desk, retrieving Eleanor's application form. "Dolly Mason tells me that this young lady would like to become a Seasider," he says.

Liz glares at Eleanor crossly, unable to believe she could waste Louis Peytons time like this. "What are you playing at?" says Liz, a little embarrassed.

The colour has quickly drained from Eleanor's face; she definitely wasn't expecting this. Louis knows he can't give her a job of course, no matter how neatly her form has been filled in and how keen she is, but like Dolly and everyone else, is happy to let her down gently. Colin is also looking at Eleanor. She looks like she will burst into tears any second.

"I just wanted to ask something," says Louis, with a glint in his eye, "You have given your father's name as a reference, and so if I was to employ your 12 year old daughter, what could you tell me about her, as a recommendation."

Colin knows that Louis is only kidding, and is happy to play along. "Well," replies Colin, "She's not afraid of hard work, helps me in the garden, keeps her bedroom tidy, and helps her mum around the house."

"I see, that's very good," nods Louis, "Well, thank you for that Colin, but unfortunately Eleanor, I am not able to offer you a job." Eleanor, tries not to start crying, but fails, as two big tears escape. Liz puts an arm around her in support. "The problem is, well, you're too young right now. Because of the nature of the work, and things like insurances, I am only allowed to employ Seasiders at age 18," confirms Louis.

"Can't you make an exception for me, I work hard, you heard what dad said," says Eleanor, pleading.

"I'm very sorry. If anything should happen to you, well I wouldn't be insured for that and I might have to close the park down," says Louis, "But in a few years time, when you are old enough, please apply again, ok?" Eleanor nods sadly, her dreams shattered.

"It's alright," says Liz, "There'll be other chances in the future, you heard Mr Peyton. Just need to be patient."

They get up to leave. Louis shakes Colin's hand one final time. "If you ever change your mind, the offer will always be open, that is a promise," says Louis. Ruth shows them out of the apartment.

As they head back into the centre of the camp towards the amusement arcades, they happen across Johnny, on his way to his first engagement of the day, hosting a quiz in the Family Centre. Completely unaware, he bounds across in his usual enthusiastic manner, as his final Uppers have just taken effect.

"Hello there you lot, Colin, Liz, how's it going, having a good time?" he asks, "I hear Louis has offered you extra work, big money, job for life!"

"I've turned him down," states Colin.

"You did what? What was it, not enough money? If you pitched for double what he offered you'd get it, probably treble, or even more than that if you asked," says Johnny, disbelievingly.

"The thing is, I love and respect my wife and my children more than anything, and money means nothing to me," says Colin, in a deliberate swipe at Johnny's attitude to both. He takes Eleanor and Jamie by the hand and strides off in the direction of the amusement arcade, leaving Liz alone with a stunned Johnny.

"What was that about? Did I say something wrong?" he asks.

"Last night. We saw you with Johanna. How could you, she's so vulnerable," says Liz, bitterly unhappy.

"What? She was drunk and threw herself at me, I'm not interested in the girl," splutters Johnny.

"Don't make me laugh, you knew exactly what you were doing, how could you," states Liz.

"Why don't you believe me? Why would a happily married man like me want to get involved with a young girl?" he protests.

"Spare me your lies, Johnny, you did because you knew you could, knew she would be an easy catch, I am so disappointed in you," replies Liz, walking off in the same direction as Colin, while Johnny stands still, unable to believe he'd been found out.

Chapter Eighteen

Johnny looks on as Liz marches purposefully in the same direction as Colin, Eleanor and Jamie, feeling very guilty indeed. If they saw him with Johanna last night, how many more people did, he wonders.

To satisfy his guilt he decides to call Olivia, on the premise of making sure she and their boys are coming to see him at Happy Daze on Saturday afternoon.

At their home in the valleys, Olivia is in bed with her much younger neighbour Rory, the pair of them enjoying a post-coital cigarette. The children are all at school, and Rory's unsuspecting fiancée is at work. This arrangement, where Rory comes around to spend time with Olivia during his dinner hour, is becoming a regular habit.

When the telephone rings downstairs her first instinct is to ignore it, knowing it's probably Johnny, however as it could just as easily be the school or her mother, decides she needs to answer it. She quickly puts on a dressing gown and gets to the phone just as Johnny was about to ring off.

"Oh, you are there then," says Johnny, "Thought you must have gone out."

"I was down the garden putting out the rubbish if you must know," lies Olivia, "What do you want, Johnny?" Rory creeps quietly down the stairs behind her, while doing up his shirt. He gives Olivia a quick kiss on the cheek while mouthing 'love you', before heading for the front door and back to his job at a local car dealership. She smiles seductively as Rory looks back at her, while he opens the door.

"I'm just making sure you're still coming to Portwynne tomorrow, I miss you all so much," says Johnny, guiltily.

"Yes, we'll be there," sighs Olivia, not looking forward to their trip one bit, only for the fact that she knows how much the boys enjoy Happy Daze and spending time with their father.

"Good, good, I can't wait to see you," replies Johnny, "So, what else have you been up to lately?"

Olivia tries not to giggle. 'If only you knew' she thinks, while reliving about her latest encounter with her hunky next door neighbour. "Nothing much," she continues to fib.

As ever, this conversation is becoming hard work. "I know I keep asking, but are you sure everything is alright? You would tell me, wouldn't you, if something was troubling you?" says Johnny.

Olivia sighs. Here we go again, she muses, and wondering if 'I think we should divorce' ought to be her next line. "How many more times Johnny, stop fussing. I'm fine, the kids are fine, everything is fine," she snaps.

Johnny looks at the receiver, unhappily. Becoming a habit this, he thinks, one way conversations, Olivia having little or nothing to say. "Ok, then, I just wondered that's all. And I want to tell you, I won't be staying on here another season," he confirms, "Haven't told Louis Peyton yet, but I will." He knows it's doubtful he'll make it to the end of this one, now his supply of stimulants has evaporated, but is committed to stay for now.

This isn't what Olivia wants to hear, quite happy with Johnny staying out of the way, allowing her adulterous affair to continue undisturbed. "Surely it's too early to make any decisions like that," she says.

"No, I mean it. I don't want to put our marriage under any more strain than it is already," he says, "I love you, Livvy."

"I know," sighs Olivia, not caring.

For the first time in living memory Trevor is dragging his own cases, with Muriel following close behind, as they make their way solemnly to the minibus. People are staring at them but Muriel doesn't know if it's because they are leaving early on a Friday morning, or if these bystanders know he two of them are being thrown off the site by Louis Peyton. From a safe distance Alun is watching, on his boss's orders, making sure the Maynards leave

Happy Daze as instructed. As the minibus splutters its way to the gate, he goes to the payphone and puts in a call. "They've gone," he says down the receiver.

"Good," replies Louis, "I feel far better now."

Once off the telephone to Alun, he calls Elvis in the betting lounge. "Elvis? Only me," confirms Louis.

"Afternoon boss," says Elvis, trying to balance the receiver under his chin while paying out a customer.

"I need a favour from you," says Louis.

"Anything, boss," replies Elvis, while not particularly appreciating the interruption.

"Will you pick me up Sunday, first thing? I have somewhere I need to be, I'll pay you overtime, I know it should be your day off," he replies. Elvis doesn't mind this request, but is wondering where Louis wants to be on a Sunday.

At the other end of the line Louis is looking at the framed picture Johanna drew and smiling fondly.

Johanna and Charlotte head back to the camp late morning, despite Charlotte trying to talk her out of chasing after Johnny, doing all she can to get her to visit Louis first. Johanna won't be dissuaded so they go over to the cafeteria where he she knows he always spends his lunch break. They're in luck as they can see him through the window with his coffee and sandwiches, but at the same table is Alun so any chance of a private word would be all but impossible.

"That's the end of that then," states Charlotte, "You can't speak to him privately when he's not on his own."

"Let's wait for him, he won't be with Alun forever," says Johanna, determined. They sneak in through the side doors unnoticed, taking the table that backs onto the one where the two Seasiders are having their lunch. The partition between the tables means they can't be seen, but it's low enough for conversation to be overheard. Johanna gets an unwelcome surprise.

"I've been a total idiot, Alun, don't know what I was thinking, should have left her well alone," says Johnny, gloomily.

"Surely the young girl doesn't think it's actually going anywhere," replies Alun, "She isn't getting daft ideas like that, is she?" Johanna catches her breath at the realisation that Johnny is confiding in Alun about her.

"Nah, I trust her to say nothing," admits Johnny, "She's a smart girl, no way will Livvy get to find out. Might be best if I stay out of her way tonight though, to be on the safe side."

"Might be for the best, you're right," agrees Alun, "How did it happen in any case?"

"I asked her to come to the Midnight Cabaret with me, to see Colin, you know," confirms Johnny, "She was on her own, it seemed like a good idea at the time, and I fancied company. Afterwards we walked back, I was supposed to be walking her half way. She made a play straight for me, caught me totally off guard." Johanna starts to feel a little emotional, hearing the previous night being played out again, but completely horrified at the blatant lie he's just brazenly told.

"It can happen to anyone I suppose," says Alun, having no reason to disbelieve Johnny.

"Well, I only went along with it because I'm not getting any at home, and here was a pretty girl handed to me on a plate," Johnny continues, "Who wouldn't have crumbled in my position." Johanna feels a tear fall, not happy that Johnny is making it sound like she threw herself at him when that was far from the truth. She shakes her head in despair, while Charlotte is horrified to hear Johnny telling fibs.

Alun looks up at Johnny in alarm. "You didn't, you know, end up giving her one?" he says, sheepishly.

"Hell no, just a drunken fumble, a quick snog, nothing else," says Johnny, as Johanna and Charlotte silently listen on. "Not saying I wasn't tempted though, she was definitely up for it I could tell, didn't want to let go of me," he admits, "Perhaps if she'd been a girl

with 'previous experience' then maybe we would have, a quickie, no strings, if you get me. When it came down to it I just couldn't."
Johanna completely breaks down at the realisation that Johnny wouldn't sleep with her because he knew she was a virgin, and not out of any concern for his wife, as she had been made to believe at the time. That had she been most other girls her own age, one who had been with other boys in the past then he would have, but not wanting the burden of being her first lover.

Charlotte puts a comforting hand on Johanna's arm, feeling so sorry for her.

"Anyhow, it'll be soon forgotten, she'll be off home tomorrow, no doubt," says Alun, draining his coffee cup, "Right that's me done."

"And me," says Johnny, finishing his sandwich and coffee at the same time. They get up to leave together taking the far doors, not having to walk past where Johanna and Charlotte are sitting. She continues to sob quietly, not believing that Johnny could say such things about her. Yes, she knew she was a quick ego boost for him, and that he would never be serious about her, but to be made out to be cheap and up-for-it is devastating. He clearly had no idea of the depth of her feelings, that 10 minutes in his embrace meant everything.

"How could he," says Charlotte, shaking her head, "I had no idea he was such a creep."

Liz, Colin, Eleanor and Jamie come into the cafeteria, with the two youngsters both mithering for a cold drink as the rain has stopped and warm sunshine sun has once again has broken through.

They see Johanna with her hands covering her face, shaking with distress, with Charlotte sitting across from her. "Go and get whatever Jamie and Eleanor want, I'll go and see if those two are ok," says Liz, walking over.

Johanna looks up with a tearstained face. "Are you alright," asks Liz kindly, sitting down alongside Charlotte. Johanna feels ashamed. She starts to cry again, while Liz hands her a tissue. "Is this about something that happened last night?" asks Liz.

Johanna nods, while more tears fall. "Johnny thinks I'm a cheap slag, up for it," she says.

"Don't be daft, whatever makes you think that?" asks Liz.

"We heard him talking to Alun," confirms Charlotte.

Liz panics for a moment, wondering exactly how far their romantic encounter actually got. "Look, you don't have to tell me, but did you, umm, go back to his chalet?"

"No, I thought we might, thought things were happening, it seemed that way, how he was towards me," admits Johanna, "But he pushed me off, said we had to stop, and reminded me he was a married man."

"Then what did you hear him say to Alun?" asks Liz.

"That I chucked myself at him, and I was a 'pretty girl on a plate', and that he didn't want to sleep with me because..." wails Johanna. Liz guesses.

"Hey, it's ok, and probably for the best," says Liz, "He shouldn't have said that though, more than a bit thoughtless."

"He started it, Mrs Chesters, it wasn't me," Johanna sobs, "He offered to walk me back, but that was all I expected, you must believe me."

"Of course I do," nods Liz, having no doubt that Johnny started everything because he knew he could, and probably get away with it.

"He kissed me, ok I responded, perhaps I shouldn't have," explains Johanna.

"You're not to blame here," states Liz, "He took full advantage of the situation."

She looks up and sees Colin returning with Jamie and Eleanor in tow, both slurping on a large Slush Puppy. "Look, I've got to go, but don't worry about it ok?" says Liz, smiling.

"Ok, and thanks," says Johanna, as Liz gets up to join her husband and the two children on their way to the Games Room for the afternoon.

Johanna makes a decision. "If I can't speak to him, I can write him a message, put it under his chalet door, what else can I do?" she says. She delves into her handbag, getting a piece of paper and a pen out, and quickly writes a note.

'Dear Johnny. Thank you for last night, for ten minutes I felt special, loved. That has never happened to me before. I'm no fool though, I know it meant nothing to you, but to me it was everything. I overheard you in the cafe talking to Alun, making me out to be a drunken slut who threw myself at you. You know that isn't true, you invited me to the cabaret, and offered to walk me back. If nothing had happened, then that would have been fine. I expected nothing. But you kissed me, you initiated everything. So right now I am hurting. Not for the fact you don't care about me, I already knew that. But for you to be making me out to be something I'm not, and never was. Take care, Johanna x'

She folds the note up and puts it in her handbag. Retrieving her new make-up bag she reapplies her eye liner and mascara and leaves the cafeteria with Charlotte, heading straight for the staff accommodation, praying that Barnaby is in and that he knows which chalet belongs to Johnny.

Charlotte knocks loudly on Barnabys door. Luckily he's in, getting a lie down before his busy evening shift in the dining hall. He can't believe his eyes seeing both her and Johanna standing there, like all his Christmases have come at once. "Whoa, wasn't expecting you!" he says, smiling widely, "Come in!"

"No, we can't, I need you to tell me what chalet is Johnny's, if you know?" asks Johanna. Barnaby frowns, looking a little hurt. Charlotte feels guilty, like they're using him. He'd been so kind to her and Johanna this week, even after suffering at Trevor's hands.

"Ok, we'll come in just for a minute then," says Charlotte. Barnaby opens the door to allow them past, and they sit on the end of his bed.

"I do know which one is Johnny's chalet, for what it's worth, but why do you need to?" he asks.

"I've got something for him, that's all," says Johanna.

"Well, he won't be in at this time of day, will he, it's all the indoor sports finals this afternoon, he'll be in the Games Room," replies Barnaby.

"I don't actually need to see him, I just need to pop a note under his door," admits Johanna.

"A note? You'll see him later won't you? Hang on, you're not leaving today?" asks Barnaby, aware that Trevor and Muriel are on their way home.

"No, tomorrow, but I need to let him have this note, it's really important," confirms Johanna.

"Ok, well he's on the row facing this one, on the first floor, number 107," says Barnaby, "Can you tell me what this is about?".

Slowly she admits everything, from the dance, to Christy and Neil leaving her in the Family Centre on her own, Johnny inviting her as his guest to see the cabaret, their walk back and what happened after. Barnaby can't help but feel a little crushed, would have given anything to have been in Johnny's shoes, anything to get that close to Johanna himself. Looking at her now with her new makeover, any chance of that would be gone, even though he knows he would take such good care of her given half a chance, as he would Charlotte. Must let these thoughts go, he thinks.

Both Johanna and Charlotte give Barnaby a fond hug before leaving his chalet, dashing across the chalet line and up the metal staircase to the first floor facing, looking for 107. They have a quick look through the window, although not doubting Barnaby's information. Just making sure it's the right one.

They can just make out a photo on the bedside cupboard, looking like a woman and three children. Johanna sighs. Just as well we didn't come back she thinks sorrowfully, unaware that Johnny had only put it out there through guilt after he had returned the night before. She shoves the note under the door and they scurry away, heading for a planned visit to see Louis.

Chapter Nineteen

The two girls head up to Louis's apartment, with Johanna wanting to see him one last time as she'd promised Elvis the night before. The large gates that front the apartment are tightly shut, but they can see his front door wide open, and the Mercedes parked up, so it's obvious Louis is in.

Inside, Louis is on the telephone again. "Yes Mr Briscoe, you have my word, when have I ever let you down," he says, smiling down the phone. Johanna presses the intercom by Louis's gate, and this buzzes inside his study. "One moment, Mr Briscoe," he says, covering the receiver, wondering who it can be. "Hello, yes?" he says, into the speaker on his desk.

"It's me, Johanna, and Charlotte too," comes the reply.

"Oh how lovely," beams Louis, "Come right in, I'm in the study." He presses a button under his desk to open the gates and allow them both through. He goes back to complete his telephone call. "Sorry about that, Mr Briscoe, visitors," he says, "Now, I will get the information you need on Sunday, and will call back first thing Monday morning if that suits." Johanna and Charlotte come into Louis's study and take two seats across from his large oak desk. He smiles at the pair of them fondly. "That's fine then, I'll do that, thank you so much Mr Briscoe, good day to you." The call concludes. "Sorry about that ladies, just some business I needed to tidy up, and goodness me is that really you Johanna? Elvis did tell me, but I was keen to see for myself," says Louis.

Johanna smiles confidently for a change, and Louis finds himself beaming adoringly in return. He candidly thinks about his own childless life, wondering if he had ever had a daughter if she would have turned out as pretty and talented as Johanna is. 'Oh well,' he thinks, 'No point in reflecting on something that wasn't meant to be'.

"I wanted to say thank you, Mr Peyton," says Johanna.

"For what?" asks Louis, quite bemused. "Well, thanks to

you, and Christy of course, I know now that hiding my drawings away is not the thing to do, I have so much more confidence now," admits Johanna.

"Should have happened long ago, if it wasn't for your wretched parents. I am told they have gone home now," replies Louis.

"Yes, thankfully. My Nan is staying in Christy's chalet with me tonight," says Johanna.

"Well, it ought to be me thanking you," states Louis, "For that." He points at his framed portrait on the wall. "And for making me a little bit of money thanks to your stunning artwork, which reminds me." He reaches for his wallet and counts out five twenty pound notes. "There you go, your share," he says. Reluctantly Johanna takes the cash, putting it into her purse.

"I'll be getting some new pens and some more sketch books when I get back home," she says, "I'm going to live with Christy and Neil, until I find my own flat, and I'm going down the local Poly to sign up for art classes, night school."

"Really," says Louis, "Good for you."

Meanwhile, clambering through the hole in the fence at the back of the staff chalet line, is Robert 'Bo-Bo' Boston. One of the conditions of his bail was to not be within a two-mile radius of the perimeter of Happy Days. That was one condition he had no intention of adhering to, determined to get his revenge on Louis. Already aware he is likely to be sent to prison for his previous misdemeanours, Bo-Bo now believes he has nothing left to lose.

As he quickly strides down the chalet line, he taps the front of his jacket, feeling the outline of the sawn off shotgun hidden beneath.

As he reaches the apartment, he is astonished to find the large gates wide open, having expected to have to make his presence known from the outside. The front door is also open, as Johanna and Charlotte hadn't bothered to close it behind them. "How easy is this," smirks Bo-Bo, going inside. He retrieves the gun from under his jacket, and makes his way towards the study, unaware that Louis has visitors. He stands framed in the doorway, and raises the gun. Louis had been laughing and joking with Johanna and Charlotte a moment ago, now a stony silence replaces it. A petrified Louis raises his hands in surrender.

Johanna and Charlotte turn around and squeal. Bo-Bo lowers the gun slightly, annoyed that Louis has two young girls for company. Hostage taking wasn't part of the plan, frightening Louis was. "What do you think you are doing?" splutters Louis, scared out of his wits.

"You're finished, Peyton, no one gets the better of me," sneers Bo-Bo, menacingly. He glances briefly at the two petrified youngsters, and recognises Charlotte as the girl he saw Barnaby with earlier in the week. A sly smile creeps across his face. "Well, not only do I get the chance to finish you off, Peyton, but I can take that Irish bastards girlfriend as well. I know it was him who came running to you, telling tales."

"Let the girls go, I beg you," says Louis, "It's me you want, not them, let them go."

"No," shouts Bo-Bo, "We're all staying here. Do you know something, Peyton? With one pull of this trigger I will be doing so many people a favour."

"I don't understand," says Louis, quivering, and still with his hands above his head.

"Well, your staff will be grateful for a start. You do realise I had over half of them queueing round the block for what I had. You're killing them Louis, they are all totally knackered thanks to you running them into the ground, you're a no good slave driver. They depended on me just to keep going," states Bo-Bo.

"It wasn't just drug dealing though," seethes Louis, "You had been stealing money off me big time, even got your job here under false pretences."

"If it wasn't for that nosey rat Mansfield, I'd have got away with it," Bo-Bo replies. He raises the gun again, as Johanna and

Charlotte cower, both shaking. “I’ll bring your empire tumbling down,” says Bo-Bo, “Like those ramshackle chalets – all fall down.”

“Let the girls go,” pleads Louis, again, “Please, it’s me you want, let them go.”

“No,” repeats Bo-Bo, looking like he’s going to shoot Louis any second now. “I can give you a way out, though,” he says, starting to put his real plan into place, “Get on that phone, ring your bank and have them transfer £20,000 from your account to mine. Then me and Krystal can get away, and you will never see or hear from us again.”

Louis can’t believe it. To add to the stealing, and the drugs, it’s blackmail. “Haven’t you had enough of my money already,” he replies, incredulous.

“Just do as I say, and then no-one will get hurt,” replies Bo-Bo, pointing the gun directly at him.

While in bed the previous night, Elvis stated to Marissa that the two of them should put on a united front, be totally upfront with Louis and to hell with the consequences. Marissa, however, wants to stick to her original plan and see Louis for herself, announcing her pregnancy but not revealing the identity of the father. She uses a half hour break in her busy schedule to go and see him, unannounced. She too is surprised to see the front gates wide open, knowing how security conscious Louis usually is. She sees the Mercedes parked up, so knows he’s about somewhere, but completely oblivious to the dangerous situation currently unfolding inside the apartment.

She peers through the front door, listening out for any signs of where Louis might be. She hears a voice she’s sure she recognises, but isn’t Louis. She nearly turns around, believing her employer would not thank her for disturbing what might be an important meeting. In a split second, however, she recognises the voice as belonging to Bo-Bo. ‘What the heck is he doing here?’ she thinks, walking down the hallway towards the study, fully aware he isn't supposed to be anywhere on the site.

Silently she hovers behind the doorway. Bo-Bo is lifting the gun again, pointing it menacingly towards Louis. Marissa hears what sound like frightened sobs, definitely female. She is frozen to the spot in fear, unable to believe she has walked in on what appears to be a hostage situation. What to do? Quietly leave and alert the police? They might got get here in time, she thinks, and stays silently in the shadows instead.

"No, I will not hand you a penny piece of my hard earned money," spits Louis, silently praying that Bo-Bo is bluffing, and the gun isn't real. It is a real gun, but isn't actually loaded, with Bo-Bo stupidly thinking that scare-factor alone would force Louis to do as he asked.

"Hard earned?" laughs Bo-Bo, "You've never done a tap in your whole career, always getting others to do your bidding." This retort makes Louis even more determined to not give in. Panicking, Bo-Bo grabs Charlotte by the arm, forcing her to stand, pointing the gun at her head, while she whimpers and trembles with fear. "Do as I say, or Walsh's girlfriend gets it."

Louis's instinct is still that Bo-Bo is bluffing, that he would never shoot a young girl, no matter how desperate he is. That he's just a chancer, an opportunist, up to his eyeballs in debt, and seeing Louis's wealth as his way out. He looks at Charlotte shaking, scared beyond comprehension. The last thing Louis wants to do is give into Bo-Bo's threats, but seeing a young girl not knowing if she'll get out of his study alive is tipping the balance. Slowly Louis goes to lift the receiver.

Bo-Bo throws Charlotte to the floor, once again training his gun on his ex-employer. Both Charlotte and Johanna are frozen with fear, neither daring to move in case it looks like they are trying to make an escape.

"Go on, call the bank, I'm waiting," says Bo-Bo, while Louis stares down the barrel of the shotgun. He picks up the handset.

"I don't know the number," splutters Louis. Even if he did

know it off by heart, he would have pretended otherwise.

"Don't lie to me, Peyton," sneers Bo-Bo, putting his finger on the trigger, "Someone with all your dough, you'll be on first name terms with the Bank Manager, so stop lying and call them. Now."

Marissa is still quietly taking in these unbelievable events, barely breathing. Knowing she cannot simply stand by doing nothing, and that raising the alarm might make things worse, takes matters into her own hands. She quietly lifts up one of Louis's prized Ming vases from a small display table just outside the door, and smashes it violently over the back of Bo-Bo's head. He drops to the ground out cold, as the priceless porcelain antique shatters into a million pieces.

He drops the gun as he falls; quick thinking Charlotte scrambles to her feet and kicks it away, in case he comes to. Louis is wide eyed with shock, while Marissa stands there, hands trembling.

"Oh my god," she says, as the shock of what she has just done dawns on her. Almost immediately though, all thoughts of disarming a dangerous criminal disappear as a sharp pain in her stomach makes her double over in agony. Johanna and Charlotte go straight to her, while Louis quickly dials 999, hoping that Bo-Bo stays unconscious long enough for the authorities to arrive.

"Police," he says down the phone, "And two ambulances. This is Louis Peyton, Happy Daze, Portwynne."

Marissa is in so much pain she can't tell the girls what the trouble is, what exactly is causing her such agony. With Louis also unaware why Marissa has fallen unwell, assuming it's just shock, and not knowing about her pregnancy, or her ongoing relationship with Elvis, he doesn't bother ringing the betting lounge, just wants the emergency services to arrive swiftly.

Over in the Games Room, Liz is standing with Rodney, Sandra, Neil and Christy, while watching Jamie, Mikey and Karl playing 5-a-side soccer. Eunice is having a quiet sit down with a cup of tea, while Colin and Eleanor are having a round of indoor crazy golf. Christy turns around to look out of the window, checking to see if the rain was still holding off, when she sees two ambulances and a police car with their blue lights flashing, speeding up the road leading to Louis's apartment. She's totally unaware that this involves Johanna and Charlotte of course, believing them to be spending the afternoon in the arcades and shops on the seafront, so turns back again.

"Guess what I've just seen," she tells Liz, "A police car and two ambulances going past, looks like they were going up to Louis Peyton's place."

"Two ambulances? Blimey, if Louis Peyton had took ill, then he wouldn't need two ambulances, wonder what's happened there then?" says Liz, looking up to see Colin and Eleanor coming back. Curiosity gets the better of Christy.

"I think I might just take a quick wander up there, see what's going on," she says.

"Tell you what, I'll come with you for a nosey," replies Liz.

"Did I just see some blue flashing lights outside?" asks Colin.

"Yes, ambulance and police," confirms Christy, "Me and Liz are just going to see what's happening."

"Yes, you two stay here, we won't be long," says Liz.

By the time they get to Louis's apartment a small crowd, also alerted by the lights and the sirens, has gathered. The gates and the front door remain open, but it's impossible to tell what has happened. First out of the apartment is Marissa, lying on a stretcher under a blanket.

"Oh my god," says Liz sadly, not knowing how she is going to tell Eleanor that her favourite Seasider has been taken ill.

Next out, also on a stretcher, is Bo-Bo. The paramedics managed to bring him round, and with Louis telling the police exactly what he did, handcuffs are swiftly applied, while his head was bandaged up.

"Blimey, wonder who that is?" wonders Christy, as neither she nor Liz have ever seen Bo-Bo before, having never been in the

Betting Lounge.

"Oh well, that solves the mystery of the two ambulances, but I wonder what actually happened?" says Liz, getting ready to walk off again. Just as she is about to turn around, out come Charlotte and Johanna, either side of a policewoman, who has her arms around the two of them protectively. Just behind them is a policeman, with the gun in an evidence bag. Both Liz and Christy gasp with shock, hastily pushing past others in the crowd to get to the girls.

"Mum," cries Charlotte, flinging herself at Liz, "I thought we were going to die."

"Oh my lord, what the hell happened," implores Liz, while hugging her distraught step-daughter tightly.

"The man from the betting shop turned up, he wanted to shoot Mr Peyton, and threatened to shoot me too," confirms Charlotte, tears streaming, leaving Liz to wonder how Charlotte knew who the man was. "He was selling drugs, and stealing, I think Mr Peyton must have given him the sack, and he wanted revenge," she continues.

"How do you know all this?" asks Liz.

"Barnaby tricked him into selling him some drugs the other day, he took them to Mr Peyton as proof," Charlotte replies.

"I assume Barnaby has told you all this, then," says Liz.

"Not quite, I was with him when he went to the betting shop, the man thinks I'm Barnaby's girlfriend, and it's because of that he wanted to kill me as well," wails Charlotte.

Christy has her arms around Johanna, comforting her. "I was so scared, he was waving a gun around. He asked Mr Peyton to give him money and then he would go away, he even pointed the gun at Charlotte, I was petrified," says Johanna, "Marissa hit him over the head to stop him. And now she's ill as well, I can't understand what's happened."

"It's ok now, all over," says Christy kindly, barely believing that Johanna, Charlotte and Louis had all been taken hostage.

The policewoman approaches the four of them. “I’m sorry to bother you,” she says, “I know it’s a bit soon, but we will need witness statements from the girls. Can you tell us what chalet number you are staying in, so we can send someone round later on?” This information is readily given, allowing Liz to take Johanna and Charlotte straight back, while Christy goes back up to the Games Room to tell everyone else the news.

Quickly, the boys are rounded up and everyone returns to Primrose Block.

Back inside the apartment, and after Louis had given a full statement, the police leave. Just as they do, Elvis is making his way to the apartment, after closing the Betting Lounge for the day. He’d heard some of his punters muttering about police, and sirens, but as Louis hadn’t called him assumed it was something and nothing. Using his pass key to get into the apartment, he finds Louis in his living room sitting in a leather armchair, knocking back a large glass of brandy.

“What’s going on? Why were the police here?” Elvis asks.

“You wouldn’t believe me if I told you,” says Louis, quietly, thinking he was lucky to escape with his life not too long ago.

“Try me,” says Elvis.

“I have been held up at gunpoint by Robert Boston,” states Louis, “along with Johanna Maynard and her friend.”

“You what?” splutters Elvis, “How did that happen?”

“I was careless enough to leave the gates open, and the front door was also open, I was letting in some fresh air, made it easy for him,” sighs Louis, “Tried to blackmail me, wanted £20,000 or he was going to shoot.”

“Oh my god, how did it end up, don’t say the girls got hurt,” says Elvis.

“No, they are fine, it was Marissa Black who saved the day, would you believe, I don’t even know why she was here, but she was, she crept up and hit him over the head with one of my Ming vases,” confirms Louis.

Elvis starts to panic. “Marissa? Well, where is she? Louis, where the hell is Marissa?”

“Gone to hospital, stomach pains, I think the shock got to her,” says Louis, unknowingly.

“The shock? Oh my god Louis, it’s not the shock – she’s pregnant!” shouts Elvis.

“Is she? How do you know?” asks a mystified Louis.

Elvis gets very emotional. “How do you think I know,” he replies, grabbing the keys to the Mercedes.

“What? You mean.... you and her? It can’t be, you know my rules,” says Louis, in total astonishment.

“Stuff your rules,” splutters Elvis, quickly leaving the apartment and hastily speeding off to the hospital.

Louis pours himself another large brandy in disbelief.

Chapter Twenty

By the time Elvis gets to the hospital, good news is waiting. After being thoroughly examined, the doctor confirms that both Marissa and her unborn baby are going to be fine, that the pains may well have been phantom ones brought on by the shock of felling an armed assailant. The doctor goes onto joke that in future she should consider leaving 'super-hero antics to Wonder Woman'.

Elvis is at her bedside, after being told that Marissa will be kept in overnight. "Louis knows. He knows about you being pregnant, and about me being the Father," he says.

"That's why I was going there, to tell him about me expecting a baby, I had no idea that I was walking into danger," replies Marissa.

"Well, no need to worry now," says Elvis, "That scumbag Bo-Bo won't be going anywhere, if he's breached his bail he'll be remanded in custody."

"I hate to think what might have happened if I hadn't been there, poor Louis, poor girls," says Marissa, sombrely.

"You are a hero, and I am so relieved you and our baby are alright, I was so scared coming here, was expecting the worst," admits Elvis.

Visiting time concluded, he drives back to Happy Daze to his normal Friday night task of taking Louis back to his South Wales mansion. Again he lets himself into the apartment, finding Louis where he left him, still in the armchair with his brandy glass.

"She's going to be ok, and so is the baby," confirms Elvis.

"Thank goodness for that," replies a clearly relieved Louis, "And I'm sorry. Shouldn't have snapped at you, if you and Marissa are a couple then so be it. Ummm, congratulations."

"Thank you," says Elvis, smiling, happy in the knowledge that Louis has put his loyalty to him over any personal feelings.

"The police just called me," says Louis, "Apparently the gun was genuine, but unloaded would you believe. He didn't have a single bullet on him. Seems that he just wanted to scare me, in the hope I would give him money. Unbelievable."

Elvis shakes his head, in the knowledge that Marissa put herself and their unborn child in peril for nothing.

"Are you ready to go, then?" asks Elvis.

"Yes, ready as I'll ever be," says Louis, getting up, glad to be getting away from Portwynne for a couple of days.

Over at Primrose Block, the police call round as planned, and both Charlotte and Johanna give comprehensive statements about what happened. The police praise them for their bravery, and assure them that Robert Boston will not be let out of custody for a very long time indeed.

Both families head to the dining hall, although none of them really have much appetite. For all that, the atmosphere there is a whole lot better without anyone looking over their shoulder, waiting for Trevor to make a loud and needless complaint about the food or service in an attempt to get extra portions.

The final night in the Family Centre is always a big one, and with this being an extra busy week for Happy Daze, the venue is full to bursting, with many people unable to find seats or tables. Luckily, employing a tactic that Trevor usually would, Rodney sends Mikey and Karl off to reserve a table or two big enough to house all of them and the Chesters family as well. Liz and Colin allow Jamie to go along with them, to ensure suitable space can be found for everyone. Good fortune is on their side, as they quickly find two large tables that they push together, despite this not generally being permitted. The thought of a bribe of a pound note each for doing this more than worth it, as the others soon appear.

Colin, Rodney and Neil head to the bar. "Is it true then," asks Colin, "They've definitely gone."

"Yep," smiles Rodney, "And I shouldn't say this about my own parents, but good riddance to bad rubbish."

"That goes for me too," confirms Neil, "And nice to know they won't be coming back here either. I'm already looking forward to our next stay at Happy Daze without them."

"Has anyone rang to tell them about what happened this afternoon?" says Colin.

"No, it's doubtful they'll care less in any case, probably make it out to be Johanna's fault, true to form," states Rodney.

As the room fills up very quickly indeed, a small gaggle of Seasiders gather in the corner making a plan of action. Johnny, Alun, Ruth and Big Barry are the only ones there, however. They look around the Family Centre expecting at least three more of their number to appear, knowing it will take that many at the very least to keep control of what will be a busy and challenging night. Bad news is about to arrive. Already aware that Marissa is in hospital, it's when Jed the glass collector from the Jolly Roger turns up that even more bad news is delivered.

"Sorry folks, got a message for you. The other three supposed to joining you are all unwell, stomach bug, not fit to work. Mr Peyton knows, alright?" he confirms.

"Oh well," sighs Jed's sister, Ruth, "Can't be helped I suppose."

Further problems are coming. With all available cover doing stints in the Pavilion, the Jolly Roger, Sonikz Disco and the fun-fair it looks like just the four of the will be supervising a night where almost over a thousand people are present. Already things are starting to get a little out of hand, with over a dozen youngsters running around the dance-floor in a clumsy looking game of 'Tick'.

"What the hell are we going to do," panics Johnny, "This is going to be a nightmare of the very highest order."

The other three are also extremely worried over how they can keep on top of things, knowing that Louis would be furious if the busiest night of the week became a shambolic debacle.

From her seat not far away, Eleanor has her eyes firmly fixed on the four Seasiders. She can tell something isn't right by the panicked look of concern on their faces. Seeing the young children running around, all over the dance floor and weaving around the tables and chairs dangerously and out of control, is enough for her to want to do something about this.

Without a word to her parents she jumps out of her seat. Already wearing her light blue 'Seasider in Training' blazer, that Liz had unsuccessfully asked her not to put on, she quickly rounds up the unruly youngsters, grabbing two of them by the hand and shouting “Stop! Stop running about! Stop it now!!" sternly, to the others. Seeing her, and assuming she is a real Seasider, the children quickly stand still, looking at her as some sort of authority, to the utter astonishment of the real Seasiders at the side of the floor, and Colin and Liz.

Then, without a second thought, she strides her way to the stage and can be seen making a request to the disco DJ, while holding her hand in a 'Stop' sign behind her, which the children continue to respect. Other youngsters come onto the floor, and also behave themselves impeccably.

The DJ does as Eleanor requested and starts to play some party dance records. She stands confidently in front of at least thirty under tens, including her brother Jamie, and Karl and Mikey, and starts to perform the actions to a popular party dance, which the youngsters happily copy. Ruth dashes onto the floor alongside her to join in, barely believing she can see such a young girl in a replica Seasiders outfit have complete control of so many children. The other Seasiders can now start to mingle amongst the crowd without any worry.

"I can't believe it," says Liz, smiling, "Who knew?"

"She did," says Colin, proudly, as Eleanor carries on dancing with the children happily, believing she's finally made it and that she really is a Seasider. Even when the DJ gets a little fed up of playing non-stop cheesy pop records she stays on the floor, ensuring no one is running around, and that everyone is dancing and not running about. Ruth manages to grab a quick word with her. "Well done you, you have really helped us out," she says.

"It's so easy, I love it," smiles Eleanor, in her element, "Will you tell Mr Peyton what I did, perhaps he might change his mind and give me a job after all!" Ruth laughs fondly, happy to let Eleanor have her dream of being a proper Seasider for one night only.

Johnny has spotted Johanna sat with the rest of her family, having already read her note over and over again while in his chalet. He felt ashamed while he was reading it, that his bravado and ego had been his undoing. He doesn't know what to do now. Try to speak to her at some point? Ignore her? As he makes his way happily chatting to other people, although not really in the mood, and craving Uppers, he knows he won't be welcome where the Chesters are sat for a start, and also not knowing how much Johanna had told the rest of the Maynards, believes avoiding them too may be the sensible option. Johanna herself isn't especially concerned, just glad to have got her message to him.

He decides to leave their table alone, allowing Big Barry the opportunity to ask if they are all enjoying themselves. In an unusual step, Johanna has her sketch pad out in front of everyone, and is busily drawing a picture of Eleanor in her Seasiders outfit along, with some of the other children she has dancing with her. It's taking all her resolve not to draw Johnny as she usually would.

Dave Busby and Busbys Canyon replace the DJ, allowing several dozen exhausted children to sit back down. Eleanor returns to where Colin and Liz are, to take a quick mouthful of her glass of lemonade.

"Sit down now, Eleanor," implores Liz, "You've done more than enough for one night. We're very proud of you, of course we are, but it's time to let the real Seasiders take over now."

"No mum," she insists, looking over her shoulder at the others busily talking to guests, "I've got to get back to work." And with that she vanishes.

"She won't be told," sighs Colin, putting his arm lovingly around Liz, "I think we best leave her to it." All week she has watched carefully how the Seasiders interact with the many holidaymakers in the Family Centre, and knows exactly what to do, asking people where they have come from and if they having a good time, and this is very well received. Eventually, after some persuasion from Alun, concerned that Eleanor might end up burning herself out, she returns back to Colin and Liz.

"My work is done," she smiles proudly, "This is what I want to do all the time, I wish Mr Peyton would let me, who needs school, this is so much more enjoyable!"

"Stop getting carried away," says a concerned Liz, glad to have her step daughter back where they can see her.

Ruth comes across. "I just wanted to say thank you Eleanor, for all your help," she says kindly, "I don't know what we would've done without you tonight."

"Thank you, I can help you anytime, you only have to ask!" replies Eleanor, smiling broadly.

"Maybe, one day," says Liz, determined to keep Eleanor's feet firmly on the floor.

"I've just spoken to Mr Peyton on the telephone, and he also says a big thank you," confirms Ruth, "He did go on to say that he was sorry he still couldn't offer you a proper job, but has asked me to give you this as a reward." She hands her a £20 note. "Call it wages," says Ruth.

Eleanor can't believe it. "Look at this mum," she says excitedly.

"You deserve it," says Liz.

"You certainly do," confirms Colin, proudly, as Eleanor puts the money into her small handbag.

As the night starts to draw to an end, Dave Busby announces he's slowing the tempo down to allow couples to get up to dance. Barnaby, who had been over the other side of the Family Centre with his friends from the kitchens all night, decides to try and hunt down Charlotte for one final time. He'd heard that her and Johanna had been involved with the incident at Louis's apartment, and didn't know whether they would want him bothering them. 'I won't get another chance,' he thinks, so makes an approach. He can see her laughing and chattering to Johanna, and feels a little rude interrupting them. "Sorry, Charlotte. Would you like to dance?" he asks, hopefully.

"Thank you, but no thank you," she replies. She doesn't fancy him one bit, and has no intention of building his hopes up. Barnaby looks extremely crestfallen.

"How rude, Charlotte," says Liz, a little unhappy, "That was a lovely thing to ask you. It's impolite to say no."

"It's alright," says Johanna, "I will dance with you Barnaby, if you like." He immediately perks up again, as Johanna gets out of her seat.

They go off to enjoy a slow dance together, while Charlotte thinks 'thank goodness for that'. "I don't like him in that way, I never did, mum," she quickly tells Liz.

From the side of the floor Johnny can see Barnaby and Johanna dancing closely, and gets a sudden pang of jealousy. That should have been me, he thinks, mentally kicking himself for overstepping the mark the previous night, and in no mood to ask anyone else for the last dance as a result.

As they continue their slow dance Barnaby looks intently at Johanna, realising that all along he knew she was the one. Even before the makeover, she was the one he should have asked out for a date, that he should have stood up to Trevor instead of being bullied by him. As much as he liked Charlotte, and he genuinely did, it's clear she'll never feel the same way, and probably only agreed to the date out of loyalty to Eleanor, and at Liz's behest. 'This feels right,' he thinks as he gazes at Johanna devotedly, while she smiles adoringly back.

The music comes to an end. Johanna gives Barnaby a quick kiss as a thank you. It takes all of Barnabys resolve not to kiss her passionately in return, but aware that her whole family, Johnny and many others have their eyes trained on them decides discretion is the better part of valour. He does manage to say something however. "Will you keep in touch with me, after you get home," he asks, “Would you be my girlfriend?”

A thrilled Johanna beams. "Of course I will, I'm staying with Christy and Neil for now, I'll give you the address tomorrow," she confirms, and goes back to the others.

Christy is smiling, delighted that her little sister may have found romance at last. “Well?” she asks.

“Well what?” replies Johanna, blushing.

“You made a lovely looking couple out there, he seems a very nice boy,” says Christy.

“He asked me to be his girlfriend, and I said yes,” smiles Johanna. Christy throws her arms around her younger sister.

“Good for you,” she says, “How lovely, I’m so happy for the both of you.”

To conclude the night, Seasider Alun takes to the floor. "Well, we've come to the end of the week here at Happy Daze, Portwynne, and I know that most of you will be going back home tomorrow," he says, "So to finish off proceedings tonight I would like to invite as many of you as possible onto the dance floor for a round of 'Auld Lang Syne', come on."

All the Maynard clan, along with the Chesters’ and many others, cram onto the floor alongside the other Seasiders linking arms as Alun requested, with Dave Busby and Busbys Canyon striking up a rousing rendition of this popular standard. Balloons are released from the ceiling as everyone engages in group hugs to celebrate the end of an unbelievable week.

Chapter Twenty-One

Saturday morning. Elvis is in good spirits having heard from the hospital that Marissa has had a very restful night, and is ready to be discharged. Having already made an agreement with Louis, she is to spend her days living with him in his flat, and will not be returning to her draughty chalet again. A week off work is also agreed to, with Marissa happy to see out the rest of the season provided she feels well enough.

Back at Happy Daze, and for the final time, everyone is making their way down to the dining hall for breakfast, before packing the last of their cases and heading home. Again it doesn't go unnoticed how it's a lot quieter in the hall without Trevor's booming voice.

With some other early leavers meaning a few empty tables, the Chesters' and the Maynards are able to sit all together, chatting happily, making plans to keep in touch once back in Manchester and Birmingham.

"Will you draw a picture of me?" Jamie asks Johanna, across the table.

"Don't be so cheeky," says Liz, a little horrified at her son's insolence.

"It's ok," smiles Johanna, "In fact I can do a bit better than that." She delves into her handbag, getting out a neat piece of white paper on which she has drawn a stunning caricature of young Jamie wearing a red football kit, and a football under his arm. Written underneath in neat calligraphy is 'Manchester United's Latest Signing'. Johanna has also signed it in the corner.

Jamie's eyes light up straightaway, while the others smile in appreciation. "Oh wow, look at this dad," he says, excitedly.

Colin smiles fondly. "Very nice, what a very talented young lady you are Johanna," he says. Johanna blushes, while handing over the drawing.

Liz has it out of Jamie's hand in a flash. "I'm not having you handling this, it'll get spoilt," she says, "I think this might be worth money in a few years." Johanna blushes even more.

"It's true," insists Liz, "Your designs will be on catwalks and in art galleries all over the world. And here's us, in possession of an original Maynard!"

"Liz is right," states Christy, "Once we are back home, we will get you enrolled at the college like I said, not that you need to learn anything, you'll be teaching them before long."

Johanna looks around the dining hall for Barnaby, but can't see him anywhere to her utter disappointment. In a last minute rota change, due the bug that is currently making some of the staff unwell, he's been sent to the staff canteen to serve breakfasts there instead. He too is unhappy at not being able to see Johanna, knowing there is a good chance she'll be on her way home before he can finish his shift.

Johnny is getting ready in his chalet a little slower, and with a little less enthusiasm than usual. Now completely out of Uppers, the lethargy he suffered in the early weeks of the season will soon return with vengeance, he already knows this. He also knows he's obliged to see Colin and Liz before they depart, despite yesterdays awkward encounter, but is aware of their friendship with Johanna and the others, and that they might just be all together before they go, same as they were all together the night before. He reads Johanna's letter yet again, his heart completely in bits. Must forget all about her, he thinks, today is the start of another week, she's going home, and Olivia and the kids are coming down, must get back to reality and get all thoughts of Johanna out of his head quickly. Not wanting to run the risk of Olivia discovering the letter he tears it into tiny pieces and throws it into the nearest waste bin outside, as he goes over to get his own breakfast from the staff canteen. As he sits down waiting to be served, he can see Alun and Ruth looking over in amusement, as rumours of his encounter with Johanna are being spread around the staff as gossip. He knows he's been a fool, over stepping the mark with Johanna, but is hopeful that they and the other Seasiders say nothing in front of Olivia. Barnaby appears, and throws Johnny's breakfast at him in contempt.

"I could report you for that," snaps Johnny.

"And I could say things to your unsuspecting wife, about what you did with Johanna," says Barnaby, "Such a lovely girl is Johanna, how could you. And I know about your filthy drug habit as well." Suitably shamed, Johnny says nothing else.

After a pleasant breakfast, far more relaxed than almost any other meal this week, they all go back to Primrose Block for one final time to retrieve their cases.

"As much as I can't wait to get home," admits Liz, as Colin locks the chalet door behind them for the last time, "I think I will miss this place, honest. What a week we've all had."

"Not sure I'll miss it," replies Colin, mindful of squeaky beds and doors, along with paper thin walls, "Not sure Charlotte will either, considering what happened."

"Well, I suppose so. But you got a paid gig out of it!" Liz reminds him, "That's something!"

"Well, yes, I just don't want Louis Peyton beating a path to our door wanting a repeat," he says, as they make their way down the staircase.

"You said it was money for old rope!" says Liz, chuckling.

"I know," Colin confirms, "but for all that I couldn't manage a whole summer here away from you and the kids these days. Don't know how Johnny does it, I really don't."

They arrive at Colin's car just as two taxis turn up to take the Maynards to the railway station. Johnny is stood at the top of the car park looking down towards everyone, as they engage in fond hugs and repeat plans to stay in touch. Just as Johanna is giving Liz a hug goodbye she spots Johnny over Liz's shoulder looking at them all and freezes. Liz turns around. "Oh, I see," she sighs. Johnny knows he's been seen and sheepishly makes his way down.

Johanna's eyes fill up with tears. As far as she's come this week, getting close to Johnny, even for a short time, is precious. His sly remarks when he didn't know she was listening are unforgivable, but the memory of Thursday night is still special for all that. Johnny looks a little remorseful. "I'm sorry Johanna," he says, "Should never have said those things, I've been a fool."

"It's ok," replies Johanna, "I forgive you." She goes up to Johnny and gives him a hug. He responds warmly. Liz smiles, even if in her heart she's a little dismayed that Johanna has been so forgiving, so soon. Most women would have a lifetime grudge against any man who said what he did. Just goes to show what a special girl she is, she thinks, and how much he means to her.

"Bye, Elizabeth," says Johnny, giving Liz a hug, "Give my best to your parents."

"I will," Liz confirms.

"Colin, all the best mate," says Johnny shaking his hand, "Job for life here if you want it, you heard Louis Peyton."

"I know, but I'll not be taking him up on his kind offer as I told you," admits Colin, "I love Lizzy and the kids too much to be away week after week, I just couldn't do it." Johnny thinks of the difficulties in his own marriage, and can understand fully where Colin is coming from. Had things been great between him and Olivia it is doubtful he could do it either.

"I'm sorry for being a bit off with you yesterday, by the way," states Colin.

"No more than I deserved," admits Johnny, "Anyway, bye everyone, safe journey home," he says to the others as they're putting their luggage away and getting in the taxis, "Well, I must be off, things to see to, another week begins!" And with that Johnny strides down towards the front gate, another week beckoning, more guests.

Just as Johanna is opening the taxi door she hears a shout. "Johanna, wait," calls Barnaby at the top of his voice, sprinting across the car park. Having literally only just finished his shift, he hasn't even had time to take off his kitchen-whites or his bandana, but was desperate to see her.

Johanna runs up to meet him, and with neither of them caring about anyone watching, embark on a passionate goodbye kiss. "I'm so glad I caught you in time," smiles Barnaby, "Thought I was going to miss you."

"Another 60 seconds and you would have," says Johanna, also smiling, "Here's Christy's address and telephone number, she says it's fine to call at any time." She hands over a slip of paper.

"I will most certainly be calling, soon as I can," confirms Barnaby. If he had managed to miss her, he would've had to prize the information out of Dolly or Val, which didn't appeal as it's doubtful the security conscious pair would have been particularly forthcoming. "I'm so proud that you're my girl," he says, softly. Johanna can't stop smiling at him. "I couldn't sleep last night, kept thinking about you," he continues on.

"Me neither, I couldn't stop thinking about you either," says Johanna, as they start kissing again. It crosses Johanna's mind to not go home for a split second, to remain at Happy Daze drawing pictures for Louis, and spending time with her new boyfriend. Christy shouts over, interrupting her daydream.

"Come on you two, the taxi driver is waiting and we don't want to miss the train." After a loving hug and another kiss, reluctantly the two of them part, with Barnaby promising faithfully he will call her as soon as she gets home, and make active plans to see her in Birmingham at the earliest opportunity.

"Louis owes me a favour or three," he states, "Some extra time off will do for starters!"

No matter what the next week, or the rest of the season brings, no way will it ever be as eventful as this one he thinks, as the taxi disappears into the distance.

Epilogue

Johanna is sitting in Christy and Neil's living room watching the television, while her sister and brother in law finish washing the dishes after their Sunday lunch. Feeling so much more content and relaxed, but not looking forward to returning to Budget-Buys tomorrow, knowing that her mother will most likely hunt her down to try and talk her back into returning home.

A very keen Barnaby has already been on the telephone to her three times since they arrived back in Birmingham, and plans have already been hatched for the loved-up twosome to get together again very soon indeed. Johanna glances at the telephone, willing it to ring again so she can speak to him, her mind full of nothing else but the handsome Irish boy she's fallen in love with.

An unfamiliar gold Mercedes turns into the narrow street where the Hassall's modest mid terrace is situated, causing a few net curtains to be twitched as it pulls up outside. "This is the one," says Elvis, looking out of the car window.

"Thank you Elvis, I won't be very long," states Louis, getting out. He rings the doorbell. Johanna looks up in total panic, convinced that it must be her mum and dad coming round to make trouble, wanting her to return to them. Neil strides past to see who it is, and gets the shock of his life.

"Hello there Mr Hassall, sorry for just turning up like this, without notice," smiles Louis. Neil can hardly speak for surprise. What the hell is Louis Peyton doing on my doorstep? "I understand you have your delightful sister in law living with you now."

"Yes, she's here," says Neil.

"I'd like to see her for a few moments. Could I?" asks Louis.

"Sure, come in, Mr Peyton," replies Neil. He shouts up. "Johanna? Visitor here for you."

Johanna is frozen to the chair, certain that Trevor and

Muriel have come chasing around. She is as shocked as Neil when Louis appears around the door. "Oh my god, Mr Peyton!" says Johanna.

"Good afternoon Johanna, sorry for the surprise visit, but I needed to see you, and quite urgently in fact," confirms Louis. Christy appears, also not able to believe who she can see in her living room.

"Good grief, erm, can I get you a cup of tea?" she says.

"No thank you Mrs Hassall, this won't take long," states Louis. He gets straight to the point of his visit. "Now, I understand from what you told me that you are enrolling at the local polytechnic soon," he says, "But I think you're so much better than that. So much so, that I've spoken to a contact of mine at Birmingham University, told him all about you, what an extremely talented artist you are, and he would like to see you."

"University? I can't afford anything like that on my wages, but thank you anyway," says Johanna, sadly, liking the idea, but not seeing how it can possibly happen.

"Money is the last thing you need worry about, I assure you," confirms Louis, "Tomorrow, you are going to Budget-Buys and handing in your notice."

"What? I don't understand," says a bemused Johanna.

Louis opens his briefcase and gets out his cheque book. "There you are, call it a down payment, or sponsorship, whatever you like," he says, handing over a cheque for £50,000. Johanna's eyes nearly fall out of her head.

"I can't take this, oh my god this is way too much," she says, shaking.

"That is to pay your way through University, and once you have graduated I want you to set yourself up in business, as a fashion designer," smiles Louis, "and I want to back you every single step of the way. No need for you to be working on a till any more, you will be getting the best education money can buy - not that I think you need it, you are bright enough. Your clothes will be in boutiques all over the world, I have no doubt at all."

Johanna gets emotional, showing the cheque to Christy. Christy also gets emotional, this puts the £500 she had been trying to save up, but ended up winning instead, well and truly in the shade. "You deserve this," says Christy, smiling.

"And a little something for you too, Mrs Hassall," says Louis, handing over another cheque for £5000, "And one for your brother as well, with my compliments. Look, I have no close family, no one to leave my money to, so while I can I want to share my wealth with honest people like you who deserve good fortune. Just don't mention it to your parents!" They all laugh heartily. "Right, I'll bid you good day. Mr Briscoe from the University will contact you in due course, Johanna," says Louis, getting to his feet.

"I really don't know what to say," smiles Johanna, "This is incredible. Thank you so much Mr Peyton."

"Call me Louis," he replies, "And let me know how you get on with the University, I want to know everything. I know my investment is in very good hands though."

"You have my word. Louis." says Johanna.

*

It's not just Neil and Christy's house where Louis turns up unexpectedly. Utterly determined to persuade Colin into working for him some more, he next heads up to the Chesters' residence in Manchester unannounced. Despite raising the fee to £2000 per gig or even more if he wants it, Colin still politely turns him down for the same reasons as before.

Louis looks around at the lovely house the Chesters family have, kept immaculately by Liz, and can see Jamie and Eleanor in the garden playing happily, and with that quickly realises why Colin loves his lifestyle just as it is. Comfortable, relaxed, restful, no more than he deserves after all the years of performing, thinks Louis. Eleanor spots Louis through the patio doors, and races inside full of excitement, immediately thinking he must have changed his mind and that he wants to give her a job after all! Liz is on hand to explain that it's her father he's here to see, not her, which makes poor Eleanor get very upset.

An exasperated Liz gives her a hug, and softly tells her to be patient, that the opportunity will be there once she is old enough. "I was told how well you did, but as your mum says, you need to wait a few years, that is all," confirms Louis.

He doesn't leave the Chesters' house totally empty handed, with Liz insisting he takes with him two of her home-baked sponge cakes!

Despite all his best efforts, not a single newspaper is interested in Bo-Bo attempting to dish the dirt on the Peyton Empire from behind bars, having fed all the information to Krystal. The stories about the frazzled staff of Happy Daze relying on powerful stimulants to function properly, and dangerous, ramshackle chalets, make a number of ears prick up to start with, but having looked into the background of the informant any hope of these tales seeing the light of day is quickly forgotten. One of the newspaper editors contacted happens to be a personal friend of Louis Peyton, and quickly makes him aware of the rumours being peddled about his leisure parks. Canny Louis decides to use this to his advantage, inviting his friend to see him at his South Wales mansion, and telling him he has someone he would like him to meet.

Johanna, along with Barnaby, now a permanent item, are happy to tell their story to the press, no longer feeling any need to hide. Trevor and Muriel found out about her drawings and her new relationship not long after they arrived home, and in the first instance predictably started to scoff. Once they were aware that Louis Peyton had paid her a fortune to leave her job, so she could attend university instead to follow her dream, they had deluded ideas of trying to share in her new found fortune. Sensibly, when they turned up on Christy's doorstep, they were quickly sent packing.

Johanna moved into her new flat six weeks later, and instead of returning to Ireland, once the season at Happy Daze ended, Barnaby moved in too, the besotted twosome in domestic bliss, as Johanna goes from strength to strength in her studies at university.

Charlotte is a regular visitor, as her close friendship with Johanna shows no sign of abating.

Johnny hands in his resignation at Happy Daze two weeks before the end of the season, explaining to Louis that the punishing schedule, plus the strain his marriage is under, means he can no longer remain as a Seasider. Louis tears his letter up in small bits right under his nose, to Johnny's utter astonishment. He spares no time in telling Johnny to go home and sort out his personal problems, and that he will see him in April for a second season. He also explains that for the following year he plans on employing extra staff, to ensure no one has to work any hours on a designated day off, and not only that, extra time off will also be rostered.

Johnny and Olivia are divorced six months later.

On the very same day Barnaby and Johanna announce their engagement, to everyone's delight. As an engagement present, Louis gives them the keys to one of the Beach Huts on Portwynne front that were vividly portrayed in her drawings, while promising a lifetime of free holidays at Happy Daze for them, and, cheekily, any Maynard-Walsh's that they bring into the world in the future.

Marissa gives birth to a healthy baby daughter, in the New Year. Her and Elvis naming their little girl Louise, quickly engaging Louis as her Godfather. One or two cynical types reckon 'Benefactor' might be a more apt name, once rumours of Louis setting up a very large trust fund for the new arrival are heard.

Robert 'Bo-Bo' Boston gets his deserved comeuppance, being found guilty on all charges levied. A four-year prison sentence the outcome of this, with the judge telling him in no uncertain terms that he would have got a lot less, maybe even nothing at all, had he not stupidly decided to wave a gun in Louis Peyton's face. Many of his other enemies are in the courtroom looking on, eagerly waiting for the day of his release so more of his old gambling debts can be called in.

All the while he's incarcerated he swears he will get his revenge on Louis Peyton one day........

Printed in Great Britain
by Amazon.co.uk, Ltd.,
Marston Gate.